Paul Doherty is one of the most prolific, and lauded, authors of historical mysteries in the world today. His expertise in all areas of history is illustrated in the many series that he writes about from the Mathilde of Westminster series, set at the court of Edward II, to the Amerotke series, set in Ancient Egypt. Amongst his most memorable creations are Hugh Corbett, Brother Athelstan and Roger Shallot. Paul Doherty's newest series is set around the mysterious order of the Templars.

Paul Doherty was born in Middlesbrough. He studied history at Liverpool and Oxford Universities and obtained a doctorate at Oxford for his thesis on Edward II and Queen Isabella. He is now headmaster of a school in north-east London and lives with his wife and family near Epping Forest.

Praise for Paul Doherty:

'Paul Doherty has a lively sense of history . . . evocative and lyrical descriptions'   *New Statesman*

'Teems with colour, energy and spills'   *Time Out*

'Doherty is a master storyteller, his skills honed through an incredibly prolific literary career . . . terrific'
Nottingham Evening Post

'Masterful   *ood Book Guide*

By Paul Doherty and available from Headline

The Rose Demon
The Soul Slayer
The Haunting
Domina
The Plague Lord
The Templar

Mathilde of Westminster mysteries
The Cup of Ghosts
The Poison Maiden
The Darkening Glass

Ancient Roman mysteries
Murder Imperial
The Song of the Gladiator
The Queen of the Night
Murder's Immortal Mask

Ancient Egyptian mysteries
The Mask of Ra
The Horus Killings
The Anubis Slayings
The Slayers of Seth
The Assassins of Isis
The Poisoner of Ptah
The Spies of Sobeck

Hugh Corbett medieval mysteries
Satan in St Mary's
Crown in Darkness
Spy in Chancery
The Angel of Death
The Prince of Darkness
Murder Wears a Cowl
The Assassin in the Greenwood

The Song of a Dark Angel
Satan's Fire
The Devil's Hunt
The Demon Archer
The Treason of the Ghosts
Corpse Candle
The Magician's Death
The Waxman Murders
Nightshade

The Sorrowful Mysteries of Brother Athelstan
The Nightingale Gallery
The House of the Red Slayer
Murder Most Holy
The Anger of God
By Murder's Bright Light
The House of Crows
The Assassin's Riddle
The Devil's Domain
The Field of Blood
The House of Shadows

Egyptian Pharaoh trilogy
An Evil Spirit Out of the West
The Season of the Hyaena
The Year of the Cobra

The Canterbury Tales of murder and mystery
An Ancient Evil
A Tapestry of Murders
A Tournament of Murders
Ghostly Murders
The Hangman's Hymn
A Haunt of Murder

THE **SPIES** OF **SOBECK**

PAUL DOHERTY

headline

First published in Great Britain in 2008 by
HEADLINE PUBLISHING GROUP

First published in paperback in Great Britain in 2009 by
HEADLINE PUBLISHING GROUP

1

Cataloguing in Publication Data is available
from the British Library

ISBN 978 0 7553 3847 4

Typeset in New Century Schoolbook by
Palimpsest Book Production Ltd, Grangemouth, Stirlingshire

Printed in the UK by CPI Mackays, Chatham ME5 8TD

Headline's policy is to use papers that are natural, renewable
and recyclable products and made from wood grown
in sustainable forests. The logging and manufacturing
processes are expected to conform to the environmental
regulations of the country of origin.

HEADLINE PUBLISHING GROUP
An Hachette UK Company
338 Euston Road
London NW1 3BH

www.headline.co.uk
www.hachette.co.uk

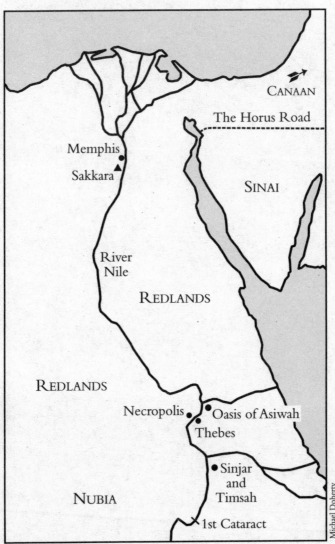

EGYPT C.1477 B.C.

CANAAN

The Horus Road

Memphis

Sakkara

SINAI

River
Nile

REDLANDS

REDLANDS

Necropolis ● ● Oasis of Asiwah

Thebes

● Sinjar
and
Timsah

NUBIA

1st Cataract

Michael Doherty

List of Characters

THE HOUSE OF PHARAOH

Hatusu:	Pharaoh-Queen of the XVIII dynasty
Senenmut:	lover of Hatusu; Grand Vizier or First Minister, a former stonemason and architect
Valu:	the 'Eyes and Ears' of Pharaoh; royal prosecutor
Omendap:	commander-in-Chief of Egypt's armies
Tuthmosis:	Hatusu's younger half-brother

THE HALL OF TWO TRUTHS

Amerotke:	Chief Judge of Egypt
Prenhoe:	Amerotke's kinsman, senior scribe in the Hall of Two Truths
Asural:	captain of the temple guard of the Temple of Ma'at in which the Hall of Two Truths stands

Shufoy:	a dwarf, Amerotke's manservant and confidant
Norfret:	Amerotke's wife
Ahmase and	
Curfay:	Amerotke's sons

THE HOUSE OF THE FOREST

Imothep:	retired veteran, formerly chief scout in the Spies of Sobeck
Parmen:	Imothep's steward
Neferen:	Parmen's daughter
Rahmel:	Imothep's bodyguard
Sihera:	housekeeper

THE TEMPLE OF NUBIA

Khufu:	high priest
Busiris:	Khufu's wife
Mataia:	chief heset
Maneso:	chief priest of the Chapel of the Ear

MEDJAY SCOUTS

Hennam:	chief scout
Kaemas:	Medjay scout
'Dog':	skilled in detecting scents

THE THEBAN UNDERWORLD

The Churat: Eater of Foul Things; gang leader in the Abode of Darkness

The Lady of the Dark: mistress of poisons

The Mongoose: former Member of the secret sect of Arites

The Breaker of Bones:
The Devourer of Hearts:
The Drinker of Blood: gang leaders
The Gobbler of Flesh:
The Flayer of Skins:

THE OASIS OF SINJAR

Nebher: chaplain priest of the Oasis

Isala: his daughter

OTHER CHARACTERS

Nadif: standard-bearer in the Theban police

Amtef: imperial courier

HISTORICAL NOTE

The first dynasty of ancient Egypt was established about 3100 BC. Between that date and the rise of the New Kingdom (1550 BC), Egypt went through a number of radical transformations, which witnessed the building of the Pyramids, the creation of cities along the Nile, the union of Upper and Lower Egypt and the development of Egyptian religion around Ra, the Sun God, and the cult of Osiris and Isis. Egypt had to resist foreign invasion, particularly by the Hyksos, Asiatic raiders who cruelly devastated the kingdom.

By 1480 BC, Egypt, pacified and united under Pharaoh Tuthmosis II, was on the verge of a new and glorious ascendancy. The pharaohs had moved their capital to Thebes; burial in the Pyramids was replaced by the development of the Necropolis on the west bank of the Nile as well as the exploitation of the Valley of the Kings as a royal mausoleum.

I have, to clarify matters, used Greek names for cities,

etc.; e.g. Thebes and Memphis, rather than their archaic Egyptian names. The place name Sakkara has been used to describe the entire pyramid complex around Memphis and Giza. I have also employed the shorter version for the Pharaoh Queen: i.e. Hatusu rather than Hatshepsut. Tuthmosis II died in 1479 BC and, after a period of confusion, Hatusu (daughter of Tuthmosis I; half-sister to Tuthmosis II), held power for the next twenty-two years. During this period, Egypt became an imperial power and the richest state in the world.

Egyptian religion was also being developed, principally the cult of Osiris, killed by his brother Seth but resurrected by his loving wife Isis, who gave birth to their son, Horus. These rites must be placed against the background of the Egyptians' worship of the Sun God and their desire to create a unity in their religious practices. They had a deep sense of awe for all living things: animals and plants, streams and rivers were all regarded as holy, whilst Pharaoh, their ruler, was worshipped as the incarnation of the divine will.

The Egyptians also had a great reverence for life, which had to be enjoyed both before and after death. They expressed this in exquisite paintings and poetry. Their existence was bound up with the life-giving Nile, that broad, turbulent ribbon of fertility that cut through the searing heat of the eastern and western deserts. They had a fascination with the sun, its rising and setting, which, for them, were mystic events to be watched and worshipped in awe. Such occasions were to be celebrated and described in poems and hymns. This balance of sun and water, the fount of life, was embodied and worshipped in the form of their pharaoh, appointed by the gods to keep human affairs in harmony.

By 1480 BC, the Egyptian civilisation joyously expressed its richness in religion, ritual, architecture, dress, education and the pursuit of the good life. Soldiers, priests and scribes dominated this civilisation, and their sophistication is expressed in the terms they used to describe both themselves and their culture. For example, Pharaoh was the Golden Hawk; the treasury was the House of Silver; a time of war was the Season of the Hyaena; a royal palace was the House of a Million Years. Despite the country's breathtaking, dazzling civilisation, however, Egyptian politics, both at home and abroad, could be violent and bloody. The royal throne was always the centre of intrigue, jealousy and bitter rivalry. It was on to this political platform, in 1479 BC, that the young Hatusu emerged.

By 1477 BC, Hatusu had confounded her critics and opponents, both at home and abroad. She had won a great victory in the north against the Mitanni and purged the royal circle of opposition led by the Grand Vizier Rahimere. A remarkable young woman, Hatusu was supported by her wily and cunning lover, Senenmut, also her First Minister. She was determined that all sections of Egyptian society should accept her as Pharaoh-Queen of Egypt.

Egypt's foreign policy was built along the Nile. Sea invaders from the north, landing in the Delta, could easily be repulsed, whilst Egypt often sent chariot squadrons across the Horus Road into Canaan. The country's real fear was a war on two fronts: a hostile force in the north occupying the Delta and a revolt in Nubia. Nubia was an independent kingdom until annexed by the Egyptian pharaohs. It was the source of gold, silver and precious materials. If Egypt lost Nubia, it would not only lose its treasure house but also expose itself to attacks from the south. A great deal of evidence exists from Hatusu's reign to indicate that the Pharaoh Queen placed great importance on retaining Nubia as part of the Great House of Egypt. However, the danger always remained. Nubia not only wanted its independence, an end to the export of its treasures; it also dreamed dreams of counterattack against Thebes, and the expansion of Nubian power. Conspiracies and revolts in Nubia were commonplace. Hatusu had to face her fair share of them. This novel concentrates on one . . .

PROLOGUE

Netch: almond tree

Kaemas, a leading Medjay scout attached to the Anubis regiment, licked his dusty sunburnt lips and crouched on the hillock of sand. He squinted his eyes, searching the horizon for any sign of life, and tried to ignore the strange pulling sensation in his belly as he scratched his curled, oiled hair. He went back to searching, looking for any movement here in the Redlands, the haunt of the Seth creatures and the devourers from the Amduat, Egypt's macabre Underworld. The sun was setting, playing tricks with the colours of the dying day. Kaemas stared. Was it the sunset or something else? Everything seemed red and tinged with black, even the birds swooping swiftly against the sky. In the distance, a black herd of wild camels were weaving their way around the mastabas, derelict tombs and memorials, those dry desires of long-dead men. Kaemas glanced up. Soon the sky would turn pale and the sun disappear, leaving nothing but a bar of red with a hint of brown, and Ra would sink into his nightly voyage through the darkness of the Underworld. Kaemas sipped from his water bottle, then, fingering the pouch on his belt, took out a small natron pellet and pushed it between his lips to keep his mouth fresh and wet. The desert truly was the house of fire. The ground was hot, as if heated by a fiery glow from the earth's bowels. In the far distance to his right curled the Nile, the life-giving river. Kaemas peered in that direction, unaware of the death seeping through him. He glimpsed the twinkle of water, the movement of lush yellowing grass bowing under the evening breeze. He fingered the necklace of agate pebbles circling his neck, then the black horn brooches around his wrist. He felt so strange, a light-headed sensation, as if he was dreaming, yet he was very much awake.

Kaemas glanced to his left and glimpsed his companions, scouts sent out from the camp to search for any signs of the Arites, the killers from the slaughterhouse. He wondered once again what was really happening. He was of the Medjay, a tribe that had eaten the Pharaoh's bread to become Egypt's police, spies and bowmen. The Medjay had nosed the ground before the Horus in the South, Pharaoh, the God Incarnate. They had been gathered into the Great House, and yet now? Kaemas fought against the growing discomfort in his belly, the tingling along the muscles at the back of his neck. All was changing. The Nubians had risen in revolt, taking advantage of the Divine One's absence in the Delta and along the Great Green. A treacherous, malevolent conspiracy

2

fired by Seth creatures from the blackness. The Nubian rebels had driven Hatusu's viceroy back to the fortress of Buhen, near the Second Cataract. They had seized the other cataracts further south as well as the Sobeck roads through the oases, or so said Chief Scout Hennam. Worse, the Arites, dedicated to the great destroyer Nema, their hyaena goddess, had also joined the revolt, slipping out of their hidden fortress at Bekhna. Killers to the bone, the Arites! A secret religious sect devoted to strangling their enemies with so-called sacred red cloths blessed by their hideous goddess. Rumours about these and other frightening events had swept General Omendap's camp like desert breezes.

Kaemas heard a whistle and turned. The desert heat shimmered, twisting and distorting shapes. Kaemas could see Hennam beckoning to him. Kaemas rose and stared up at the sky. Why was it turning blood red, with black clouds? Would the arrows of the god, the lightning shafts, be hurled? Kaemas felt both hot and cold. The blood drummed in his ears; his stomach was bubbling like a fiery pot. He could feel the sweat on his face, the beat of his heart. Colours shot up from the ground. A whirl of light caught his eye and he stared in horror. The jackal god Anubis, a black and gold mask hiding his face, was striding towards him like a warrior harnessed for battle. He was dressed in a leather kilt with a silver and gold medallion gleaming on his breastplate. The god wore the brilliant red gloves Pharaoh always bestowed on her Maryannou, the Bravest of the Brave. In one hand he carried an oval-headed mace and in the other a curved scimitar drenched in blood. The jackal god rose in stature as if to black out the garishly coloured sky. A chariot rattled. Kaemas turned. The god Seth, garbed in crimson, horses of the same bloody colour, was thundering towards him. The chariot was of gleaming purple electrum, the harness black and silver, whilst fiery standards flowed from its pennant poles. Was he dreaming? Kaemas wondered. The horizon had disappeared, replaced by walls of writhing cobras. The sand was now a torrent of blood flowing across a black meadow of twisting scorpions and snakes. Pains flared up from Kaemas' belly. He was trapped. Anubis to his left, Seth to his right. He spread his hands. He turned and twisted, the terrors gripping his body, until he collapsed lifeless to the ground . . .

'Hatusu, Mighty of Amun-Ra, She of the Two Ladies, Flourishing in Years, Golden Horus, Divine of Diadems, King of Upper and Lower Egypt, Lord of the Two Lands . . .'

The voices of the massed temple choirs in the holy of holies, Ipet-sut, the most perfect of places, rang out across the Nile. The powerful words glorified Hatusu, Pharaoh, the Pride of Montu. She sat like the war god incarnate on her Throne of Glory beneath a gold-blue awning at the centre of the massive war barge *The Power of Amun*. The craft moved majestically, its curving prow cutting the water. The rowers along each side and the rudder men in the high stern paid careful heed to the shouted cries of the skilled imperial steersmen and pilots. *The Power of Amun* rocked gently against the strong pull of the Nile, a glittering mass of wood, metal, precious stones

4

and all the weapons of war. The sunlight picked out the armour, jewels, rings, bracelets, the ostrich plumes and awnings across Pharaoh's great war craft. On either side of the prow the Wadjet, the ever-seeing eye, made the barge even more ominous. From the mast floated coloured pennants. On the top of the prow the carved lioness head of Sekhmet the Devouress lunged in a fierce snarl. On either side of the prow, head down, hung the struggling naked bodies of eight chieftains of the Sea People whose power Pharaoh had shattered in the Delta and along the Great Green.

Hatusu sat, her beautiful eyes hard as flint, her lovely face under the blue war crown carefully painted. She was clothed in the finest linen, carefully starched and gauffered, her sleeves projecting slightly beyond her hands. Over her shoulders hung the brilliantly bejewelled Nenes, the Cape of Glory; around her waist was the golden cord of Isis. Her impeccably manicured feet were enclosed in gilded leather sandals, and circling her neck was a heavy collar of glittering jewels, lapis lazuli and carnelian. Pharaoh's purple-gloved hands tightly grasped the flail and the rod. On either side of her, stiffened pennants displayed the Uraei, the spitting cobras who protected the Crowned One, the Golden Horus, the Beloved of Osiris. Had they failed her now? Hatusu gazed unblinkingly; her sensuous eyes, carefully ringed with black kohl, did not reveal her doubt. Despite her agitation, she hardly moved, except for her mouth as she quietly dissolved the natron pellet her lover, the Grand Vizier, and First Minister Senenmut, had provided to wet her mouth against the sand-tinged spray and salty breezes.

Senenmut stood slightly behind the Throne of Glory, his burly body garbed in the finest robes, his shaven head and rugged face gleaming in the sun as his dark eyes carefully scrutinised the approaching quayside. Senenmut was tense. He could feel the same from his imperial mistress. She'd journeyed north beyond the bend of Dendera, up to Memphis, then further north to crush the seaborne invasion. A triumphant display of military power. They had surged solemnly along the Nile, watching the banks on either side change in both colour and texture; the arid desert where the Sheshu, the sand-dwellers, roamed giving way to open countryside fringed with acacia, tamarisk, sycamore, date and fig trees. They had docked along quaysides thronged with boats of every description, packed with fruit, cedar and pine from Lebanon, barrels of oil, precious goods and cages of exotic birds. In the evening they'd sometimes moored off villages from where the people hastened down, splashing through the papyrus groves and sedge that flourished along the banks: they'd left their cranes, listless above the precious wells, to greet their all-powerful Pharaoh. Images and scenes! White-walled Memphis with its mysterious ancient temples. Further north the pyramids and mastabas of long-dead pharaohs towering above the huddled villages of the poor as well as the gorgeously walled, cedar-wooded mansions of the wealthy. Ships, boats and barges, punts, galleys and rafts had turned to greet them. Now and again they would catch sight of the

6

rolling dust of their regiments marching alongside, their standards brilliant in the sun, and beyond these the sparkling flashes of the chariot squadrons.

Eventually they'd entered the Delta to deal out judgement and death by sword and fire. Hatusu had turned the camps and ships of the Sea People into their funeral pyres. Now she was returning home, crowned with victory by Horus of the Red Eye. Or was she? Senenmut shifted to steady himself as *The Power of Amun* began its final turn. He looked swiftly over his shoulder at the other war boats taking up their positions. He moved his gaze and glimpsed Khufu, high priest of the Temple of Nubia, that sprawling fortified complex of black stone to the north of Thebes. Beside Khufu, the high priest's lovely-faced wife, Busiris, and her equally appealing principal heset or handmaid, Mataia. Senenmut caught Khufu's eye and smiled, even though the land of Nubia, and everything about it, now threatened Hatusu. Khufu and his party had joined the royal barge earlier in the day so as to affirm the loyalty of their temple as well as explain what was happening in Thebes. The Arites were on the loose, threatening even the Divine One, leaving their cursed scarabs as a warning of impending dangers around the gold-plated obelisk raised to Hatusu's glory in the centre of Thebes. The Divine One was impatient to return. Senenmut blinked and licked his lips. Thebes, the Waset, the Many-Gated City, its basalt-paved thoroughfares lined by brooding sphinxes, lions and winged wyverns carved out of stone, waited to greet them. It would be good once again to walk the city streets.

Senenmut glanced again at the quayside where the music of the lute, lyre, zither, oboe, drum, tambourine and castanets abruptly stilled at the blowing of horns, the shrill cry of bronze trumpets and the lowing of battle horns that heralded Pharaoh's imminent arrival. All was ready. The fragrance of incense floated across to mix with the frankincense, cassia, aloes, myrrh and kiphye that billowed from the costly robes of the courtiers. *The Power of Amun* turned sideways to the clash of cymbals. Small punts appeared manned by Medjay scouts in their leather kilts and baldrics, bare chests sheened with sweat, crimped hair decorated with ornaments fashioned out of ostrich eggshells. These craft now clustered on either side of the prow, cutting down the prisoners who were to be sacrificed a short while hence, their brains smashed out by the ever-victorious Pharaoh Queen in the Place of Victory at the top of steps of the Temple of Montu. Other moon-shaped boats appeared, thronged with Nubian mercenaries. Senenmut's eyes clouded, he watched these warily. They and their province had provoked Hatusu's dark mood, for rumours, soon proved to be true, had swept up the Delta. Nubia was in rebellion! A dark stormcloud of menace troubled Pharaoh's heart and sent her hurrying south to confront new perils closing in like scavengers for the kill. The Arites, that secret religious sect of Nubia, were truly on the hunt. They were even in Thebes! Little wonder this day's glorious victory of eternal jubilee was greatly dimmed. Already the House of War was busy, with General Omendap assembling the regiments at Farinal – the Field of Mustering.

Senenmut breathed in deeply as the war barge slipped along the quayside, its rowers bringing up their oars in salute. The gangplank was lowered, and members of the Nubian regiment, chosen as a mark of confidence, hurried on board to grasp and raise the palanquin bearing the Throne of Glory. Along the quayside the musicians and choirs fell silent under the blinding blue sky. Senenmut gazed at the throng of courtiers, flunkeys, administrators, generals, priests and scribes clustered to meet them, a field of white robes. Beyond these were the citizens of Thebes, rapturous to look upon the face of their Pharaoh. Senenmut felt uneasy, but the moment passed. They were committed. Hatusu had made it very clear that she would show no fear or apprehension in public. The palanquin was raised and taken off along the processional road towards Ipet-sut, lined either side by its row of awesome stone sphinxes and rams. As the palanquin left the quayside, the entire crowd fell to its knees and nosed the ground. A troop of Nakhtu-aa, together with the Maryannou, guarded the palanquin; all of these were veterans who'd taken a head in battle and cut off the penis of their enemy. These hand-picked warriors were garbed in snow-white kilts, their heads covered by the royal blue and gold headdress. They were well armed. A dagger, with its straight double-edged tapering blade encased in an embossed gilded sheath, was tucked into each of their waistbands; in one hand was a spear, in the other a long shield decorated with leopard skin.

Conch horns wailed, a sign that the people could look upon their Pharaoh, 'Fair of Face and Lovely of Form'.

9

The air became a blizzard of scented petals thrown from countless baskets. Officers in padded tunics and jerkins sewn with leather or metal scales walked ahead of the palanquin. Each of these was armed with a bronze mace carved in the shape of the head of a cobra, to keep the more enthusiastic spectators back. Hesets, dancing girls from the temples, swirled in front of the palanquin to the rattle of sistra, the clash of cymbals and the tune of flutes. Behind the palanquin thronged priests in their gauffered robes and leopard-skin shawls, chests and throats glittering with heavy necklaces, collars of gold and silver pectorals, festooned with jewels. After these came the court. Senenmut briefly glimpsed the sallow-faced Amerotke, Chief Judge in the Hall of Two Truths, then the judge disappeared in the sea of faces. Senenmut grimaced to himself. They would need Amerotke, but not just yet.

They entered a forest of stone, the temple complex of Karnak, the courtyards of pinkish-red limestone and black basalt broiling in the blistering heat. They passed through pylons stretching up like twin towers, their double gates thrown back; on the top soared long, slender gilded flagpoles adorned with narrow pennants painted with sacred emblems such as the 'Ankh' and 'Sa' and proclaiming 'Peace and Protection': these now hung limp in the dry, windless noonday air. Further along, rows of blood-red obelisks, capped with bronze, silver and gold, shimmered and gleamed above square pools of purity sprinkled with fat pink water-lilies. The procession entered the Mansions of the Gods, the hypostyle halls lined with columns, their tops decorated with capitals representing papyrus buds. On the rounded, squat columns the petals and buds were open; on the more slender ones they were closed. Light slanted through clerestory windows to illuminate the walls decorated with frescoes extolling the deeds of the gods, who were always depicted with blue-green skins, their hair of the purest lapis lazuli. Other paintings proclaimed the wonders of long-dead pharaohs, the memorials of mortal men who dreamed of being immortal. Torches flared. Ornamental lamps of calcite and alabaster glittered from countless wall niches. Oil stands carved in the shape of the blue water-lily gleamed through the murk. The light ebbed and flowed, sparkling in the cedarwood overlaid with gold or inlaid with precious stones. Fans of ostrich plumes, mingled with those of palm fibre, wafted back and forth, all drenched with costly perfume, though this did little to mask the stench of spilt blood and woodsmoke.

The cortège entered the imperial robing room, its walls decorated with the most delightful pastels. The palanquin was lowered and Pharaoh stepped out; the bearers picked it up, then walked to the far doors, beyond which they would wait. Hatusu was now alone except for Senenmut and a few chosen advisers. Priests came out of the dark to greet her, their faces hidden behind masks of the jackal of Anubis, the hawk of Horus, the curved beak of Osiris and the lioness of Sekhmet. They brought the robes of glory, short skirts embossed with cloth of gold; a long gown of transparent linen. A beautiful pectoral was looped over Hatusu's head, the blue war crown replaced with one displaying the spitting cobra. Around her neck the priests clasped a collar of gold and carnelian, along her arms bracelets of twisted pure silver. An acolyte anointed Hatusu with sacred water and perfumed her mouth with scented natron tablets pushed between her lips. The robing room remained silent; only the faint chanting from the choirs outside echoed through along the light-dappled hall.

At last Hatusu was ready. The doors at the far end were opened, the entrance to the central courtyards of Karnak a hymn in stone to the strength, vigour and power of Egypt. Hatusu once again took her seat on the Throne of Glory; the palanquin was raised. Outside in the sunlight were mustered the crack regiments, the college of priests, the officials of various houses. Senenmut sighed and wiped a bead of sweat from his neck. The palanquin moved majestically into the blinding light as the choirs intoned a hymn of praise:

Earth shines as you rise in the land of light.
You dispel the dark,
You cast your rays,
The sky is yours,
The lightning, your arrows.

Senenmut followed, wrinkling his nose at the fragrant clouds of perfume. Abruptly the procession halted. The palanquin swayed, then was hastily lowered. Senenmut went forward. One of the Nubian bearers at the front had apparently fainted. The man was being dragged away when another Nubian, holding one of the rear poles, sprang forward, a blood-red cloth draped over one hand. Senenmut's heart skipped in horror as the man climbed up to the back of the throne. Hatusu was turning. Senenmut drew his dagger and lunged forward. Khufu, the high priest, was faster: grasping a spear from a bewildered guard, he ran and thrust the blade deep, twisting the would-be assassin away as if he was a skewered fish. The Nubian who had fainted scrambled to his feet. Other bearers were moving, but the Maryannou and the Nakhtu-aa swiftly recovered from their shocked surprise. Swords, daggers and spears whirled as the bodyguard clashed with the assassins.

'Kill them!' Senenmut screamed. 'Kill them all!'

And that elegant courtyard in that most perfect of places became nothing more than a bloody slaughterhouse, as red-haired Seth swept in from the desert, the House of Fire to the south.

Three days after the attempted assassination of Hatusu, late in the evening as the sky turned a dark sapphire blue, Seth also visited the House of the Forest to the north of Thebes. The stately mansion had been given its name by Imothep, its owner, to evoke memories of his military service in his own province of Nubia, the Land of Burning Faces. Imothep had been chief metru, or scout, in the Spies of Sobeck when Hatusu's father, Tuthmosis I, had brought fire and sword to the People of the Bow. He and his tribe had decided to shelter under the old Pharaoh's shadow, and Imothep had been richly rewarded for his loyalty with the plump, comely daughter of a Theban nobleman in marriage as well as extensive estates outside Thebes, a short walk from the soaring pylons of the Nubian Gate. Imothep had waxed fat and prosperous. True, his wife had died childless, but Imothep did not marry again. Instead, he withdrew into himself, dependent on Parmen his steward, Parmen's daughter Neferen, his loyal bodyguard Rahmel and his old housekeeper Sihera.

Life, until that evening, was serene in the spacious House of the Forest. Imothep had allowed the extensive gardens, protected by a high curtain wall and double-barred gates, to run wild, except for the vegetable plot, where peas, lentils, onions, lettuce and cucumbers grew next to a row of conical beehives woven out of fibre. The rest of the estate, however, remained unattended, including the small orchards of pomegranate, date and other fruits. Imothep equally neglected the sacred sycamore and holy willow as well as the palm, oak, acacia and tamarisk trees. These had sprouted and grown over the years, their branches intermingling above the long grass, banks of weeds and green-slimed ponds and pools. He maintained that such wildness reminded him of the jungles of his native Nubia. Imothep was fond of pointing out how the foxes, marmosets and monkeys would feel more at home there, as well as the rock pigeons, doves, swallows and brilliantly coloured kingfishers that nested in the green darkness to feed on the myriad of insects and gorgeously winged butterflies. Such neglect wasn't because of money. Imothep was certainly no miser. The house itself, with its colonnaded porticoes, was approached by a wide sweeping ramp with steps cut on either side. It was an impressive building, with its flat garden-terrace roof, square windows with decorated wooden lintels and double-fronted door fashioned out of costly cedar. A spacious dwelling built on a stone platform, the main house contained a pillared hall, bedrooms, private quarters, storerooms, offices, latrines and bathroom, whilst in the sizeable courtyard beyond stood an open kitchen and bakehouse beneath a protective awning. However, for all its grandeur, it was not the main house that was Imothep's pride and joy; rather what he called his Mansion of Silence at the far end of the garden: an elegant residence built on stone foundations, its gleaming limestone walls pierced by six clerestory windows, two on each side of the square edifice. The mansion was entered by a double-gated door in the shadowed front portico, flanked on either side by pillars that glowed eerily red as if swollen with blood. The Mansion of Silence, some claimed, was modelled on the ancient mastabas, the funeral homes of Nubia. Others said that the building, with its elegant cornices and pillared front, reminded them of a Nubian temple. Whatever, to Imothep it was his Ipet-sut, a place of refuge where he could write his memoirs and brood on the past. Little did he realise such a place of consolation would be his death shroud.

The harmony of the House of the Forest had been brutally shattered seven days earlier when the bloated corpse of a man, his hands severed, had been found deep in the overgrown garden. A stranger whom no one could recognise, he had been strangled and stripped naked, the red cloth still tied tightly around his throat. Rumour and

15

gossip claimed he must be a victim of Imothep's old enemies, the Arites. Perhaps it was a warning? Everyone in Imothep's household recalled the stories and legends about the Arites. If their master had been singled out for execution, then Seth, like some giant bat, would glide swiftly and secretly into the House of the Forest and there'd be no escape. Such gossip, together with the news of the recent assassination attempt on the Queen Pharaoh, had swept through Thebes like fire through dry stubble. Other news followed about the slaughter of the Nubians, the emissaries of the Arites, in the courtyard of Karnak and the excruciating torture of those who had survived. All of this must have provoked Imothep's memories about his own fighting days, when Pharaoh Tuthmosis had swept into Nubia to eradicate that sinister sect once and for all.

Accordingly, late that particular afternoon, Imothep had retired to his Mansion of Silence. He had lowered the bar on the inside of the door whilst Rahmel his faithful servant had done the same outside, sealing his master away from any turbulence or disturbance. Imothep's household and retainers expected that their master would leave the mansion just before sunset, as usual, to catch the last golden burst of light and whisper his own poem to Ra. However, when the sun did set and the darkness swooped in, that owl-wing time when Imothep's garden became alive with the shrieks of night creatures and the wild gorse shook as the hunters emerged, he still had not left his mansion. The housekeeper, Sihera, lay sick of a mysterious ailment in her own narrow chamber, but even

16

she became agitated when the whispers reached her. Hours passed. Rahmel beat on the door with his mace and called his master's name, but to no effect. The Mansion of Silence became ringed with servants holding flaring torches. Parmen the steward, openly agitated, gave the order to break in. The outer beam was removed, then used to pound the door until it buckled, the inside clasp breaking free and the bar within slipping out. The servants pushed open the doors. Inside, a dark well of silence greeted them. Parmen entered, Rahmel following behind. The others remained clustered at the bottom of the steps as the steward had ordered them to. These witnessed the lights flare inside the mansion, followed by the most heart-rending cry. Parmen came stumbling out, his wig all askew, he stood at the top of the steps tearing his clothes. His daughter Neferen tried to console him but was unable to; Parmen simply dragged her into the darkness of the mansion to show her the horror within. The servants waited a while, then Rahmel appeared and lifted his hands.

'Our master is dead,' he proclaimed. 'The Arites, the killers from the slaughterhouse, have visited here.'

On the same evening that the ka, the soul, of Imothep began its awesome journey through the Am-duat to confront the Devourers, the Shadows and the Swallowers of Life, Amtef the royal courier was about to begin a similar journey. Amtef truly thought he was safe. After all, he was Uptui-Nes, a royal messenger, an imperial courier under the divine protection of both Pharaoh and

Apui the messenger god. Amtef prided himself on the imperial cartouche or seal strapped to his right wrist, and wallowed in the pompous grandeur of his status, the imperial barge with its royal Horus pennant and his escort of rowers, ten burly veterans from the Anubis regiment. They had journeyed all day from General Omendap's camp outside Thebes to reach this oasis. In the main it had been a pleasant journey. The Inundation had finished, so peasants and villagers had been frantically busy in the basins and pools formed by the generous rush of water, men, women and children eagerly raking the rich black mud back over their fields, which they would dry out and later sow. Children astride oxen lifted their canes to Amtef in salute. Fishermen and farmers called for their families, basking in the shade near their small square houses of sun-dried brick, plastered with manure and sand against the elements, to come and see Pharaoh's messenger. Amtef had gloried in this. He drank deep of the sights: crocodiles basking in the early-morning sun, jaws open in the direction of the east; hippopotami sheltering deep in the papyrus groves or playing noisily in the thick riverside sedge. His barge had surged past such scenes, its prow cutting through the flotsam and jetsam, even the occasional corpse of some animal trapped in the flood that the river beasts were already nosing. The scenes would change as they passed rocky outcrops shifting in their colours as they caught the light, but always the Nile, full and rich, its breezes thick with the various odours of the desert and the villages along its banks.

They had eventually reached the Oasis of Sinjar, just

as the sky changed to that pale primrose colour before sunset. Sinjar! A strange place! A dense cluster of palm trees and long, sturdy grass around a well providing the sweetest water. Pharaoh's armies and messengers always used this during the journey south. Tuthmosis I had set up a stela, carved from rock, praising the fragrance and abundance of the pool whilst giving thanks to the Red-Eyed Horus for his munificence. The Oasis of Sinjar was a lonely, fertile enclave, a welcome escape from the Redlands with their gravel paths, dry, dusty air and sand-strewn winds.

Amtef shook off his cloak, struggled to his feet and looked around. His companions were fast asleep, the dark shapes of their bodies faintly outlined in the poor light. The fire of dried dung had spluttered out. The moon was hiding behind drifting clouds that also cloaked the stars, those blossoms of the sky. It looked as if the heavens had retreated, not hanging down as usual like a jewelled canopy above them. Amtef felt slightly sick, and wondered if he should drink from the pool glittering in the pale light. He walked across the oasis, pushing his way through the scrub, and stood at the water's edge, resting against a towering palm tree and staring out at the great fortress of Timsah, a long huddle of rocky black ruins, a sprawling, desolate testimony to the wars of previous pharaohs.

The oasis priest Nebher, who lived in his small hut at the top of the high bank overlooking the river, claimed that the fortress was ghost-ridden. People kept away from Timsah, except for the Sheshu, the desert-wanderers and sand-dwellers. A haunted place! Amtef shivered. He recalled the sinister stories about the mysterious disappearance of other royal messengers, merchants and envoys; even Nebher's own daughter. He thought of his old friend Maneso, a priest of the Chapel of the Ear in the Temple of Nubia, who always maintained that the desert housed demons. Did such fiends lurk here? Amtef felt a prickle of cold, then startled at a deep, throaty roar. The night prowlers were awake! The breeze whipped cold air about him and he stood back from the trunk of the tree. Something was wrong. The hyaena bark was distant; it should be closer. The night prowlers must have smelt the human presence; they always closed in, even just to watch. Amtef rubbed his eyes. He must be more vigilant. He became aware of soft, slithering sounds and glanced around. The breeze soughed through the gorse and the hardy plants of the oasis, rippling the water of the pool. What was wrong? Amtef glanced across the desert at the ghostly ruins of Timsah. It was too quiet, too placid, as though the prowlers of the night had withdrawn before a greater menace. He quietly whispered a prayer to He-Who-Stares-From-the-Shadows. He recalled his conch horn and hastened back to his sleeping mat, only to confront a terrifying shadow that seemed to rise from the dust. A grotesque, a Devourer with an evil face; was it a mask? And that red cloth strung between his hands? Amtef screamed and turned to flee. It was a fatal mistake, for it left him vulnerable to the red cloth that snaked around his throat to choke off his breath.

CHAPTER 1

Ar: to strangle

The sky rains down fire,
The vaults of heaven quiver,
Earth's bones tremble,
The stars stand still
As all-seeing Horus moves in power.
A god who lives on his worshippers,
Who feeds on those who adore him,
Who feeds on the lungs of the wise,
And gluts on the hearts of the foolish.

The dramatic voice of the Chaplain of the Stake, the execution priest, carried through the hot air of the Place of the Skull. The priest stood before the line of condemned men, hands extended, head thrown back so that his oiled fat face glistened in the torrid sunlight. The prisoners, six in number, shifted in a clink of chains and stared in

21

terror at the potholes dug in the dirt, a sharpened stake beside each one. These were the Nubians, the Arites, those who had survived the massacre in the temple courtyard of Karnak. They glanced at the Chaplain of the Stake, then at Lord Amerotke, Chief Judge in the Hall of Two Truths, present at the Divine One's order to see sentence carried out. Beside the judge stood Lord Valu, the Eyes and Ears of Pharaoh, the prosecutor of all offences against the Great House. Amerotke, clothed in pure white robes, stared pityingly at the prisoners. They were to die here, dispatched into the Eternal West, devoid of the rites of Osiris, impaled alive on this rocky escarpment. The stakes would be driven up into their bowels and the condemned men would writhe in agony as the desert wind clogged noses, eyes and throats with sand. Their hideous screams and the stench of blood would lure in the carrion-eaters, the feather-winged vultures, the short-haired jackals, the striped hyaenas and the savage lion packs. A gruesome death in a hideous place here on the dry burning plains of hell.

The prisoners were already a mass of open wounds. Former bearers of the imperial palanquin, they and their now-dead comrades were Arites, killers from the slaughterhouse, dedicated to their sinister goddess, stranglers who murdered their victims with sacred red cloths. Valu had established all this. He had tortured them in the House of Chains until their bodies oozed blood. In the end, they had not broken or confessed to anything except that they were under orders from the Sgeru, their leader, the Silent One, to offer Hatusu as a sacrifice to their goddess. Now it was all finished. They had been condemned by Amerotke, and the execution procession had left Thebes just after dawn for the Place of the Skull, where they would face hideous death.

'My lord.' The Tedjen in charge of the chariot squadron escorting the execution detail left the huddle of prisoners and saluted Valu. 'My lord,' he repeated, 'sentence is to be carried out?'

'Immediately!' Valu, small and fat, turned and, moving his parasol, squinted up at Amerotke. The prosecutor's piggy eyes were black and hard as agate despite the smiling crinkles around his mouth. 'My lord Amerotke?'

'Sentence is to be carried out immediately,' Amerotke confirmed.

Valu lifted a hand. The torturers moved, grasping a prisoner, lifting him high above the squat, razor-sharp stake driven into the rocky ground. The first man was brutally impaled to horrid screams and yells. Blood splashed out. Amerotke glanced towards his chariot. The groom was trying to control the magnificent pair of bays who now reared, pulling the glittering embossed chariot, rattling the brightly embroidered javelin and arrow sheaths. The man struggled to keep the ornamental brown harness free of the axle and the six-spoked wheels. Other attendants were having similar problems. The air was riven by blood-chilling sounds as the second prisoner was impaled. Amerotke felt his gorge rise, and a sheet of sweat dampened his bare chest. He removed his carnelian pectoral and slipped it into the bag fastened to the broad sash around his waist. He impatiently scraped one leather-sandalled foot against the pebble-strewn ground as his horses bucked and reared again, the golden and red plumes fixed between their ears swirling in the hot breeze. Amerotke knew he had to be gone. He turned away, but Valu grasped him by the wrist.

'My lord, the Divine One said we must watch the execution. We are official witnesses. I am her Eyes and Ears, you are her Chief Judge.'

'Lord Valu,' Amerotke flinched at the tight grip, 'I have witnessed. Now let go of my wrist.' He thrust Valu's arm away. 'I witness,' he hissed, 'but I do not relish. Tell me when it's done.' He strode away, even as fresh harrowing screams raked the air. He glanced upwards. The sky was a brilliant blue, and already Pharaoh's hens, the grey-winged vultures, were appearing, floating high, ominous black heralds, whilst in the distance came a mocking harsh bark. Fresh blood was being spilt! The desert prowlers were alerted.

Amerotke reached his chariot and climbed in, kicking off his sandals to allow his feet a better grip on the wickerwork floor. He smiled at the groom, who stood back. Amerotke grasped the reins, clicking his tongue, talking gently to the bays, who were still moving restlessly in a jingle of harness. He urged the horses on, leaning slightly to the left going down the slight rise from the Place of the Skull and on to the rocky escarpment fringing the desert, which stretched as far as the eye could see, a plateau of shimmering light and eerie undulating shapes. A scream cut the air. Amerotke fingered the lock of hair that fell down one side of his face, an eccentric reminder of an oath to the memory of his long-dead brother. He blinked away the tears caused by the stinging sand and the hot glare, then shifted the reins to one hand and lifted the folds of his robe to protect his head and face. He grasped the whip and flicked it hard above the bays. The horses responded vigorously, moving from a trot to a canter. Again the whip cracked. The chariot moved to a full war charge, horse, rider and carriage swaying as one, speeding like an arrow across the hot sand, wheels skimming the ground. Amerotke shifted his feet to secure a better balance, guiding the horses, rejoicing at the ferocious fury of the charge, which cleansed his mind of the horrors he'd just witnessed. He allowed the horses to run, then slowed down as he glimpsed two old palm trees twisting out of the desert floor, relics of some ancient oasis overcome by the desert. He curbed the horses to a canter, aware of the sand clogging the carriage wheels, then reined in under the meagre shade of the trees and climbed down, steadying himself against the chariot, quietly cursing the hot sand burning his feet.

Amerotke hobbled the horses, then went and sat cross-legged in the shadow of the oasis, his back to a tree trunk. He freed his head and face from the folds of his gown and gazed across the desert. He steadied his breathing, and in his soul cried out to those he loved: Norfret, his wife; Ahmase and Curfay, his two sons; Shufoy, the disfigured dwarf, his messenger, friend and companion. He closed his eyes and called on his dead, his parents, his brothers and sisters who'd gone into the Far West to rest in the eternal fields of never-ending dreams. Amerotke spread his hands and intoned his own prayer to the One Who Sees All, the Eternal Being, the Most Fitting of Forms, the Cause and Source of All. He thought fleetingly of the creature-headed statues of Anubis, Seth and green-skinned Osiris. He found it hard to accept such beings as gods, granite statues with their dead eyes and dry ears. He recalled the preaching of Medinet, the priest-prophet from Akhmin who'd swept into Thebes with his theory of one eternal being. Medinet had been proclaimed as a heretic, but Amerotke had been fascinated by his ideas, which had certainly found a home with him.

The neighing of his horses broke his reverie. Amerotke smiled. 'Sorry,' he whispered, 'but you had to cool.' He rose, walked across to the chariot, put on his sandals, grasped the small gazelle-skin of water and took it round to the horses. He cupped his hand and poured a little in, allowing them to drink, then brushed their muzzles with his wet hand. He lifted the waterskin to his own lips, took a mouthful and returned to squat beneath the shade. He recalled the verdict he'd passed on the Nubian assassins and tried to make sense of the blizzard of events that had swept Thebes, disturbing the harmony of the Great House. He recalled the recent meeting of the Divine Circle: Hatusu, eyes blazing with anger, Senenmut agitated, Valu inquisitive, his black eyes constantly moving. Amerotke always wondered about Valu's loyalty, a man who could be venal and took to politicking as a bird to flying. Khufu, high priest of the Temple of Nubia, Busiris, his lovely wife, and her gorgeous handmaid, the heset Mataia, had also been present, together with

General Omendap and other officials. Hatusu's fury knew no bounds. She'd swept north to deal with one danger, and while she was away, another had emerged. The present threat was ominous. The southern province of Nubia was a source of great riches to Egypt: wood, ivory, ebony and precious stones. More importantly, Nubia controlled the lower regions of the Nile. A rebellion there would cause hideous problems for the Great House. Amerotke recalled what he knew. The people of Lower Nubia were lighter-skinned; those of Upper Nubia dark, almost black. In all they were a powerful collection of clans and tribes whom the pharaohs of Thebes always kept under tight subjugation. Hatusu's father Tuthmosis I had defeated them decisively in battle, besieged and taken their fortresses and accepted Nubia into his love. The Arites, the keepers from the slaughterhouse, had been a different problem. Dedicated to their hyaena goddess, they had withdrawn into their secret fortresses at Bekhna, refusing to accept the flail and rod of Thebes.

Amerotke breathed in, willing himself to relax, as he sifted through the various problems. First, Hatusu had swept north to deal with the Sea People. A victorious campaign, but almost immediately Nubia had risen in rebellion. Not surprising: that rich, powerful province was always ready to test the power of Pharaoh. So what was new? Amerotke wiped his face. The emergence of the murderous Arites was a shock. He blinked. He had no time for such assassins and their bloodthirsty creed. In the past, he and others had counselled that Bekhna be besieged and destroyed, leaving not one stone upon the other: such advice had been ignored, and Hatusu would now pay a heavy price. They had advised that Bekhna was simply a pimple on the skin of Egypt, to be dealt with very quickly, arguing that an attack might provoke further unrest in the province as a whole. Now it would seem the Arites had spent the last twenty years licking their wounds and fostering their influence. The attack on Hatusu in Karnak proved they had infiltrated the Nubian regiment, yet there was more. The Medjay, the skilled scouts of the Egyptian army, the Eyes and Ears of General Omendap, were being gruesomely poisoned in their camp at Farinal or out in the Redlands. No one could say why or how the victims were chosen. They hallucinated and glimpsed dreadful visions before dying horrible deaths. But how were they being poisoned? Water supplies and provisions had been rigorously checked, yet still the murders occurred. Amerotke suspected the deaths were random, to cause as much chaos and consternation as possible; they must be the work of the Arites. The Medjay were an elite corps of the army. If their morale was sapped before the campaign began, what would happen when Omendap marched?

The army had also been deprived of vital information, deepening further the atmosphere of unease, suspicion and distrust. Imperial couriers, using either the Nile or the Sobeck roads through the oases, had disappeared like the morning dew, leaving no trace or sign. Individual envoys, even couriers with armed escorts: none seemed safe. Shortly after the attack on Hatusu, the Pharaoh Queen had dispatched Amerotke south to the Oasis of

Sinjar on the road to the First Cataract, where a number of the vanished couriers had last been seen. Amerotke leaned his head against the tree and stared up at the vultures circling above him. A true mystery! That lonely, haunted oasis with its dark clump of palm trees and tangled wild gorse circling a spring-fed pool. The oasis chaplain, Nebher, who lived in his mud-brick enclave on a bank overlooking the Nile, had been of little help, being more concerned about his own daughter, Isala, who'd also vanished. A strange one, Nebher, with his dusty, care-worn face, lanky frame and scrawny hair. A former priest of the Chapel of Tears at the Temple of Isis, he had been given the benefice of Sinjar to act as a chaplain to those journeying south. Amerotke wafted away an insect. Nebher seemed not only anxious, but deeply frightened. About what? The disappearances? Amerotke had made careful enquiries in the villages to the north and south of the oasis; nobody had seen or heard anything untoward, no sign of violence detected. Asural, captain of Amerotke's guard and his cohort of troops, cunning old veterans, had swept the area. Amerotke eventually accepted their conclusion – nothing! The desert and the river might be wild and endless, but a corpse was difficult to hide. The Nile always gave up its dead, whilst the desert was the feeding ground for a horde of scavengers, yet not a scrap or a sign of any of those who had disappeared had been uncovered. Eventually Amerotke had wandered over to the fortress of Timsah, a range of buildings behind crumbling walls and towers, deserted except for sand-dwellers and desert-wanderers encamped in their shade. He had found nothing unusual. In the end, Amerotke had stayed two full days at Sinjar, camping in a nearby village. He'd established that some of those who had disappeared had definitely visited the oasis. Nebher kept a careful register of the expenses incurred by official visitors, which would be reimbursed by the House of Silver in Thebes. Despite his searches, Amerotke had detected nothing suspicious: the couriers had apparently visited Sinjar, then journeyed on.

Amerotke and his escort had returned swiftly to Thebes to discover that there had been more deaths amongst the Medjay scouts, with no clue as to who or what was poisoning them. At the same time, Lord Valu had the Arites captured at Karnak brutally interrogated. On his return, Amerotke had visited the House of Chains, but Valu, despite the skill of his torturers, had been unable to elicit anything. Amerotke had no choice but to pass sentence of death, then witness punishment being carried out. He took another sip of water. Hatusu's victory in the Delta had certainly been overshadowed by the growing crisis, yet there was worse. Imothep, an old servant of Tuthmosis I, chief of the Spies of Sobeck, who had fought against the Arites in Nubia, had been found strangled in his Mansion of Silence with no clue as to how the assassins had struck. Even more strange were reports of a naked, unidentified corpse discovered in Imothep's garden, also strangled with the damnable red cloth the Arites used. Such mysteries awaited Amerotke's investigation once he returned to Thebes.

The judge had reached one definite conclusion. He

believed that the perpetrator of the present unrest was lurking in Thebes. Somebody was deliberately creating chaos, disturbance and unrest, with brilliant results. Hatusu had been attacked. The Medjay were demoralised. Loyal Nubians had been put under lock and key. Messengers and couriers dispatched south disappeared into thin air. The latter was truly dangerous, a threat to the Divine One's communications with Nubia. Amerotke picked up the waterskin and wetted his face. He stared out across the desert. Faintly on the breeze trailed a thin, piercing scream. He closed his eyes. Where was he to begin? Omendap wanted to hurry south immediately, bring fire and sword to Nubia and burn the fortress at Bekhna, then the disturbance would disappear. Amerotke disagreed. He strongly advised that the army should not march until the crisis in Thebes had been resolved, arguing that whoever had organised the attack on Hatusu was also responsible for the deaths amongst the Medjay and the disappearance of the couriers, not to mention the infiltration of the Nubian regiment. Hatusu had person-ally asked for those Nubians to carry the palanquin; all had records of bravery and loyalty, yet someone, some-where in time, had turned their hearts, waiting for the right opportunity. Amerotke also argued that the Sgeru, the Silent One who directed the Arites, must be in Thebes. Naturally suspicion had fallen on the Temple of Nubia, that dark stone complex of buildings, supposedly a symbol of Nubia's loyalty but now a place deeply distrusted. Yet there again, Lord Khufu, the high priest, had been instru-mental in frustrating the attack on the Divine One.

31

Whoever was responsible, Amerotke reflected grimly, was succeeding beyond their wildest expectations. Hatusu and Senenmut were distracted. The Great House didn't know which way to look. The army was undecided about whether to march or stay. Amerotke heard a sound and glanced up. A chariot was thundering towards him. He sighed, got to his feet and walked out of the shade. The driver reined in, pulling the chariot round, its horses restless to begin the journey back.

'Lord Amerotke.' The officer shaded his eyes against the sun. 'Lord Valu says that all is finished.'

'All dead?' Amerotke asked.

The man shook his head. 'One of the traitors watched the others being impaled; he offered to trade for his life. Lord Valu,' the officer grinned, 'because of your sensibilities, has moved away from the Place of the Skull. He asks you to join him.'

Thankfully Valu, his escort of troops and retinue of torturers had left the execution ground, which was now transformed into a gory shambles almost blanketed by a flurry of bloodstained feathers as a host of vultures and buzzards came floating in to feast. The Eyes and Ears of Pharaoh had withdrawn to a small oasis on a trackway leading down to the main road into Thebes. He had made himself comfortable on a small portable stool of acacia wood, sipping at a jewelled beaker of crushed fruit a servant had poured for him whilst another held a brilliantly hued parasol above his master's head.

'Ah, Amerotke.' Valu plumped the cushion beside him.

The judge walked into the shade and sat down. A

strange sight: Valu drinking delicately, a servant squatting near him. A little further away, the soldiers and other retainers tried to secure whatever shade they could find, while directly opposite Valu squatted one of the Arites, hands tied by his wrists above his head. A black-skinned veteran from Upper Nubia, the prisoner's crimped hair was dusted with grey, his blood-splattered face weather-worn, his naked, wounded body wrinkled with age. He gazed unblinkingly at Amerotke, then stared back at Pharaoh's prosecutor.

'This is?' Valu gestured at the Arites.

'Nema.'

'Nema?' Amerotke waved away Valu's proffered goblet. 'Surely that's the name of your hyaena goddess?'

'We are part of her,' the man replied, 'mere hairs upon her back.'

'But once you were part of Egypt? You nosed the ground in front of Pharaoh!' Amerotke exclaimed. 'You ate her bread and swore loyalty to our gods.'

'A mistake,' the Nubian whispered, wincing in agony.

Amerotke, ignoring Valu's exclamations, drew his dagger, leaned forward and sawed at the Nubian's bonds. The rough cord snapped, and the prisoner sighed with relief, lowered his arms, then rubbed them vigorously. Amerotke shouted for a waterskin. The prisoner was allowed to gulp before Amerotke snatched it away. The judge stretched forward, resting the blade of his dagger against the prisoner's neck.

'You fear impalement?' Amerotke withdrew his dagger. 'You want to live?'

33

'Yes, lord.'

'Why?'

'As you say, I broke faith.' The Arites' reply held a hint of cynical amusement. Amerotke wondered if his repentance was truly genuine or mere pretence. 'I wish to be gone,' the Arites continued. 'I have told my lord,' he nodded at Valu, 'that for some ounces of silver, a waterskin, a dagger and a staff, something to wrap around my body, and a little bread and dried meat, I will speak.'

'That depends,' Valu snapped, 'on the worth of what you say. If you mislead or deceive, you will join your comrades on the stakes! The vultures are just whetting their appetite. This day will end. Dusk will fall. More flesh-eaters will come. I can impale you tonight just before sunset, then withdraw to listen to your screams.'

For a brief moment, a few heartbeats, Amerotke saw the hate blaze in the prisoner's eyes. This man, he thought, was not finished yet, even if he wished to confess.

'Tell me,' Amerotke smiled, 'whatever your true name is, tell me your story.'

The man cleared his throat. He looked hungrily at the waterskin. Amerotke let him take a few gulps.

'I come from a village deep in the south. My father fought alongside Pharaoh's father, so with other young men, I journeyed north as a mercenary. For a while I served in the armies of the Viceroy of Nubia, then I travelled on, working for this lord or that. Eventually I came to Thebes. I made my mark, took the bread and salt, swore the oath, and became a member of the Imperial Nubian regiment.'

'And you were happy?' Amerotke asked.

The prisoner pulled a face. 'At night I'd dream of my village, of a young woman I knew, but, as you know, lord, days pass into weeks, weeks into years. The sun rises, the sun sets. Life imprisons you. Like a man walking in the dark, you put one step in front of the other, not knowing where the road might lead.'

'Did you fight for Pharaoh?' Amerotke asked.

'I did, and when his daughter assumed the crown, I took the oath again.'

'So what changed?' Amerotke asked.

'I faithfully served the House of War,' the prisoner shrugged, 'against the Tejenu and the Sheshu. I went by barge and fought in bloody struggles along the bitter waters near the Great Green as well as out in the Redlands, but like my comrades, I dreamed of Nubia. I witnessed the power of Egypt and the vast hoard of tribute it exacted from my native land. We also learnt about the Arites, legendary warriors who held out in their fortress at Bekhna. At night we told tales from our country and our hearts would grow heavy and sad. We wondered why we ate Egyptian bread and slept under foreign skies.'

'But all soldiers do that,' Amerotke said softly. 'Be they mercenary or Egyptian, they always dream of a home that doesn't exist, of a wench who's grown crinkled with age, of a family they never really wanted. So what changed you?' He offered the waterskin again. The man took it. 'You became an officer?' Amerotke persisted. 'You speak with clear tongue. You are intelligent. Pharaoh must have advanced you, bestowed collars of gold and bracelets of silver.'

'I have had those.' The Nubian lowered the waterskin and thrust it back. 'That's why I was chosen to carry Pharaoh's palanquin when she returned to Thebes.'

'Your story,' Amerotke insisted. 'What changed, and when?'

'It was before the Inundation.' The Nubian squinted at Amerotke. 'The weather was very hot in Thebes. The city stone burnt. We knew Pharaoh was gathering her forces to march north, but we had done our military duty. For most of the time we were allowed to relax in the barracks or wander the city. I'd heard whispers about visitors from Nubia. Men slipped away at night. Meetings were held in hot, airless rooms that fell silent when I walked in. Then I was approached, like the others were.'

'How?' Amerotke asked.

'One of my comrades you have just impaled.' The prisoner laughed bitterly. 'He came to me. He said that at a certain wine shop in the Necropolis, I would meet someone from Nubia with a story to tell me. Of course I was curious, I knew something was happening, so I agreed. I went with him at night, long after the lights had been doused and the curfew imposed. Which wine shop, my lord? To tell the truth, I can't remember where the place was. I was taken down worm-thin trackways and streets, up and round, deliberately confused, then I was pushed under an awning and through a doorway. The room was dark and nasty-smelling. One solitary lamp burned. At the far end a figure waited.'

'Man or woman?' Amerotke asked.

'Man,' the Nubian replied. 'He knew my name and called me forward. I knelt, my companion behind me. I realised my comrade had drawn his dagger.' He smiled. 'I would either have to accept what was offered that night or die.'

'Some did refuse,' Valu interrupted. 'Not all of your comrades would betray Pharaoh.'

'True, true.' The Nubian shrugged. 'We are men of our word. Such comrades just disappeared. Our superiors thought they'd deserted or been slain in some knife brawl. No questions were ever asked. A story was always fabricated. Nobody became curious.'

'But many of you accepted what that stranger offered?' Amerotke demanded. 'Which was what?'

'Oh, at first just a story,' the Arites replied wearily, 'a story I'd heard so many times before. The beauty of Nubia, the nobility of its people, the way it had been oppressed and plundered by Egypt. How Nubians yearned to be free. I listened and nodded in agreement, for what he said was true, common talk around Nubia's campfires. I asked what it had to do with me. I was Pharaoh's slave. I served in the garrison of Thebes. What was he offering? The man then introduced himself as the envoy of the Sgeru.'

'The Silent One?' Amerotke asked urgently. 'Who is he?'

'Our leader,' the man replied. 'The living incarnation of Nema. He preaches her faith, he accepts the oaths of those devoted to her. The stranger claimed he had travelled from Nubia to meet me, then he talked about my family.'

'Ah,' Amerotke interrupted,' of course. He would offer a dream with one hand and a threat with the other. You have relatives, kin?'

'Of course,' the Nubian replied. 'I am a tribesman. My village is well known, as are those related to me.'

'And Nema?' Amerotke asked. 'I know something of your goddess.'

'She is both destroyer and creator,' the Nubian replied flatly. 'She pervades all things and sees all things: that is what the Sgeru proclaims. My allegiance should be to her, not to Pharaoh. If I became her devoted follower, so I was promised, I would realise true happiness both in this life and in the next. I would journey back in glory to Nubia. I would be hailed as a hero. When I died, there would be no need for the priests of Osiris or for those who wear the dog mask; my corpse would be left for the vultures, my soul enraptured in Nema's embrace.'

'And you believed that?' Amerotke asked.

'As much, my lord, as you believe that when you die, your ka travels into the Eternal West. Why shouldn't I? The cult of Nema is popular in Nubia; many practise it secretly.'

'But there is more to it than that, isn't there?' Valu interjected. 'You have to make sacrifice to Nema?'

'Yes, the Sgeru's spokesman declared that a victim would be chosen for me. I would use the sacred red cloth to send that victim as a holocaust to our goddess.'

'But you weren't told who?' Amerotke asked.

'Of course not! Such information would be given to me later, once I'd accepted.'

'And did you accept?'

'What do you think?' The Nubian smiled cynically. 'I was alone in a darkened room away from my other comrades, a man stood nearby ready to kill me at a given sign. I have kin back in Nubia; they were threatened, whilst the envoy talked of dreams I also shared.'

'Then what?'

'He asked me to take the oath. Was I prepared? I said I was. I was given a goblet of wine, the finest I've ever tasted. I was told to drink it quickly and I did. There must have been some potion in it, because I felt as if I was floating. The sensation wasn't painful, but deeply sensuous, like when you lie with a young, vigorous woman. I lost consciousness. When I awoke, I was back in that dirty street, my comrade grinning down at me.'

Amerotke leaned forward. He was no longer aware of the murmur and chatter of the escort, the dust and the wind or the gory sights he'd witnessed. He studied his prisoner carefully, wondering if he was telling the truth: his answers had a logic all of their own, but why was he confessing now?

'So you became one of the Arites?' Amerotke asked. 'A member of that secret sect. How could you tell those who were fellow members from those who were not?'

'We had codes and signs, symbols we would sketch in the dust or in wine spilt on a table. We were organised into units of ten. I became the leader of mine.'

'But you never made the blood sacrifice?' Amerotke asked. 'The strangling of another?'

'Didn't I?' The prisoner smiled. 'Oh yes, I did. There were those comrades who perhaps could not be trusted. Those who took the oath, then became reluctant, as well as those who, regrettably, grew too curious. We were vigilant for spies and traitors. Life is cheap. Bodies can be bought and sold. Some of us made the blood sacrifice; others were told to wait for their orders. Of one thing we were assured: what we did was for the glory of Nubia, and one day we would topple Pharaoh's power. We were to wait for a sign.'

'What sign?' Amerotke asked.

'We were told that we would recognise it when it came. In the meantime, I lived my new life.' The prisoner braced himself. 'It was as if the years had fallen away. I was no longer part of Egypt, but Nubia. My allegiance was to Nema, not to Pharaoh. I had already distinguished myself in battle. Four times I've taken an enemy's head. I was told to organise the bearers for Pharaoh's palanquin. The rest was so easy. We would have succeeded if it had not been for Khufu.' The prisoner spat the name out.

'You despise him?' Amerotke asked. 'The high priest of the Temple of Nubia?'

'A traitor, Pharaoh's lapdog, her creature. He noses the ground before her. What does he know of Nema, of the true religion of Nubia, of the people he betrayed? Oh, he may parade around his temple like a pharaoh in his court, but Khufu has been judged a traitor. He and his bitch of a wife, Busiris, may be Nubians by birth, yet through treachery they are more Egyptian than any Egyptian.' The prisoner turned away, hawked and spat.

'Are Khufu and Busiris listed for sacrifice?' Valu asked.

'They are traitors and heretics; they worship Egypt's gods, eat Pharaoh's bread and drink her wine. They are flunkeys at her court! Like the rest of her priests, tame dogs! Above all,' the Nubian's voice turned to a snarl, 'they do not have pure blood!'

'Pure blood!'

'Ask him!' The Arites gestured at Lord Valu.

'My lord?' Amerotke turned to Pharaoh's Eyes and Ears.

The prosecutor just sat chewing the corner of his mouth, staring at the Arites.

'Tell him!' the prisoner declared. 'Tell him what you asked us.'

'During the interrogation,' Valu replied slowly, 'I put forward as a hypothesis that the Sgeru could be someone in the hierarchy at the Temple of Nubia.'

'You mean Lord Khufu or his wife?'

'It is a possibility,' Valu replied. 'It has been known for those in power to plot secretly against Pharaoh. After all, treason remains hidden, and if it succeeds, it's no longer treason, is it?'

'And what was your reply?' Amerotke turned back to the prisoner.

'Oh, I'll tell you that,' Valu intervened quickly. 'Apparently the Sgeru is of the pure royal blood of Nubia, an aristocrat. It is forbidden for anyone of mixed blood, what they term half-caste, to be admitted into the circle of the Arites. Lord Khufu and his wife Busiris are of mixed parentage. Their fathers were Egyptian soldiers, their mothers Nubian. You may recall,' Valu continued drily, 'how Lord Khufu and his wife were sent as envoys immediately after the revolt broke out in Nubia. They were rejected as half-breeds, underlings, unworthy to meet Nubia's chieftains. No, no, my lord Amerotke,' Valu rocked himself gently backwards and forwards, 'according to this man and others, the Sgeru must be not only of pure blood but of royal lineage. Is that not so?'

The prisoner, eyes half closed, nodded.

'So who could the Sgeru be?' Amerotke persisted.

The prisoner shrugged. 'An officer,' he replied, 'a priest, a beggar on the street . . .'

'And the attack on Pharaoh,' Amerotke continued remorselessly, 'how did the Sgeru organise that?'

The prisoner wetted his lips and stared up at the branches of the tree. 'It was well known in Thebes,' he replied slowly, 'that the Divine Bitch—'

Amerotke raised his hand to stave off Valu's objection to the insult.

'Pharaoh,' the Arites smirked, 'wished to show confidence in the Nubian regiment. We were chosen to bear her palanquin. Once that happened,' he shrugged, 'it was easy. At the dead of night I was summoned to a meeting and given strict instructions. We agreed that once we entered the temple, the heart of their godhead at Karnak, we would carry out sacrifice, send Pharaoh into the West, a blood offering to Nema.'

'But you must have known that others would be vigilant?'

'Have you ever seen a cobra strike, a snake, a viper?' The prisoner half laughed. 'That's how swift we were.'

'But not on that day,' Amerotke insisted. 'You fumbled, you made a mistake.'

The man nodded. 'The Arites we sent forward to strangle the Pharaoh was killed immediately. He made a mistake; he delayed slightly. That was fatal, for Khufu the lapdog was swifter.'

'And why strangulation?' Amerotke asked. 'Why do the Arites believe that their victims have to be strangled with a red cloth?'

'The red cloth is a symbol of blood. When we strangle someone we trap both the soul, the ka, and the spirit in the body and offer it as a complete sacrifice to our goddess, mind, body and soul.' The prisoner leaned forward, wagging a bony finger. 'My lord judge, you should be careful, as should you, my lord Valu: your work in the House of Chains has not gone unnoticed. You'd make suitable victims for our goddess, an offering, a libation to those you executed this morning.'

'And how many Arites are there amongst the regiment?' Amerotke asked, refusing to be cowed.

The Nubian spread his hands. 'How many grains of sand in a cup? We were organised into units of ten. What each unit knew was kept to a strict minimum. I met my superiors, strangers in the darkest night. We continued to act as if . . .' He paused.

'You were the loyal servants of Pharaoh?' Valu snapped.

'But really you were traitors. Perhaps I should still impale you?'

'You gave me your word, Lord Valu: food, silver, a knife, staff and clothes. I will be gone.'

'But where will you go?' Amerotke asked. 'You cannot return to your own people.'

'I can wander the face of the earth,' the Nubian replied, 'assume a new name and disappear.'

'So why are you confessing?' Amerotke asked. 'You have lost everything: your people, your tribe, your dream, your Nema. Surely her vengeance will pursue you?'

'I am a soldier.' The Nubian stretched, easing the cramp in his neck and shoulders. 'I am first a soldier. This morning I did not wish to be impaled. Perhaps tonight I might regret that, but now I seek life. You, Lord Valu, gave me your word!'

'Tell me.' Amerotke rubbed his hands; he felt hungry and thirsty. He also believed this man was a liar, but he wished to play the game to the end. 'This Sgeru, what do you think he is like?'

The prisoner pulled a face, blinked and looked away.

You are lying, Amerotke thought. You are deliberately leading us along false paths, but to what end?

'My lord judge asked a question,' Valu snapped.

'I don't know,' the prisoner replied, 'but he must be a man of power, of true words, of great physical and spiritual strength.'

'And the future?'

'The future?' The prisoner laughed softly to himself. 'What future, my lord judge? You face rebellion in Nubia.

The Arites are loose in Thebes; they almost killed your Pharaoh. The future is in the hands of Nema. She will decide.'

Amerotke clambered to his feet, snapping his fingers as he called for the guards.

'You promised me my life,' the Nubian warned.

'And life you shall have.' Amerotke smiled down at him. 'But not just yet. You will be taken back to Thebes, to the House of Chains; there'll be other questions for you. Is that not so, Lord Valu?'

The prosecutor nodded.

Amerotke noticed the nervous look in Valu's eyes and wondered if the prisoner had frightened him. He walked from under the shade of the tree, then came back.

'Did you know the old soldier Imothep; formerly chief scout in the Spies of Sobeck? I received reports before I left Thebes that he was also visited by the Arites. They strangled him in his Mansion of Silence at the House of the Forest.'

'I know of Imothep,' the man replied, 'and his household retainers.'

'And?' Amerotke asked.

'They are collaborators, apostates; such renegades will be swept away on our day of great vengeance.'

Amerotke crouched down and stared at the prisoner. You are lying, he thought. Everything you have told us has been rehearsed, prepared, except for that question about Imothep: you didn't know what to say; you didn't expect it.

'My lord Amerotke?'

The judge glanced up and joined Valu out of hearing of the prisoner.

'It's time we returned to the city,' Valu hissed, hands on hips. He was staring crossly at Amerotke. 'We have our confession; I'll append it to my report for the Divine One's eyes. I will send a copy to you.'

'And where shall we take our prisoner?'

Valu smiled thinly. 'You!' He beckoned at one of his escort. 'Go into the city, find my Lord Khufu at the Temple of Nubia. Tell him I am bringing an Arites for him to question in the House of Chains. Leave now.'

The man raised a hand in salute and raced off down the dusty trackway.

'Why the Temple of Nubia?' Amerotke asked.

'Lord Khufu must listen to our prisoner. Khufu is the high priest, a physician, a Nubian. He is skilled in the history and customs of his country. So come,' Valu walked over and kicked the prisoner's leg, 'let us return to Thebes.'

'You promised!' The man glared back.

'I said I would free you.' Valu grinned. 'I never mentioned when and where. Come on!' He clapped his hands. 'It is time we were gone.'

CHAPTER 2

Nek: murder

A horn sounded. The cortege formed up, the escort taking the lead. Valu joined Amerotke in his chariot whilst his cohort of torturers, the prisoner manacled between them, brought up the rear. They went down on to the highway leading to the soaring pylons of the double Sphinx Gate. Valu's herald, armed with a conch horn, and another retainer carrying a blue and gold pennant proclaiming the Djed hieroglyph for 'Domination' went ahead to clear the way. The escort pushed to either side the donkeys, litters and two-wheeled carts, as well as the horde of peasants, farmers and fishermen, bowing under their baskets and slats brimming with produce of every kind. Even an execution party of Medjay, dragging a condemned grave-robber wrapped in a sheepskin on a hurdle through the dust, paused. They kicked the bloodstained, dusty covering with their calloused feet to silence the groans and moans of their

47

prisoner. A travelling troupe of players, their masks and props piled high on a sledge, were too drunk to move quickly and were driven off the road under a hail of blows from the sticks and cudgels of Valu's escort. Amerotke noticed how the usual clamour and bustle of such crowds abruptly subsided at their approach. Nothing sullen or threatening; the mood was more watchful as people glimpsed the manacles on the naked, bruised Arites. It was the same when they entered the city gates to a clash of cymbals and braying of horns. They passed on to the great Sphinx Road, darkened by the shadows of a long row of soaring black sphinxes carved out of basalt, which gleamed in the sunlight. People from the city and beyond thronged noisily about, pushing their way down to the various markets that housed the principal trades: the carpenters, coppersmiths, perfumers, weavers, linen-makers and silver- and goldsmiths. These all paused to watch Amerotke's party, as did the unlicensed enterprising traders from the City of the Dead. The latter had crossed the Nile from the Necropolis with their trays and baskets full of models of funerary caskets, coffers, shabtis, tomb furniture, canopic jars, amulets and even examples of wall paintings and frescoes for those wishing to purchase a sepulchre in preparation for their final journey across the Far Horizon. They stopped to gape at the procession, then grabbed their baskets and hastily withdrew. Even swifter were the scorpion and lizard men who threaded the crowds looking for easy pickings amongst the bemused and unwary. Amerotke glimpsed a few faces he recognised from his own court. Such villains and illegal hawkers were usually careful not to let their curiosity get the better of them. Nevertheless, the predators were out in force, hunting in packs, especially as the Nubian police had been withdrawn to their barracks.

The noisy din around the market stalls further down the thoroughfare subsided as Amerotke's retinue passed. Now and again there was the occasional yell or catcall, but then it was back to business as usual. A group of young women in flamboyant robes, their necks, wrists, arms and fingers all shimmering as the light caught the beautiful brooches, collars, pectorals, ear-studs and finger rings, had paused by a fortune-teller's booth. A young man, his face painted green, and dressed in a multicoloured cloak, offered to tell their fortunes by throwing the bones. A ballad-seller tried to entice these customers away with a rendition of his love poems, only to be greeted with a litany of curses. Further along, a group of roisterers fresh from some party and as inebriated, as one of them shouted, as 'Hathor the goddess of drunkenness', were baiting a man with a string of pet monkeys, which could, for a gift, perform the most amusing antics. Priests in white robes and leopard-skin shawls pushed arrogantly by. Mercenaries and strangers from across the Great Green, conspicuous by their light-coloured hair and strange eyes, moved uncertainly through the crowds.

Further along, at the corner of the Sphinx Road, a dromedary had sat down. A group of sand-dwellers, heads and faces almost masked by twisted white cloths, were remonstrating noisily with an itinerant food-trader who refused to move his cart full of platters offering a range of foods. Despite the foul odours and the swirl of other smells, Amerotke caught the tang of bean salad with its distinctive lemon flavour, as well as that of stuffed cabbage leaf soaked in garlic. He reined in and smiled. Such kitchen smells made him think of home. He wondered idly what Norfret would serve for dinner that evening, and absent-mindedly watched the soldiers approach the noisy squabble. He glanced around at the crowd, then back at the line of torturers now stepping out of line to see what was going on. Valu got down from the chariot to summon one of his officers. Amerotke caught a disturbance in the crowd to his right. He glanced quickly towards it. Sand-dwellers, hooded and masked, were forcing their way through. Amerotke's throat went dry. This was no accident!

'Valu!' he yelled. He threw aside the reins and jumped down, even as two of the sand-dwellers broke through, darting like hunting dogs towards Pharaoh's prosecutor, red cloths whirling in their hands. Amerotke drew his dagger and hurled it at the leading one; a lucky throw, it struck the attacker deep in the throat. He staggered back, then collapsed, blocking his companion, who stumbled and made to rise, only to be cut down by Valu's officer. A third assassin now sprang out of the milling crowd even as the rest of the escort were attacked by more sand-dwellers desperate to break through. Valu, recovered from his surprise, met his assailant by lunging forward and ripping the man's belly with his knife. Abruptly the ambush faded. The crowd had fled, and those Arites not cut down simply melted away. Amerotke, chest heaving, face laced with sweat, climbed back into the chariot, then whirled around at a raucous bark of laughter from the Nubian prisoner.

Valu wiped his dagger on the fallen man, rose, pushed

his way through and punched the prisoner with the pommel of his knife, squashing the Arites' nose to a bloody pulp. He then moved amongst the fallen Arites. Three had been killed outright; two were bubbling blood. Valu quickly cut their throats and stormed towards the corner, but those who'd caused the blockade had vanished, though not before strangling the itinerant food-trader. He lay sprawled amongst his platters of aubergines and sesame cakes, a red cloth tied tightly around his throat. He was a gruesome sight: popping eyes, tongue thrusting out, his face mottled an eerie bluish-red. Valu glared around as if the Arites still lurked close by.

'Come, my lord,' Amerotke called.

Valu reluctantly rejoined him. The soldiers now ringed their chariot, the Tedjen loudly insisting that until they reached the Temple of Nubia, the escort would stay close. Amerotke did not demur. He got down, moved to the nearest corpse, crouched and pulled away the head cloth to reveal the Nubian face beneath.

'Very serious.' He glanced up at Valu. The prosecutor was still seething with rage. 'These attackers are undoubtedly from the Nubian regiment,' Amerotke murmured. 'Soldiers who once swore allegiance to the Divine One. I wonder why they attacked?'

'To kill our prisoner.'

'Perhaps.' Amerotke rose and touched Valu gently on the side of his face. 'Or something worse. An audacious assault in the City of the Sceptre, the residence of the Pharaoh God, on the Divine One's chief judge and prosecutor, who were to be brutally and publicly sacrificed to their hyaena goddess.' He glanced back at the prisoner, now nursing his injured face. 'They never killed or rescued him,' he murmured.

'They were beaten off!' Valu scoffed. 'Now it is time we were gone.'

The cortege moved swiftly through the city. Amerotke now had no time for the sights and sounds, the swirl of conflicting odours and smells; everything was just a blur of colour, an indistinct hum of noise. How, he wondered, had the Arites known they were bringing a prisoner back into the city? He smiled thinly. They couldn't have, until Amerotke and Valu left the Place of the Skull. The judge was certain the object of their attack was Valu and himself, as well as an insulting snub to Pharaoh. Yet the Arites hadn't sent their warning scarab, that small piece of blackened stone with a crude white drawing of a prowling hyaena. Amerotke abruptly startled, pulling so quickly at the reins that Valu lost his balance and clutched at the sides of the chariot.

'My lord judge?'

'The scarab!' Amerotke declared. 'The Arites never sent their warning, yet they always do. Not to us personally,' he added bitterly. 'I am sure it went to our houses, threatening us and our families.'

Valu immediately shouted for his officer, who came hastening over.

'Take six men,' Valu barked, 'three to Lord Amerotke's house and three to mine, and ensure all is well. Ask if a letter or gift, anything unexpected, has been delivered.

52

The men are to stay there until our return.' The officer saluted and hurried off.

Valu took the hem of his robe and vigorously mopped his sweaty face.

'My poor daughter,' he whispered. 'If those hyaenas have threatened her . . .'

Amerotke clicked his tongue and snapped the reins. Valu was deeply agitated about the one and only person he cared for. The prosecutor spent any time away from his official duties with his beloved daughter, whom he called 'the true heart of my heart'. Amerotke remained calm. Norfret was of sharp mind and keen wits, while Shufoy, despite his current dabbling in magic and prophecies, would be alert to any danger. Nonetheless, Valu's litany of curses deepened Amerotke's unease as they broke free from the frenetic bustle of the coffer-makers' quarter on to the approaches to the Temple of Nubia. The complex was ringed by a lofty curtain wall; soaring pylons, surmounted by flagpoles, flanked either side of the great gateway, which was now closely guarded by units of the Royal Isis regiment. They passed by these into the spacious temple grounds and buildings surrounding the central chapel dedicated to Amun-Ra of Thebes. Amerotke had visited the place before, and whereas other temples were, in the main, a forest of white, gold and pinkish stone, the Temple of Nubia enjoyed a unique appearance. Many of its buildings were of darkish hue, a stark contrast to what Amerotke called 'the other places of light'. Nevertheless, like other temples, that of Nubia was a small city in itself, with lush gardens, shaded walks and open courtyards where statues and obelisks gleamed in the sun. The grounds were fed by specially dug canals brimming with sparkling Nile water; these refreshed the rich black soil, specially imported from Canaan, the source of the brilliant flowers, green lawns, herbs, plants and lush orchards of various fruit. It was a busy place, with its House of Life, chapels, House of Myrrh, offices, garden pavilions, bakehouses and breweries, stables and granaries, storerooms and smithies. Priests chattered to pilgrims visiting the shrines. Traders laid out their goods, whilst Chaplains of the Ear squatted in shady porticoes waiting for those who wished to purge their souls of any offence against the gods. The harmony was broken only by the lowing of animals and the screeching of birds being herded in for the evening sacrifice. This cacophony almost drowned the chanting of choirs rehearsing their hymns and the rattle of sistra as hesets practised their sacred dances. Odours trailed from the stables and fleshing houses to mingle with the pungent smoke of sacrifice as well as the sweetness of oil, perfume and fragrant incense. Amerotke sensed no fear or apprehension here. Hatusu herself had reassured the Temple of Nubia of her love, whilst High Priest Khufu had solemnly informed the Divine One of the undying loyalty of his temple, despite what was happening further south.

In the Sycamore Courtyard, the arrival place for important visitors, grooms, acolytes and servants clustered round to unharness their horses. Beautiful heset girls, their thick, oil-drenched wigs festooned with flowers, skimpy kirtles around their waists, gauze veils draping their full breasts, glided forward in a clink of bangles and bracelets with bowls of perfumed water for them to wash their hands and faces. Other hesets offered beakers of the most delicious crushed-fruit drinks. Amerotke and Valu refreshed themselves. Mataia, the principal heset, stood apart, tall, elegant and strikingly beautiful. A full oil-rich wig framed a face as black as ebony, large lustrous eyes, perfectly formed features, her full lips parted in the most welcoming smile. She was dressed in a pleated linen robe, silver-chased sandals on her feet. She wore little jewellery except for delicate gold bracelets and a necklace of the purest carnelian. Mother-of-pearl drops hung on silver chains from her earlobes, and when she walked gracefully forward, her robes exuded the delicious fragrance of the blue lotus. She stopped in front of them, joined her hands and bowed.

'My lords, I welcome you in the name of High Priest Khufu and Lady Busiris. They await you in the Chamber of Audience; they have visitors here with urgent cause. You have heard of the hideous death of Imothep, former chief scout?'

'We have a prisoner,' Valu interrupted rudely, gesturing at the now crouching Arites, a piece of coarse sacking thrown about him. 'He must be confined in the House of Chains.'

'And I have a visitor for you, my lord Amerotke.' Mataia tactfully ignored Valu's open insult and beckoned to one of the servants, who hurried across the courtyard and in through a shadowy doorway. When he re-emerged, Shufoy, Amerotke's diminutive manservant and friend, was trotting beside him. The little man hurried across clutching a small black casket, a golden hyaena with fiery red eyes painted on its concave lid.

'Shufoy!' Amerotke knelt down and clasped the little

man's shoulders. Shufoy, his grey hair parted down the middle, stared sadly at his master, his shrewd eyes all concerned, a look so dramatic it almost diverted attention from the hideous wound where his nose had once been.

'Master, I heard from the herald that you were coming here.'

'Is everything well?' Amerotke took the small casket from Shufoy's hands.

'Lady Norfret and the boys are well.' Shufoy smiled. 'But this arrived. I have not broken the seal. I heard about the executions, the attack on you. I should have been—'

'No, you should not.' Amerotke snapped the seal and took out the scarab curse, the polished black stone inscribed with the white-lined drawing of a hunting hyaena, its huge head and gaping jaws making it look even more fearsome. On the small scrap of papyrus beside it, the ominous warning clearly proclaimed: 'The Nema hunts.' Amerotke handed this to Valu, whose fat face paled. The prosecutor simply shook his head, more distracted by the threat that must have been delivered to his own mansion.

'Lady Mataia.' Amerotke took the warning and handed it to the heset. 'Do you know what this means?'

She breathed out noisily and gave it back, all good humour drained from her face. She glanced fearfully at the Arites prisoner, then at Shufoy, who gazed adoringly back.

'My lord Khufu waits,' she stammered. 'Your prisoner, we received your message, the House of Chains is ready.'

She led them out of the Sycamore Courtyard. They walked quickly. Shufoy, jumping like a Danga dwarf beside Amerotke, spluttered out breathless questions, which

Amerotke just ignored. Valu was muttering to himself, now and again looking back at the prisoner ringed by his torturers. Mataia seemed distracted. She apologised for the walk, offering to call the keeper of the House of Chains, but Valu insisted they lodge their prisoner personally. Mataia led them on through walled gardens with trees of every kind surrounding pools and lakes; nearby stood sun pavilions for those who wished to enjoy their shady coolness. They crossed courtyards with elaborately sculpted fountains decorated with gorgeous flower arrangements, then into a darker, more neglected area, where the temple prison, the House of Chains, built of black basalt, stood in its own walled courtyard. The smelly guardroom was merely the entrance chamber to steps stretching down to a narrow, ill-lit passageway with small dungeons leading off. Each of the cells was sealed by double doors with a small grille high in the wood, kept fast by heavy beams placed in clasps in the middle and at the bottom. It was an evil, foulsome place, too narrow to accommodate them all. Amerotke and Valu stood with Mataia and Shufoy as the burly Nubian keeper took the prisoner and pushed him roughly down towards the last cell, its doors already flung open.

'Wait!' Valu stepped forward. He beckoned Amerotke to follow him, and they both went into the cell. Valu called for light, and a pitch torch was handed in. The flickering flame illuminated what was nothing more than a filthy box of sheer stone with a rock-hard floor. The heat was cloying, the smell of decay and rottenness almost unbearable. Valu kicked the dung jar with his foot. He picked up the cracked water bowl, sniffed it, then put it back on the ledge.

'Bring him in!'

The prisoner was pushed in and sent sprawling to the floor in a clink of chains. Valu kicked him viciously in the ribs, then left, plucking at Amerotke's sleeve for him to follow. The keeper remained, as he said, to settle the prisoner, then he too came out into the passageway. The cell doors were slammed shut and the bars lowered. Valu ordered his own soldiers to stand guard, then he and Amerotke followed Mataia back out into the sunlight, choosing to ignore the mournful chant of the prisoner locked in the darkness. Mataia led them back along narrow paths, apologising breathlessly for the delay. A maze of needle-thin alleys and stark corridors abruptly gave way to halls and porticoes filled with light. Doors plated with gold and silver, their lintels flashing with malachite and lapis lazuli, opened up to elegant chambers, their light-painted walls displaying glorious frescoes of eye-catching images. The floors they crossed boasted mosaics of shimmering colours, gorgeous scenes of birds, golden wings spread, swooping over meadows rich with lotuses of every colour. They passed through an enclosed garden into the private quarters of Lord Khufu, an elegant antechamber with pastel-coloured walls, stamped tiled floor and painted roof beams of palm and acacia wood. Pots of smoking perfume placed next to baskets of brilliantly coloured plants and gorgeous flower bouquets fragranced the air. Guards waved them through, and they were halfway across when Amerotke heard his name called. Four people left the stone seat along the far wall and hurried towards him.

'My lord.' The rather plump, overdressed leader paused.

'My lord Amerotke, I heard you were coming. My name is Parmen, steward to Lord Imothep, who was so recently foully murdered.'

'Ah, yes.' Amerotke smiled. 'I am to visit you later today. I—'

'My lord, we have brought our master's corpse here. We seek an audience with Lord Khufu.'

'Impossible,' Mataia intervened. 'As you can see, High Priest Khufu must first speak to Lord Amerotke. Your business will have to wait.'

Parmen stepped back, swallowed hard and spread his hands. Amerotke felt sorry for this large, pompous man, his shaven head and chubby cheeks stained with the dust of mourning, which trickled down on to his rent robes. Parmen's companions seemed similarly distressed. Neferen, his daughter, was a petite woman, her pretty face unadorned with any paint and devoid of all jewellery. Behind her was Rahmel, the bodyguard, a burly veteran of athletic build with a crinkly face and greying hair. Finally Sihera, also garbed in mourning, was an old woman with a youthful face; light-skinned and clear-eyed, she wore no wig but allowed the tresses of her grey hair to fall uncombed to her shoulders. Amerotke courteously introduced himself, ignoring Valu's whispers that they should move on.

'Stay here if you wish,' Mataia touched Parmen on the wrist, 'but my master is very busy.'

Parmen and his party withdrew. Mataia led Amerotke and Valu into the opulent audience chamber, a small hall of columns, the latter painted a refreshing green, their gold capitals carved in the shape of lily buds. The columns ringed a pool of purity; beyond these a small ramp with steps on either side led up to the dining area, where Khufu and Busiris were waiting for them. Amerotke and Valu sat down on blue and gold cushions around polished cedar tables. Introductions were made, hands washed in bowls of rosewater before being anointed with small drops of perfume. Amerotke used the occasion to study his hosts. Khufu was lean and aristocratic, a hooked nose over thin lips, sallow-skinned, with sloe-shaped black eyes. At first glance a hard, cold-hearted man, yet he had a dry sense of humour, gently teasing both Amerotke and Valu about what he called their 'miraculous escape'. Busiris was soft and pretty; her laughing eyes and snub nose gave the impression of a woman who'd drunk deep of the cup of life. Amerotke was touched by how both the high priest and his wife fussed little Shufoy; most priests treated the dwarf as some abomination from the House of Fire. Mataia also showed him favour, and every time she glanced at Shufoy, the little man would look away and blush.

The servants served platters of fowl in pomegranate, strips of lamb cooked in coriander and rosemary and goblets of delicious white wine. Valu, between hurried mouthfuls of food, stridently condemned the recent treacherous attack on them in the city. If Amerotke had not tactfully intervened, the prosecutor would have launched into the most vitriolic diatribe on Nubia and all its inhabitants. Valu quickly realised where he was, and to whom he was speaking, and his voice trailed away. Khufu sipped at his goblet, staring inquisitively over its rim at Amerotke. The judge winked back, a swift, silent apology for Valu's ill-mannered vociferousness. The high priest nodded understandingly. He put down the goblet and snapped his fingers. Once the servants had withdrawn, he leaned forward.

'My lord, the loyalty of all Nubians is now suspect. We understand that. On behalf of this temple I have sworn the most solemn oaths to the Divine One that our allegiance to the Great House is unswerving. However, I cannot confirm the allegiance of everyone in this temple, nor can I guarantee the loyalty of the Nubian regiment. This is a matter for you, my lords, to bring to an end.'

'Then let's start at the beginning,' Amerotke declared. 'The attack on Pharaoh. You were there. You killed the traitor who tried to assault her. You acted more swiftly than any of the guards.'

'My lord Amerotke, go to the House of Books, the royal archives; you will find letters from me and my lady wife warning the Divine One's ministers, members of the royal circle, that the Nubian regiment should not be allowed near even the Divine One's shadow. True, I understand why she was insistent.' Khufu paused, choosing his words carefully. 'Pharaoh wished to show her confidence in Nubian troops, hence they selected men whose loyalty to Pharaoh had been proved in Thebes and on the battlefield.'

'Yet you acted more swiftly,' Valu repeated Amerotke's question, 'than any of the Divine One's bodyguard?'

'Because my suspicions about the Nubian regiment were still vigorous, doubt gnawed at my heart. I watched the palanquin leave the robing room, and the bearer collapsed. I've never heard of that, a young warrior, fit and able, fainting? Then the assassin moved. Think, my lords: the attack on you this morning? I am sure you became suspicious before the first Arites appeared.'

Amerotke ruefully agreed.

'So it was in the temple courtyard,' Khufu continued drily. 'Bearers are supposed to keep their position, not dart forward. Once that happened, I snatched a spear and killed Pharaoh's assailant.' He laughed and spread his hands. 'If I had not, I'd now be under suspicion myself. I saved Pharaoh's life: am I still to be depicted as an accomplice? Either way . . .' Khufu pulled a face.

Amerotke clapped his hands softly. 'My lord Khufu,' he declared, 'your allegiance is not in question.'

'So why have you brought your prisoner here?'

'Because we want you to listen very carefully to what he told us,' Valu snapped, 'then question him.'

'So tell me.' Khufu raised his goblet.

Amerotke looked at the royal prosecutor. Valu stuffed more food into his mouth, shrugged and returned to his platter. Amerotke took a sip of wine, then, in clear, precise sentences, described the Nubian's confession. Khufu listened, head slightly turned as if his hearing was impaired. Busiris and Mataia sat fascinated. Once Amerotke had finished, the high priest glanced at his wife, then shook his head.

'The greatest lie,' he said, 'is often the truth slightly twisted. Your prisoner has certainly not told you the truth. Let me explain. Most Nubians come to Thebes to fight for the Divine One. They are good soldiers, loyal and trustworthy. The Arites are a notable exception: they can, and do, exert great influence. I've heard about the debates in the royal circle, my lord Amerotke. The Arites' fortress at Bekhna should have been destroyed, its ground polluted.' He paused, breathing in deeply through his nose. 'Let me be succinct. First, most Nubians are loyal subjects of the Divine House, but once they convert, become members of the Arites, they take the blood oath and there is no going back.'

'Blood oath?' Valu barked, spitting food.

'Every neophyte, convert to the cult of Nema,' Khufu replied, 'must strangle three victims. That is the blood oath. Your prisoner was correct. They believe that the most perfect sacrifice is a person slaughtered by strangulation, so that the ka, the very essence of the victim, is offered whole to their hyaena goddess.'

'But such deaths would become commonly known,' Valu declared. 'I'd understand if the occasional mercenary disappeared, but wholesale slaughter by strangulation?'

'You are not saying that, are you?' Amerotke asked. 'It doesn't really matter whom they kill.' He turned to the prosecutor. 'Think, my lord, of the Necropolis, the slums of Thebes. Who would miss a beggar, a cripple, an orphan, an old man or woman living by themself? It doesn't really matter, does it, Lord Khufu? They just choose their victims at random and strangle them.'

The high priest nodded. 'You are correct. Life in Thebes is very, very cheap, and to the Arites, even cheaper still. Second,' he held up a hand, 'no Arites ever breaks or betrays his sworn faith.'

'So our prisoner is lying,' Valu hissed. 'I'll torture him. I'll get the full truth.'

'I don't know why he is lying,' Khufu replied. 'You'll not torture him, Lord Valu, not here in our House of Chains.'

'And the Sgeru?' Amerotke asked quickly.

'It could be anyone,' Khufu replied. 'The Silent One must be of the ancient royal line and be full-blooded Nubian. Lady Busiris and I are not; we have mixed blood, and despite the colour of her skin, so has Mataia. More importantly, none of us, as you know, Lord Valu, and I am sure you've checked the records, comes from the aristocratic line of Nubia. Our mothers were Nubian but our fathers were Egyptian soldiers, whilst Mataia is of village stock, presented as a gift by her father, who could not afford her upkeep. Lady Busiris took her into our retinue and we have treated her as our daughter.'

'And this Sgeru?' Valu insisted.

Khufu gestured at Mataia to explain. Valu sniffed in disdain.

'I am literate, my lord.' Mataia smiled at the judge.

Amerotke nodded understandingly: as chief heset of a principal temple, Mataia could be as learned as any priest physician.

'I have studied the kingdom of Nubia, its folklore, customs and traditions,' the heset continued. 'The Sgeru, the Silent One, is always secretive. He or she is of the ancient royal blood of Nubia. Whoever is Sgeru wields total power.'

'How?' Valu asked. 'I mean, if I, a Nubian, was brought into your presence, how do I know you are the Sgeru?'

'Again your prisoner lied,' Mataia declared. 'He would have been taken to a shadowed place. He would have seen not the Sgeru but one of his officers; he would also have been shown the Shesher.'

'A cord?' Valu asked.

'The same word means "to govern and rule", doesn't it?' Amerotke asked.

'True, my lord.' Mataia smiled quickly at Shufoy, who sat transfixed by this beautiful woman. 'The Shesher is, according to legend, a cord of the purest gold used by the goddess Nema herself during the Dazzling Time when she waged war on the gods of both the north and south. It is the symbol of ultimate authority amongst the Arites and is carried only by the Sgeru or whoever he delegates. The Shesher, according to tradition, is about a yard long, pure gold medallions linked by a silver chain; each medallion is stamped with the head of a hyaena, the eyes of precious stone, a veritable fortune in itself. Once the convert has the Shesher placed around his neck, there is no going back. He must perform the blood oath or face the most excruciating death, being buried alive in the wild places. I suspect the ceremony is short and swift. The candidate is brought in and given a choice. He invariably accepts, because the Arites choose well. He is then given the sacred red cloth and a certain period of time within which he must perform the blood oath and carry out his three sacrifices. Once he has done that, all doors are closed. He cannot go back. If he confesses the truth to someone like yourselves, he faces execution as a traitor and an assassin. Worse, he has betrayed Nema, and both he and his kin will be anointed for death.'

Amerotke stared around this elegant dining place. The

mosaic on the wall, vivacious and eye-catching in all its details, showed a fowler hunting in the papyrus reeds. Yet Amerotke felt a pall of fear, as if the chamber had grown a little darker, despite the beautiful lamp lights glowing in their alabaster jars.

'And the scarab Shufoy brought?' he asked.

The dwarf handed the casket to Mataia. She opened it, took out the scarab and the roll of parchment, studied both carefully, then handed them back.

'I did not wish to answer you in the courtyard, my lord, but if the Sgeru has proclaimed your death, then you must be very careful. He always carries out his word. You and yours are in great danger.'

Valu cursed quietly, beating his fist on the table. 'Nubia is treachery,' he breathed.

'My lord,' Mataia's voice grew harsh, 'do you think you are the only one?'

'You have received a warning,' Khufu agreed, 'but, Lord Valu, so have I, so has my wife, the Lady Busiris, the Lady Mataia and other officials in this temple. We are all singled out for sacrifice. Don't you realise that? In the eyes of the Arites we are traitors, apostates, worthy of execution.'

Valu lifted his head in surprise. 'All of you?' he whispered.

'All of us!' Mataia confirmed.

'And this Sgeru?' Amerotke asked. 'Is he here in Thebes or in Nubia?'

'My lord,' Lady Busiris spoke up, 'he could be anywhere: Thebes, Memphis, Nubia. He could be a guard outside or a beggar at the gate. We don't know.'

'Why?' Valu asked. 'Why now?'

'Why not?' Mataia replied. 'Nubia has always dreamed of being an independent kingdom. Can you imagine, my lord Valu, Nubia driving out Egyptian troops, ejecting the Divine One's viceroy; Nubian troops moving up the Nile? There are those who dream not only of an independent kingdom but of an Egypt dominated by Nubia.'

'But why now?' Amerotke persisted, sipping at his goblet, wishing he could ease the tension.

'They think it's the appropriate time,' Khufu replied. 'Outside, my lord, everything follows the seasons: seeds are sown, they lie dormant, then burst into life. So it is with this. The Divine One has been on the throne for over two years. Look at your history. In every pharaoh's reign Nubia musters a challenge, only this time it is more serious.'

Amerotke shook his head: a Nubian revolt he could understand, but why the pre-eminence of the Arites?

'And they are willing to risk death?' he asked. 'Those Arites impaled this morning?'

'They are assured of immortality,' Mataia replied. 'Whatever pains they undergo, they will be gathered into Nema's embrace and live in happiness for all eternity.'

Amerotke closed his eyes in concentration. He recalled himself and his brother in the family garden, the saluki hounds they had tried to train racing about upsetting everything. That was what was happening here, he reflected: the Sgeru was planning chaos and confusion. An attack on the Divine One at her moment of triumph, an assault upon her chief prosecutor and judge as they brought an Arites prisoner into Thebes. Medjay scouts mysteriously dying; imperial messengers not reaching their destination. He breathed in. Soon Omendap's army would move south. If there was one setback, one reversal, the situation could escalate into a crisis. Some Theban aristocrats resented Hatusu. They were totally opposed to a woman wearing the double crown. Such treason would spread like dirt through a pool. Whispers at the court, then in the mansions along the Nile, would gather strength. Pharaoh should abdicate or even be removed. Hatusu's younger half-brother Tuthmosis should wield the flail and the rod over the People of the Nine Bows.

'My lord Amerotke?'

The judge opened his eyes. Khufu was staring at him.

'Are you well?'

'I am,' the judge replied, 'and I speak with true heart and true voice when I say that what is planned here in Thebes comes directly from the Evil One. Everything could break down. Do you want that, my lord Khufu? Can you imagine an unsuccessful war in the south? The Libyans watch, as do those in Thebes who do not support the Divine One, whose allegiance to the Great House is suspect. Think,' he said, 'the Sgeru is like someone who grasps a pole and digs deep into a pond, twisting and churning the mud until the water is polluted. What is frustrating,' he continued bitterly, 'is that there are those in the Nubian regiment who could tell us the truth, but torture is useless. All we might do is harm the innocent and alienate those loyal to us.'

'Precisely!' the high priest agreed.

Amerotke stared down at his wine goblet. He thought of Parmen and the others waiting in the antechamber outside. 'And the death of Imothep?' he asked. 'What can you tell us about that?'

'Imothep was a favourite of the old Pharaoh. He was born in Nubia,' Khufu explained. 'When Tuthmosis I invaded that country, Imothep sided with Pharaoh. He proved to be a redoubtable warrior, a skilled scout, and his advice and support for the old Pharaoh was invaluable. A Nubian holy place was stormed and taken. Imothep was rewarded lavishly. He was given a statue sacred to the Arites, a hyaena of solid gold suckling its young, the base studded with precious jewels, as well as boxes of silver and gold ingots. He was brought back to Thebes to be covered with further honours; that was years ago. His allegiance to the Divine One has never been questioned. He lived in the House of the Forest, his kinfolk with him. All are Nubian.'

'Of pure stock?' Valu asked.

'Of pure stock,' Khufu agreed, 'but hostile to the Arites. Imothep was very concerned about this crisis. On one occasion he visited me to discuss the situation in Nubia; he studied the old map and charts stored in our House of Books. He was particularly interested in the Sobeck Road through the Oasis of Sinjar.'

'Imperial couriers have disappeared near there,' Amerotke said. 'Did Imothep discuss that?'

'Not really. I just thought he was an old soldier recalling his own glory days. Now, some days before the assault on the Divine One, a corpse was found in the overgrown gardens of Imothep's house; the head was shaven, the body completely naked. He'd been strangled with the red cloth of the Arites, his hands severed, only the gods know why, and his body hidden beneath some bushes. Imothep was deeply disturbed by this. No one knew where the man came from, what he was doing or why the Arites had killed him in the grounds of Imothep's estate. Yesterday afternoon, as you may know, Imothep retired to his Mansion of Silence, a grand garden house rather than a pavilion, with six clerestory windows high in the wall; these are narrow and covered by grilles. There are no other entrances or passageways except the double doors at the front. Imothep sealed this from the inside whilst his bodyguard Rahmel barred it from the outside. The household expected their master to come out just before sunset.'

'And?' Valu asked.

'Imothep never re-emerged. Parmen ordered the outer beam to be taken off, the doors were forced and they found their master inside, slumped over some cushions. He'd been strangled, a red cloth tightly around his throat. The golden hyaena statuette and the small boxes of ingots had disappeared . . .' Khufu was about to continue when the door was abruptly flung open. A servant rushed in and fell to his knees.

'My lords,' the man wailed, 'you must come now. The prisoner, the one taken to the House of Chains? He has been found strangled in his cell.'

70

CHAPTER 3

Hamu: sin

When Amerotke and his colleagues reached the House of Chains, all was confusion. The antechamber and the narrow passageway were so crowded, the judge had to order everyone out into the courtyard, instructing the officer of his escort to ensure that no one left. Then Amerotke, followed by Shufoy, Khufu, Busiris and Mataia, went along the murky passageway into the cell. The Arites lay sprawled on the ground, head slightly to one side, his face a gruesome bluish-grey, eyes popping, tongue slightly thrust out, spittle staining his lips. The red cloth around his throat was tied as tightly as a ligature. Amerotke cut it loose; for a few heartbeats the body jerked in the most macabre way as the air was expelled. Amerotke felt the side of the man's face: it was hard and cold. Valu picked up the pieces of red cloth and tossed them away, then paced the cell, ignoring Khufu's assertion that there was no secret entrance. The cell was a stone box, the double doors secure on their pivots and the beams that had kept them fast lying on the ground in the passageway outside. The judge inspected the water bowl. It was empty, encrusted with filth, and reeked of the same foul odour as the cell. Amerotke stared down at the corpse, ignoring Khufu's whispers and Valu's litany of imprecations. He picked up the pieces of red cloth. The coarse linen was twisted so closely it was as strong as a length of rope. The knot, which must have been positioned behind the dead man's right ear, was as hard as a link in a chain. One corner of the cloth was sewn over. Amerotke picked at this with his dagger and stared at the small pebble it concealed.

'How?' Valu asked, placing himself in front of Amerotke.

'I don't know,' the judge whispered. 'Lord Khufu, excuse us.'

Amerotke and Valu walked out down the passageway. They swiftly questioned the keeper, Valu's torturers, then the officer in charge, but their answers only deepened the mystery.

'My lord,' the officer protested, 'I am a loyal member of the Isis regiment.' He lowered his voice. 'I have no dealings with Nubian traitors.'

'Hush now!' Amerotke warned.

'I am loyal,' the officer repeated, his hard eyes and snarling lips eloquent testimony to the fog of suspicion this crisis was causing. 'I was in the passageway outside all the time. The keeper was in the guardroom upstairs. You left. Those doors were never opened until I gave the order.'

'And why did you do that?' Valu asked.

'For a while the prisoner was singing softly to himself – it sounded like a death lament – then all went quiet. I heard a sound but I thought he was clearing his throat or coughing, nothing suspicious. Everything remained quiet. I thought I should check. I called the keeper down, the bars were taken off, the doors flung open, and that is what we saw.'

Amerotke closed his eyes. He recalled the cell, hard stone and brick with no other entrances. Where had the Arites' killer come from? Flying like some ghost through the air? That red cloth whirling, the weighted piece wrapping around the man's throat. But why didn't he protest? Struggle, shout out, scream or yell?

'How?' Valu snarled. 'How did it happen?'

'I don't know.' The officer shook his head. 'I questioned my men. The prisoner's hands were manacled. He had a piece of coarse sacking thrown about him, for decency's sake, but apart from that . . .'

Amerotke and Valu questioned the keeper and others, but their story was the same as the officer's. The prisoner had sung his death chant, then all went quiet. The officer eventually decided to check and had the doors opened. The prisoner lay sprawled on the floor, the cloth around his neck; he had apparently been strangled. The officer was most insistent that no one had touched anything. No one had glimpsed anything suspicious. Amerotke beckoned at Valu and they returned to the cell. The prosecutor sniffed at the cracked water bowl, then handed this to Amerotke, who inspected it again: nothing but a filthy piece of pottery.

'So what happened?' the prosecutor breathed. 'Here is a man imprisoned in a stone box, the doors heavily fortified and guarded. No one came in and no one went out, whilst there are no secret entrances. The water bowl is empty; that's logical, the prisoner must have been thirsty, but I inspected it before he was sealed in and detected nothing but dirt. The red cloth?' Valu continued as if talking to himself. 'Yes, he could have smuggled that in, or it might have been handed to him during the attack on us in the city.'

'But could he strangle himself? His hands were manacled but it is still possible,' Amerotke said. 'Lord Khufu, you are a physician: is that feasible?'

The high priest went and crouched by the corpse, turning the man's head, beckoning at Amerotke to join him.

'Look at the marks on the skin,' he said, indicating with his forefinger. 'The throat is badly bruised; that red cloth was tight as a noose.'

'But could he do it himself?' Amerotke insisted. 'Is it possible a cloth was given to him, along with whispered instructions, during that assault when our attention was diverted, or when he arrived here?'

'It is possible,' the high priest conceded. 'But highly improbable. When a man is strangled he first lapses into unconsciousness before death occurs.' Khufu picked up the longer piece of the severed red cloth and twisted it into a rope. 'I can do that, tie it around my neck, form a knot here behind the ear, then simply start turning the knot as you would if there was a stick slipped through

74

it. Keep twisting and you'd fall into a faint, but the life breath is very strong, impatient to return. The slightest weakness and the tightness slackens; the victim can still breathe just like a man who is unconscious.'

Amerotke took the piece of cloth from the high priest, weighed it in his hands then threw it on the floor. He grasped the dead man's hands, filthy and callused, his fingernails dirt-rimmed. He studied the fingers and the hands most carefully but could find no trace of red thread, no sign of any fresh contusion caused by tightening that knot. He rose to his feet brushing his robe and left the cell.

'Very clever,' he murmured, 'very clever indeed! Here is an Arites who openly confessed, said he wished to seek Pharaoh's pardon. He is brought into the city and our escort is attacked, only for the assailants to be driven off. He is then brought into the heart of the Temple of Nubia, imprisoned deep in the bowels of the earth, in this secure stone cage, and yet the power of Nema reaches him, to cut off his breath. Can you imagine what will happen when this story is known in the city? The sinister reputation of the Arites will be enhanced, the power of their goddess will appear even more formidable. No one is safe from them! Oh yes, whoever is causing this has brewed a potion very bitter to drink.' Amerotke stared down at the ground, wondering what he should do. He wanted to be home with Norfret and the boys, assure himself that all was well. He abruptly recalled Shufoy, glanced around and called out his name.

'I am here, master.'

Amerotke grinned and walked back into the cell. Shufoy sat on a plinth in a shadowy corner, staring curiously at the corpse.

'Is it possible, my lord?' he whispered. 'Magic? The Arites have powers that we don't?'

Amerotke squatted down and touched the dwarf gently on the forehead.

'I tell you this, Shufoy,' he smiled, 'there is a logic to this, and logic will resolve it, but how?' He shook his head. 'I don't yet know. My lord Khufu,' he called over his shoulder.

'Yes, my lord?'

'You say Imothep's body has been brought here to be dressed for burial, as well as that of the stranger, the naked corpse found in his garden?'

'Yes. Before he died, Imothep asked me to supervise his funeral. We could not refuse. Our temple is the chief beneficiary of his will.'

'Have the prisoner's corpse taken to the House of Death,' Amerotke ordered, getting to his feet and turning round. 'I will go there shortly. My lord Valu.' He went across and clasped the prosecutor's hand. 'I think we have done enough for today.'

'And what about Parmen and the others of his household?' Mataia asked, coming forward. Shufoy left the corner to stare more fully at this beautiful woman. She smiled and stroked him gently on the top of his head. 'You talk of magic, little man: perhaps you should visit me. I will show you the magic manuscripts in our House of Books.' She made to leave. 'My lord, Parmen?'

'My lady,' Amerotke replied, touched by this woman's courtesy towards Shufoy, 'ask Parmen and his companions to return to the House of the Forest. I will visit them later. In the meantime, before we leave, let us search this cell carefully, scrupulously for anything untoward.'

They examined the jakespot, the filthy water bowl, but could find nothing amiss. Amerotke, completely baffled, shook his head. He stood aside as servants came with a makeshift stretcher to place the corpse on; they covered the body with a piece of sheepskin, then left. Amerotke followed Khufu back up out of the House of Chains into the sunlight. They returned to the audience chamber, where Amerotke and the rest washed their hands and faces, then sat around the table nibbling at the food and sipping the wine. Valu squatted, muttering under his breath and shaking his head at the crisis. Amerotke sat for a while in silence, then smiled at his hosts.

'My friends,' he declared, 'to speak with a clear heart, to resolve these mysteries, to see through the lies and establish the truth will be difficult. Is there anything more you can tell me?'

'Bitter fruit of a bitter harvest,' Khufu murmured.

'So when do you think this harvest was sown?' Amerotke asked.

'In my view,' Lady Busiris spoke up, 'and I have spoken to Mataia here,' she smiled at her chief heset, touching her gently on the shoulder, 'it was many years ago. The Arites have been preparing. Now it is harvest time, and they intend to wreak as much damage and devastation as possible.'

'And you know nothing,' Amerotke insisted, 'nothing that can help resolve these mysteries?'

'What we know,' Khufu spoke up, 'is what we have told you.'

'And Imothep?' Amerotke asked. 'He was close to this temple?'

'Very close,' Lady Busiris replied. 'According to his will, lodged with the priests of Isis, Imothep left his entire estate to our temple.'

Amerotke suppressed a smile.

'In which case, my friends, you may know the question I am going to ask. Were any of you present at the House of the Forest when Imothep died?'

'True, true.' Khufu seemed unperturbed. 'I see where your question is leading. We are the beneficiaries of Imothep's death. We are certainly not the cause. Neither I, Lady Busiris, Mataia or anyone else from this temple visited the House of the Forest.' He shook his head. 'Certainly not in the last few weeks. However, as I have said, Imothep was a frequent visitor here, particularly during recent months.'

'Why?' Amerotke asked. 'Did he suspect mischief was brewing?'

'Perhaps.' Mataia spoke up abruptly. 'Imothep was certainly interested in our House of Books. He asked for maps, charts of the land between Thebes and the First Cataract, in particular the Oasis of Sinjar and the fortress of Timsah. I asked him why, but he was an old soldier, sly and cunning: he just tapped his nose and said that he was trying to recall certain facts.'

'He was studying the past?'

'Yes, he seemed more interested in tracking the Sobeck roads, the routes down the Nile. After the revolt broke out in Nubia, he mentioned how the Arites might use these roads to thread men north. My lord, Imothep was an old soldier, full of memories.'

'And then he was killed,' Amerotke murmured, 'rather mysteriously in his Mansion of Silence. There's that other corpse, too, found in the gardens. Imothep took responsibility for it?'

Khufu shrugged and spread his hands. 'Imothep was pious. He did not know the man, nor did any of his household. However, the corpse was found on Imothep's estate, an apparent victim of the Arites. As an act of mercy, Imothep had the body sent to us for embalming and burial out in a common grave at the Necropolis. You can still view the corpse; it must lie in our House of the Dead for the stipulated time. My lord Amerotke, if there is nothing more, we have other duties. Our temple has been deeply disturbed by what has happened today. Mataia will escort you to the House of the Dead. Speak to the keeper of the corpses, the priests and the scribes there.'

Amerotke nodded in agreement. Khufu and Busiris rose, bowed, made their farewells and left.

The House of the Dead lay a short distance away, a square building of dark stone with a porticoed entrance leading down into the gloom. Mataia led them along an ill-lit passage into underground caverns where the dead were prepared for their final journey. Amerotke and Shufoy entered that chilling, sombre kingdom of twilight.

Priests in funeral masks depicting the hawk, the dog and the vulture moved amidst gusts of smoke and steam, around chambers brightly lit by torches and lamps. A ghostly place, as the spectral figures of the priests chanted spells from the Book of the Dead or busied themselves around the slightly sloping slabs where cadavers were laid out for preparation. Bowls of bubbling natron gave off plumes of salt-tinged steam, which mingled with the aromas of myrrh, frankincense, cassia oil and the juice of juniper berries. Corpses lay soaking in salted water where the fatty portions could be dissolved before the next stage of embalmment. Beside these baths stood the carefully marked canopic jars for the entrails, stomach and lungs of the dead. Other corpses were being creamed with a resin mixture into which rolls of bandages had been dipped to fill the empty body cavities. At one slab a priest stood crouched over a corpse, preparing for the incision in its side with the sacred obsidian knife. Another priest was busy with a special hook to break the nose and draw out the brains. Verses of hymns caught Amerotke's attention.

'Words spoken by Isis; I clasp my arms around him who is in me.'

'The West is a land of dreams and deep shadows . . .'

'The Great Enchantress purifies these . . .'

'Osiris of Dedju who hears all and sees all, wash away your sins.'

A graphic painting on the wall portrayed the weighing of souls before Osiris, Anubis and Thoth: these were divided into three groups. The artist had paid special attention to those of the dead who failed the weighing and were thrown to the bitch goddess Amemet, who crunched their bones, shattered their hearts and drank their blood. Shufoy, deeply interested in such macabre scenes, would have wandered away to gape, but Amerotke clutched his hand more tightly as they followed Mataia over to an alcove where the Scribe of the Dead squatted on a cushioned stool, inscribing a sheet of papyrus stretched out across his lap. He looked up and smiled when Mataia introduced the judge before jumping to his feet. He scurried away and returned with the keeper of the corpses, a lanky, hard-faced priest who took them to view Imothep's cadaver being cleansed in a salt bath. Next to this, knees drawn up to the chin, lay the body of the mysterious stranger found in the gardens of Imothep's mansion. Amerotke asked permission to examine the stranger's corpse, and the priest agreed, handing him a cloth. Amerotke knelt down by the bath and, through the sheen of pure water, studied the unnamed face carefully: an old man, wisps of hair on his head, eyes sunken, cheeks rather hollow, the body itself emaciated and bony. Even the ravages of death could not hide the fact that this victim had not drunk deep of the riches of life.

'Who could he be?' Amerotke asked the keeper.

The priest shook his head. 'No one has come forward to claim the corpse, even though our temple heralds have proclaimed that a stranger has been brought here. My lord, look at his wrists.'

Amerotke put his hand in the bath and drew up the

arm. He stared in horror at the bandages around the bloodied stump.

'The same with the right,' the priest declared.

Amerotke got to his feet and gratefully cleaned his hands in a bowl of water.

'Both hands were removed,' he declared. 'Severed?'

'After death, I believe,' the keeper replied. 'The stumps were all blood-dried.'

'But that was not the cause of death?'

'Oh no.' The keeper shook his head. 'He was strangled, same as Imothep: a garrotte around their throats cut off their breath.'

Amerotke crouched down and stared at the gruesome arm hanging over the side of the bath.

'Why?' he whispered. 'The Arites strangle their victims! They wish both body and spirit to be offered as a sacrifice. So why cut off the hands? Were they ever found?'

The keeper shrugged. 'He was brought in as you see him, not a shred of clothing upon him. I asked the same of Imothep. He said that careful search had been made in the garden but nothing else was found.'

Amerotke wafted away a gust of steam.

'And Imothep died of strangulation; you found no other wound?'

'Old scars,' the keeper replied, 'but nothing unusual.'

'And the Arites?' Amerotke asked.

'I have examined him quickly. His mouth was rather dry, but there again he had been imprisoned, tortured and taken out to the Place of the Skull.' The keeper's lip curled in disdain. 'But I saw nothing unusual. It is good of the high priest to give honourable burial to an enemy.'

Amerotke turned to Lady Mataia, who was now standing holding Shufoy's hand. She smiled serenely at him.

'My lord Amerotke, do you have any other questions?'

'No, my lady, I have seen enough.'

They left the House of the Dead. Lady Mataia said she must be busy over other matters so was there anything else? Amerotke shook his head and watched the heset walk elegantly away, pulling her linen shawl more firmly about her shoulders. For a while he just stood in the sunlight, relishing the light and the warmth: such a contrast to those dark, gloomy caverns. Then he took Shufoy by the hand, and led him through a small gated entrance and into the most beautiful temple garden.

'Let us sit for a while.'

They crossed to a small pavilion next to a pool of purity where blue and white lotus blossoms gently floated. Amerotke sat down, stretching out his legs, rubbing his face. Shufoy perched beside him, lost in his own thoughts. Amerotke stared out at the garden.

'Spectacular,' he murmured.

'Yes, master, the lady Mataia is truly beautiful.'

Amerotke laughed and patted his companion on the shoulder.

'I don't mean the lady Mataia, Shufoy, but the day itself, these gardens. It's like leaving the darkest night and entering the fullness of day: that audience chamber, full of suspicion, allegation, and mystery; the House of the Dead. What a contrast!'

Amerotke and Shufoy relaxed in the ornate garden pavilion. The judge deliberately chattered about the minor details of life: how he preferred one type of flower to another, about his plans to develop his own garden. He then moved on to the education of his sons, the prospect of a journey north to meet Norfret's parents at Memphis, the work of the scribes in the courts, the renovation of a statue of Ma'at, the Goddess of Truth, and the preparations for the celebration of the festival of Thoth, the Scribe God. Amerotke realised that time was passing, but he wanted to soothe his soul after a day of such gruesome terrors. Shufoy proved to be a good listener, even though Amerotke realised the little man was lost in his own dreams about the lady Mataia. At first Amerotke was amused as Shufoy began to haltingly praise the heset; then he wondered if this little man with such a big heart had truly fallen in love. He listened to Shufoy's hymn of praise as he watched the visitors and pilgrims stream through the garden to a shrine to fill their gazelle skins at a sacred stela washed by holy water. Others walked by: swaggering guards flirting with the hesets in their tightly fringed kilts and skimpy shawls, painted faces framed by gorgeous wigs, sinuous bodies glistening with oil. The young women moved provocatively, hips swaying to the musical jingle of heavy bracelets and bangles. Different priests, those of the Stole, of the Chapel of Waiting and the Inner Sanctuary, hurried by, chattering like a gaggle of geese. Workmen with bags of tools; porters and acolytes bearing panniers of flat bread or baskets filled with river fowl, their necks wrung, a heap of gorgeous plumage and lolling heads. Amerotke wanted to understand the essence of this temple. He watched and reflected. Shufoy became aware of how his master was now only half listening to him. He stopped halfway through a sentence and abruptly tapped Amerotke's knee with his fan.

'Master, those butterflies over there, they have just eaten a swallow.'

'Yes, yes,' Amerotke replied absent-mindedly.

'And that kingfisher above the pool is now all afire with the flame of the god.'

'Shufoy, what are you . . . ?'

'Exactly, master, you are dreaming.' Shufoy grinned. 'So am I, though more loudly than you. You are interested in this temple, yes? If the Arites have a nest, if their Sgeru has a lair, surely it would be here. Yet . . .' he paused, snapping open his fan, 'the Beloved of Horus has nothing but praise for this temple, so,' he squinted up at his master, 'how can she be so sure?'

Amerotke leaned forward. 'Of course,' he whispered. He kissed Shufoy on the forehead. 'So small, yet so cunning! Hatusu must have a spy here, someone of high rank who keeps the workings of this temple under close scrutiny, a person so exalted the Divine One does not wish to share such information even with me or Lord Valu. Well, little one, lover of Mataia, you must leave me.'

'Master, be careful!'

'I have my escort.' Amerotke glanced up at the sky. The sun was still strong, the light and warmth not yet tinged by the cool evening breeze. 'Hurry to the Divine

House, the Palace of the Malkata, seek out Lord Senenmut and give him my good wishes. Ask him two things. First, who is the Divine One's spy here at the Temple of Nubia. Second, beg Lord Senenmut to send his fastest courier to General Omendap's camp. I need to speak to the chief Medjay scout. He must come to my house this evening. I'll entertain him.' Amerotke stroked the top of Shufoy's head. 'Now go! I have my escort and I'll be safe. And,' he warned, 'if you see the Lady Norfret before I return, do not alarm her with this day's events.'

Shufoy was reluctant to leave, but Amerotke insisted. The little man hurried away.

'At least it will keep you busy,' Amerotke whispered. 'Well away from your enchanters and sorcerers.'

Shufoy was always involving himself in madcap schemes to make money as well as a name for himself in Theban society. Magic was his latest novelty, and the little man, when not attending court, had immersed himself in studying the bizarre details of the secret societies, rituals and rites widespread through the city. Amerotke thought fleetingly of Mataia. Would she also be a distraction for Shufoy? The dwarf was hideously disfigured, the result of an evil miscarriage of justice that had banished him to the villages of the Rhinoceri. Amerotke had intervened to rectify the great wrong and made Shufoy his lifelong companion and friend. Yet Shufoy had a life of his own, a heart, a mind and keen wits. Amerotke often wondered if he would marry and settle down. He smiled at the thought, then turned to what he should do to resolve these mysteries. He decided to wait a little longer. He wanted to make sure that Parmen and the rest of Imothep's household had returned to the House of the Forest.

The judge stared around the enchanting garden, a paradise with its various trees: acacia, olive, pine, almond and, of course, willow, where the Divine Osiris had sheltered. A shy heset came tripping across to offer a goblet of fruit of the southern oasis. Amerotke smilingly refused and watched the heset walk away to offer the same to a young man entertaining some visitors with a poem to Amun. Amerotke listened carefully to the lines.

> *Wake, lord of gods and men,*
> *Lord of the war cry,*
> *In peace awake, peaceably,*
> *Wake, great Ram of Splendour,*
> *Tall-plumed, sharp-horned,*
> *In peace wake peaceable.*

Amerotke leaned back. He caught the fragrant scent of fruit bread being baked in a nearby courtyard. Such a peaceful place. The flowerbeds and herb plots all neatly laid out. Was Shufoy correct? Could the Temple of Nubia be the home of treason, the heart of treachery? The judge's eyes drooped. He lifted his hand and smelt balm of Gilead, and realised he must have brushed against the ointment in the House of the Dead. He opened his eyes. He must be gone. He rose, walked out of the garden and found his escort waiting in the Sycamore Courtyard. They were squatting around the fountain watching Lady Busiris,

Mataia and other hesets help the infirm into the House of Myrrh, the temple infirmary. A long line of pilgrims, most of them Nubians who had fallen ill or been injured on their visit to Thebes.

'The poor and maimed, my lord.' The officer followed Amerotke's gaze. 'And yet,' he whispered, 'all are now suspects. You've heard the rumours?'

Amerotke shook his head.

'This temple is to be ringed by the Isis regiment. Lord Senenmut believes all visitors from Nubia should be kept in one place, preferably here.'

Amerotke nodded in understanding, but his heart sank. Every hour seemed to deepen the crisis. How was it to be resolved?

The officer of the Arites pulled the striped hood of his cloak close about him as the skiff nosed its way across the Nile towards the Place of Osiris. The sun was beginning to set. The Necropolis, the City of the Dead, was bathed in a red-gold light that transformed both the approaching quayside and the huddle of buildings, row upon row of houses, shops and temples in an elaborate maze of streets and needle-thin alleyways. The river stank of dried fish, fruit, salt and floating refuse as well as the odours from the animal pens. Food boats, fishing smacks, funeral barges and pleasure craft thronged the river, a sea of colour and noise bubbling over the fast-flowing waters. The Arites sat in the stern and watched the quayside, noting the mercenaries, Medjay police and soldiers from the city garrisons moving amongst the traders, hawkers, sailors and river people who thronged the far bank. He relaxed. He was safe. Most of the Arites were caged in their barracks, but he, ostensibly a deserter, could move about easily. It had all been planned. A tribesman from Lower Nubia, his skin was light-coloured, whilst his face was hidden by a deep hood: he would not attract attention.

The Arites moved the whisk to drive away the swarm of flies even as his other hand felt for the money belt strapped tightly around his waist and the dagger pushed through his waistband. He could not determine the precise hour, but his instructions had been very clear. The assassins would be waiting for him at a wine house on the edge of the Mysterious Abode, that living hell in the slums close to the heart of the Necropolis. The skiff made its final approach, turning so the Arites could climb on to the steps leading up to the quayside. He threw down a deben of copper and hurried up into the frenetic, dirty bustle. Pi-dogs and naked, red-eyed children scampered about, their barks and screams adding to the shouts of traders as well as the cries of the heavily painted whores and the raucous singing and shouting from the many ale booths and smelly cookshops that served the riverside. The Arites grasped his walking cane and moved quickly, dodging the piles of horrid refuse, the enticements of garishly painted prostitutes and the constant plucking of his sleeve by pedlars and hawkers. Such traders were eager to sell anything, from a statue of a god to a piece of copper fallen from heaven, a Melokhia omelette or a 'young, virginal girl' from the countryside. Beggars in rags, their mouths black holes displaying rotten teeth, their skins stained and calloused, whined for alms. Strange priests chanted hymns to grotesque statues whilst jumping up and down to the tinkle of bells. Dancers whirled to the beat of a drum. Whistles blew. Men and women screamed at each other. A funeral procession led by an Anubis priest realised they had landed in the wrong place and, already drunk, were trying to rectify matters as the mourners slouched miserably around the coffin caskets.

The Arites avoided all these distractions and sped up a dark runnel. On either side rose blind walls with only the occasional entrance door disappearing into the blackness beyond. He pushed aside a group of hunchbacked dwarfs disguised behind their macabre masks, and knocked away their importunate hands, deaf to even more wheedling from the shadows. At the top of the long street he paused and glanced quickly around. He was sure he was being followed, but there again, he also had others trailing his shadow ready to offer protection. The dirt and smell were offensive. The sense of threat from the crumbling tenements on either side was real and fearful. The Arites did not care. He was under the protection of the Nema and the all-seeing Sgeru. He came out of one dark alleyway into a square on the edge of the Mysterious Abode. Around its sides stood shabby booths under ragged awnings, where street sellers mashed their confectionery in steaming dirty bowls or cooked legs of goose, fresh from the fire and soaked in herbs. From under a cluster of dusty palm trees a barber bawled for custom, whilst thin-faced scribes sat in any shade they could find and offered to write whatever their customers wanted. Children searched the rutted cobbled surface for animal dung to be dried and used for fuel. Dogs fought over scraps. Donkeys and asses brayed for water gushing out of a broken fountain.

The Arites walked across into a wine shop, the Light of Horus, the Lord of the Sky. It was a rectangular room, its floor of beaten earth, its limewashed walls covered with coarse coloured matting. Stools and tables had been set up for customers, yet the place was empty. In the poor light from the window high in the wall, the Arites could make out only one shadow moving amongst the barrels and baskets heaped behind the counter.

'What do you want, friend?' a voice called out.

'The wine of Buto.' The Arites gave the prearranged reply.

'Then come and drink.'

The Arites crossed the room and went behind the counter. The man in the shadows still lurked there, though he'd opened a trapdoor in the floor. The Arites glimpsed a glow of light.

'Go down,' the voice instructed. 'Hurry, friend, and meet those you wish to.'

The Arites took a deep breath. There was no turning back. He went down the steep stone steps into the underground cavern, cool and musty. Pitch torches flared in wall niches to illuminate a cellar of shifting darkness. At the foot of the steps he paused to shield his eyes against the glare of a lamp on a table.

'Sit,' a different voice ordered.

The Arites did so, on the cushion before the table, placing his walking cane on the ground beside him.

'And your knife!' the voice ordered. 'And any other weapon you may have.'

The Arites obeyed. The lamp still glowed fiercely, but he was growing accustomed to the gloom.

'And the precious?'

The Arites took off his cloak, undid the leather money belt and placed it beside him.

'To us!' the voice barked.

'We have not yet reached an agreement.'

'We will. Throw it!'

The Arites obeyed.

'Good,' the voice whispered. 'Now the lamp, extinguish it.'

The Arites leaned forward and did so, using a metal cup to cover the flame.

'Good. If you had not obeyed you would have died. Now, Nubian, you have come to us for help?'

The Arites peered through the darkness. He could make out five shapes, all assassins, the most skilled murderers in Thebes.

'We are,' the voice intoned, 'the Breaker of Bones, the Drinker of Blood, the Gobbler of Flesh, the Flayer of Skins and the Devourer of Hearts. Once we were your enemies when you served the Great House and kissed the royal bitch's glossy arse. Now you come to us because she has trapped most of you in your cages. What do you want?'

'You know what we want,' the Arites replied, trying to curb his fear.

'Which is?'

'Chaos and death.'

'Against whom? The Divine One? Lord Senenmut?' The voice chuckled. 'I do not think so, not yet: you have tried and you failed.'

'Against two of her officials,' the Arites replied, 'Valu the prosecutor and Amerotke the judge.'

'Ah yes, they were out at the Place of the Skull today, impaling your friends.'

'Comrades,' the Arites replied. 'We seek vengeance.'

'Why not do it yourself? Nubians fill the city.'

'Days change, life moves on,' the Arites replied slowly. 'We Nubians are watched. Many of us, as you say, are caged for the time being.'

'And what do you offer?'

'The silver and gold I bring.'

The shadow in the centre leaned forward and picked up the money belt, weighing it in his hands.

'The agreed sum?'

'The agreed sum,' the Arites replied.

'And what else for the future?'

The Arites took a deep breath and leaned forward.

'Soon General Omendap will march south. I assure you, my lords,' the Arites' voice did not flinch at the flattery he used, 'once that happens, there will be more chaos and confusion in Thebes.'

'A revolution?' one of the shadows asked.

'A revolution,' the Arites agreed. 'The Powerful High

One will be brought low, her palaces plundered. The spoils of war will be yours. Already, because the Divine Bitch has caged the Nubian regiment, the police on the streets are few, the troops she has are stretched. Now is the time to act.'

'You mean against Valu and Amerotke?'

'Precisely.'

'They have guards?'

'Not enough.'

'I am the Devourer,' the voice declared. 'I am intrigued, Nubian, by what is happening. The deaths amongst the Medjay scouts: that is your work?'

'It is.'

'And the disappearance of royal couriers: that too is your work?'

'It is.'

'Tell me, Nubian, how do you kill the Medjay scouts?'

'Once the blood begins to flow,' the Arites replied lightly, 'then we shall tell you. Only when General Omendap marches south; the sooner the better.'

'Why wait until then?' the Devourer declared.

'We want as much distance as possible put between Thebes and Omendap,' the Arites replied. 'In the meantime, we mean to strike terror at the heart of Egypt. The Divine One has to be chastised, reminded that we are here.'

'Tell me.' Another voice spoke up. 'I am the Drinker of Blood. I look forward to the coming feast, but imperial scouts, messengers and couriers have disappeared and no trace of them, their bodies, their boats or their belongings, has been found. They took jewellery with them, weapons, precious goods, yet none of these have appeared in the markets of the Mysterious Abode or elsewhere in the Necropolis. Anything,' the voice insisted, 'stolen in Egypt eventually arrives here.'

'All will be revealed,' came the sardonic reply.

'You are confident,' the Devourer accused. 'I would say overconfident. We could kill you now, or hand you over to Lord Senenmut, keep your silver and claim the reward.'

'I would be dead,' the Arites replied. 'But I assure you of this, my lords, I have come here in good faith. I have brought the treasure you asked. If I die, I promise, within the week so will you, and when the great banquet takes place and rivers of blood pour through Thebes, you will not be at the feast.'

The Arites paused and listened to the whispers amongst his hosts.

'We have agreed,' the Devourer declared. The Arites heard the clink of the money belt. 'You have brought more than we asked. I can tell that simply by weighing it in my hands. What else do you wish?'

'Valu must die, and so must Amerotke,' the Arites replied. 'Immediately, this evening, so that by dawn, the Divine Bitch will know who truly rules in Thebes!'

'And the Temple of Nubia?'

'Khufu may also have to be chastised, but at our orders, in the way we wish.'

'The Temple of Nubia,' the Drinker of Blood taunted. 'How surprising! Your own holy place, your sanctuary?'

'Nothing more than a pile of stinking turds,' the Arites

replied. 'We have no dealings with Khufu or anyone of his kind. All those in the temple are traitors. There is but one god, Nema, and we are her humble servants. We will carry out judgement against Pharaoh. We will free our kingdom of Egyptian influence. Omendap will be cut off, the Viceroy of Nubia will die, then we will sweep north to meet our brothers. Time is passing. The sun has yet to set,' the Arites continued remorselessly. 'Do we have an agreement? Amerotke, Valu and, when we say, the Temple of Nubia?'

'You have our promise,' came the reply. 'Before the sun rises tomorrow, what you ask for will have been carried out. Except,' he paused, 'for the temple – that will come later, yes?'

The Arites agreed and made to rise.

'And this Sgeru, your leader,' a voice asked, 'who is he, where is he?'

'He is everywhere, lord,' the Arites mocked. 'For all I know he could be here in this chamber. You have men?'

'You know that.'

'Study them closely, my lords,' the Arites continued. 'How many of them are Nubians? How many have sworn allegiance to you but have secret loyalty to the Sgeru? I make no idle threats. I thank you for meeting me. Agreement is reached. Believe me, lords, once you have taken silver and gold from our Sgeru, you must carry out your programme.'

'It shall be done,' the Drinker of Blood replied. 'And now it is time you were gone.'

CHAPTER 4

Metu: Venom

Amerotke was truly surprised by the House of the Forest. A stately two-storey mansion standing to the north of Thebes, its high curtain wall overlooked broad green strips stretching down to the Nile, from which irrigation canals and sluices had been dug into the grounds. The wall was a brilliant white, the great double gate painted a glossy black. Once the porter had ushered the judge and his escort inside, Amerotke stood and gaped in astonishment at the overgrown garden, the long wild grass stretching out on either side. The path leading up to the main house was clean and well ordered, yet Amerotke felt as if he was walking through a jungle. Flowers such as the white lily grew to overripe fullness amongst the haifa grass and thick green sedge around the dirt-encrusted ponds, all overshadowed by unpruned birch, fir, cypress and palm trees. A place of contrasting light and darkness over which

97

butterflies floated like disembodied souls. The air thrilled with the whirr of insects and the flash of gorgeously plumed birds darting out from the green darkness.

The porter led him up to the main house, where Parmen, Neferen, Rahmel and Sihera were squatting in the shade of the portico eating the bread of sorrow and drinking the water of bitterness, standard fare for those in mourning. They rose as Amerotke approached. Parmen offered him refreshment, which the judge refused as he sat down on the cushions around the small cedarwood tables. He tactfully introduced his escort. Parmen, in a flurry of robes, instructed servants to take the officer and his cohort around into the kitchen courtyard for more substantial refreshments, an invitation the soldiers quickly accepted. During these courtesies, Amerotke settled himself and studied his hosts. They were full Nubian. Parmen was fat and fussy, eyes red-rimmed with crying, his face and cropped hair stained copiously with mourning dust. The steward was an imperious man with a strident voice and petulant mannerisms, his full lips all aquiver, as if expecting some crisis. Neferen, his daughter, was slender and comely, though Amerotke found her hard-eyed with a slightly solemn manner. Rahmel was the eternal soldier, old and grey, with a face well lived in, his lean, sinewy body displaying the scars of many battles. Sihera sat head down, grey hair falling over her face as if she wished to hide herself.

Amerotke gazed around the spacious portico. On either side of the front door were painted the Divine Apes, incarnations of the Spirit of the Morning defeating the

Filthy Ones, the fiends, casting them into the lake of fire reserved for the wicked. All the flowerpots and garlands placed before these images had been removed, leaving stained circles and marks. Pinned to the door lintel were prayers offered to the Gods with Knife-Like-Eyes, a powerful plea for protection for those in mourning.

'My lord Amerotke.' Parmen caught the judge's attention. 'How can we help you?' He leaned over, plucked a natron pellet from a bowl and popped it into his mouth. 'I am dry,' he apologised, his face creasing into a smile. 'All this agitation and fasting.'

Amerotke sat fascinated by that bowl of pellets. He thought of his own home, the natron pellets piled high in a bowl shaped in the form of a pomegranate. He'd seen similar bowls in the audience chamber at the Temple of Nubia. The officer of his escort carried a pouch of natron pellets for his men. What if they were poisoned, or at least some of them? No one ever looked or checked. The pellet was popped into the mouth and sucked, and if it was poisoned, it would be too late.

'My lord Amerotke?'

The judge blinked. Sihera was leaning forward. She was lighter-skinned than the rest, large, expressive eyes in a face that, despite the grey hair and wrinkles, still preserved its own innate beauty.

'My lord,' she repeated, her voice soothing. 'Are you well?'

'Yes,' he replied.

'Soon it will be sunset.' Sihera closed her eyes and quoted a poem.

And when thou goest all the world is bleak.
Houses are tombs where blind men lie in death.
Only the lion and the serpent move
Through the black oven of the sightless night.

She opened her eyes.

'You are thinking of murder, my lord Amerotke?'

'Yes, I am.' The judge felt slightly discomforted by her steady cold gaze. 'I was thinking of the Medjay scouts attached to General Omendap's army. You've heard about the murders there?' His question was greeted with nods.

'As we have of the death of the Arites prisoner,' Parmen intoned. 'We were in the temple when it happened. All a great mystery, shrouded in darkness and blood.'

Amerotke suddenly recalled the poem Sihera had quoted from, and closing his eyes, he recited the next verse.

Dawn in the east again, the lambs awake,
And men leap from their slumber with a song.
They bathe their bodies, clothe them with fresh
garments.
Then lift their hands in happy adoration.

He opened his eyes and smiled at his hosts.

'Soon it will be night. All will be dark, but dawn eventually comes. If there is a problem, there must be a solution. If there is a mystery, there must be a resolution. The death of your master Imothep, it came as a great surprise?'

'Very much so!' Neferen's voice was swift and clipped. 'The Arites have a great deal to answer for. Imothep was a good master, a veteran soldier, a man loyal to the Great House.'

'And yet he died in your care?' Amerotke pointed at Rahmel, who moved uncomfortably. The Nubian picked up a beaker of water and drank from it, grimacing at the taste.

'Many years ago,' Rahmel grated, 'I fought with the Divine One's father against the Arites. He should have burnt their fortress at Bekhna. The Arites are evil shadows; they can flit and slip wherever they wish.'

'Yet it's a mystery,' Amerotke persisted. 'I understand your master was in his Mansion of Silence? The doors barred? How could the Arites get in?' His words were greeted by silence.

Amerotke wiped his mouth with his finger and reflected. Above him rose Imothep's stately home, its beautiful white walls gleaming in the strong sunshine, yet around him, all was chaos and confusion, a jungle of a garden surrounding the Mansion of Silence with its own deadly secrets.

'Tell me,' he said, 'about yourselves, about your master.'

'We are Nubians,' Parmen began slowly, 'of the tribe of Karzai in Lower Nubia. When the Divine One's ancestor swept into our lands like the god Montu, he displayed his banner. Imothep and ourselves – we are all kin, distant cousins – immediately declared for Pharaoh, even though this made us unpopular amongst our people. Nevertheless, even then Imothep was known for his cunning and bravery in battle. He entered Pharaoh's camp and we followed.' Parmen laughed self-consciously. 'When I say we, I mean myself, Rahmel and Sihera, Neferen was born much later. My wife,' the fat steward's lip quivered, 'she has already gone across the Far Horizon.'

Amerotke nodded tactfully.

'The rest is what you read in the chronicles,' Parmen continued. 'Tuthmosis brought Upper and Lower Nubia fully under the rod of Egypt. Imothep proved to be an excellent scout. He became commander of the Spies of Sobeck, an elite corps responsible for spying out the lands, going before Pharaoh's armies. He was lavishly rewarded with collars of gold, silver bracelets, lands, a bride, marks of honour, even the coveted red gloves Pharaoh only bestows on his beloveds.'

'And the Nubians were defeated, the Arites with them?' Amerotke asked.

'It is a matter of history, my lord. After his victory, apart from against the fortress at Bekhna, other matters called Tuthmosis back to Thebes. When his army marched north, we came with him. His Excellency gave Imothep this mansion and the gardens around. My master settled here happy and content. True, we both experienced tragedy. Our wives died. I was fortunate in being given Neferen; Imothep remained childless.'

'And the Arites?' Amerotke asked. 'Did Imothep or any of you have dealings with them?'

'Never!' Parmen spat the word out. 'Is that not true, Rahmel?'

'I was Imothep's bodyguard, his man by day and night.

My soul and his,' the old soldier held up fingers locked together, 'were like that. I tell you this, my lord judge.' The man spoke like a soldier on the parade ground. 'The Arites hated us and we hated them.'

'Why?' Amerotke asked.

'Well, first,' Rahmel declared, 'my master had a hand in their destruction. Second, he plundered one of their holy places, a sanctuary dedicated to their hyaena goddess nestling deep in a jungle. As a reward, Tuthmosis gave him the sacred objects as booty: a pure gold statue of a hyaena suckling its cubs, its rim studded with precious stones, together with small capped coffers and caskets containing miniature ingots of gold and silver. These were my master's pride and joy. I am sure the Arites never forgot them.'

'And the night your master was murdered, these also disappeared?'

'Yes.'

'But how could that be?' Amerotke asked.

'It's best if you see for yourself.' Rahmel eased himself up; the others followed.

Amerotke got to his feet, then glanced at Sihera. She was still staring coldly at him, as if assessing his worth. Amerotke called for his escort and followed them out into the garden, along winding paths across which tendrils of grass and gorse trailed. It was an eerie experience. Here he was in a mansion in the richest quarter of the city, yet its garden was more like a jungle grove. A mixture of conflicting smells wafted across: rotting vegetation mingled with the scent of flowers and the oversweet perfume of decaying fruit. Small monkeys, a blur of black and white, scampered along branches. Birdsong burst out, only to fall abruptly silent. A world of sombre greenery, Amerotke reflected, only the occasional lance of brilliant sunlight piercing the darkness.

'This is how the master wanted it,' Neferen declared.

'Now he is dead,' Amerotke asked, 'what will you do?'

Parmen, trudging in front, stopped and turned, wiping the sweat from his dirt-smudged face.

'The estate and all within it has been left to the Temple of Nubia.'

'And you?'

'Very generous bequests,' Parmen quickly replied, 'very generous indeed. Imothep was thoughtful and we shall not go without, but . . .' He shrugged and trudged on. 'I'd give it all up for him to be back.'

They crossed a small glade and out on to the stretch of land before the Mansion of Silence. The square building on its stone base reminded Amerotke of a temple, with its porticoed entrance, great double doors now hanging half open and low sloping steps running up either side of the ramp. The walls were of hard mud brick, plastered then painted a brilliant white. Two clerestory windows high in the walls on either side of the door were sealed in their lintels by wooden slats. Amerotke murmured at his escort to stay, whilst he walked round to make further investigation. There were two clerestory windows on each of the three other sides, but no other door or outside steps: only the occasional small air grille, the wooden slats that filled them being set firmly in stone. Amerotke could detect no disturbance on the ground or along the surface of those sheer white walls. He walked back to the front, and up the side steps into the portico. He stopped before the paintings either side of the double door, depictions of Sobeck the crocodile god, with the body of a man but the head of a river beast. The god was decorated with a feathered crown, a sun disc prominent in the centre. The double doors Sobeck was supposed to protect were broken and splintered. Parmen went in to light lamps and torches whilst Rahmel explained how the doors were sealed.

'The night my master was murdered,' the bodyguard murmured, 'these doors were secured. Ask the servants. We had to use one bar to loosen the one inside.'

Amerotke nodded and went into the Mansion of Silence. It was musty and rather warm. Flies buzzed above a small square pool of purity. Rahmel explained how this was fed by an underground spring. Amerotke gazed around. The mansion was divided into three; a row of brightly painted columns were ranged either side of the entrance chamber. Its walls were painted a vivid green, as if Imothep wished to bring a touch of his wild garden here. Torches and lamps in a myriad of wall niches provided light. The entrance chamber was really a small shrine to the god Sobeck. The walls on either side boasted murals depicting the exploits of the god, whilst to the right stood a household altar displaying an elaborately carved naos. The doors to this tabernacle were open to reveal the crocodile-headed god carved out of some costly greenish-blue stone, which glowed luridly in the lamplight.

'Why Sobeck?'

'My master's patron god,' Rahmel answered proudly. 'Sobeck went with Imothep and his cohort of spies on all their expeditions. He won so many collars of valour, he was eternally grateful to the god.'

'Why this?' Amerotke gestured round.

'My master was a secretive man,' Parmen declared, coming over. 'The Mansion of Silence was his retreat, a quiet, serene place set in the jungle of his garden. It reminded him of Nubia, of his past. A ghostly experience in the dark, the silence broken only by the cries of night creatures, as if—'

'You were in some glade in the forest of the south?'

'Yes, very much so.'

'And the present danger, the emergence of the Arites?'

Parmen bit his lip, glanced quickly at his daughter and Rahmel then back at Amerotke.

'He said very little.'

'He believed the Arites had established a stronghold in Thebes.' Sihera came through the double doors. 'Imothep truly hated the killers from the slaughterhouse. He called them foul, filthy things who glutted themselves on blood.' The old woman's voice was strong and carrying.

'What do you mean by a stronghold in Thebes?' Amerotke shivered. This brooding place, the terrors earlier in the day, the swift, brutal death of the Arites were darkening his soul.

'He believed the Nubian regiment had been infiltrated, their hearts turned to stone, their minds away from Pharaoh.' Sihera walked forward.

'And the Sgeru?'

106

'Oh, so you know about that, Lord Amerotke?' Sihera laughed mockingly.

Amerotke wished her face was not so hidden in the shadows. He noticed how the other three had fallen silent.

'Imothep believed the Sgeru lurked like some pestilence in Thebes, had been for years, nurturing and developing like some deadly pus.'

'Where?'

'Anywhere, lord.'

'In the Temple of Nubia?'

'I doubt it.' Sihera's voice was now tired. 'Perhaps,' her tone quickened, 'in a house such as this.'

'Nonsense!' Parmen snarled.

Amerotke studied Sihera. She was sharp-witted, cynical, as if she was detached from the rest, a mere observer.

'And why now?' Amerotke asked. 'The Sgeru?'

'Everything comes to ripeness,' Sihera replied. 'A new Sgeru. Perhaps those filthy demons at Bekhna have recovered their strength, and have stormed out to spread their venom amongst the villages of Nubia, those with kin, menfolk in the regiment. Like some pestilence, once they've infested the tribes and the villages of Nubia, they spread north to Thebes.'

'Is that what Imothep believed?'

'Ask them.' Sihera seemed reluctant to continue.

'No, you tell him!' Neferen's voice was almost a taunt.

'I knew Imothep when he was a young man,' Sihera declared. 'He was never an administrator or a meddler in politics. He didn't like bureaucrats. Imothep was a soldier, a scout, a very skilled one. He always believed the Arites were secretive murderers, but that in the end they would have to deploy in the full light of day. They would, like the hyaenas they were, leave the darkness of the rocks and could then be defeated. Imothep was more interested in the battle to come, about the Sobeck roads to Nubia; he spent his last days browsing over old maps, going to the Temple of Nubia and searching amongst its archives.'

Amerotke thanked her, then walked into the second part of the Mansion of Silence. This must have been Imothep's library, with its reed baskets and panniers full of documents. Both walls were lined with pigeonhole boxes full of papyrus rolls. There was a writing desk covered with pots of red and black ink, sand-shakers and reed pens. The far end of the mansion was slightly raised, with cushioned seats and small tables for dining. Against either wall stood exquisite chests of costly wood, panelled with precious stones, carnelian and intricate designs. Some of these had their lids thrown back. Amerotke crouched beside them and peered inside.

'These were plundered?'

'Yes, yes.' Parmen stepped forward. 'The statue of the hyaena goddess . . .'

Amerotke sifted amongst the small wooden boxes, also empty, that littered the floor.

'They held ingots of gold and silver,' Parmen whispered, crouching next to Amerotke.

'But how?' the judge asking, getting on his feet. 'How was your master killed and his treasure stolen?' He gestured about. 'The walls are sealed. The windows are too small and high. No other entrance exists except the door, yet that was barred both within and without, whilst you, Rahmel,' he pointed at the Nubian, 'were on guard outside.' Amerotke paused. 'So tell me. First, the Arites, if they mark someone down for death, always send a scarab, a warning about what they intend. Did Imothep receive one of these?' His question was answered by silence, the occasional shake of a head.

'We know nothing,' Parmen confessed, 'nothing at all, my lord. If Imothep did receive one, he would give it very little attention, perhaps throw it away.'

'And on the afternoon your master was murdered, what precisely happened?'

'Nothing exceptional,' Parmen admitted. 'My master withdrew to the Mansion of Silence late in the day. We went about our duties. Sihera, ill with a stomach complaint, was confined to her own chamber. We expected Imothep to come out of the mansion before dusk. He always liked to sit on the roof of the house and intone his prayer to the dying sun. On that evening he did not. Eventually I forced the door. I came inside.' Parmen pointed to the far end of the mansion. 'The lamps had guttered low, though a few torches were still flaring. Imothep was sitting there with his back to the door. At first I thought he was asleep. I went up and touched him. When he tilted over, I noticed the red cloth fastened tightly around his throat.'

'And no sign of disturbance?' Amerotke asked.

'None whatsoever, my lord.'

'But someone came in here,' Amerotke declared, 'crept

up behind your master, tightened the cloth around his throat and garrotted him. Sihera, you said your master was a soldier, yet he never fought back, no thrashing of his legs, no attempt to defend himself?'

'I heard nothing,' Rahmel confessed, 'nothing at all.'

'And the killer then raided the chests and coffers, and escaped as mysteriously as he entered. Well, how could that happen?'

Parmen pulled a face and looked towards Rahmel. Amerotke studied the four carefully. Parmen and Rahmel seemed disconcerted. Neferen just stood, hands by her sides, staring blankly at him. Sihera had retreated back into the shadows.

'Well?' Amerotke repeated. 'How could it happen?'

Parmen refused to meet his gaze. 'I don't know,' he mumbled.

'They say,' Sihera spoke up, 'that the Arites can shape-shift. They are certainly very cunning. Perhaps the murderer was lurking in here when the doors were broken down.'

'Just what happened?' Amerotke asked. 'Tell me again!'

'We forced the door,' Rahmel declared. 'Parmen went in. The lamps had burnt low, it was very dark.'

'I went straight up to the cushions where my master was sitting,' the steward explained. 'I touched him on the shoulder and he collapsed to one side. Only then did I notice the red cloth around his neck. There was confusion. We didn't allow others in. I was frightened. I knew there were precious goods, but it was only after we'd removed our master's corpse that we discovered that the statue as well as the gold and silver ingots had been stolen.'

'So.' Amerotke sat down on a chest. He ticked the points off on his fingers. 'Your master Imothep was chief scout in the Spies of Sobeck for the Divine One's father in Nubia. He returns to Thebes, a friend of Pharaoh. He settles here and builds the Mansion of Silence. He lives a quiet life after the death of his wife. You are his kin, part of his family. Nevertheless, Imothep's real allegiance is still to Nubia; that's why he left this house to the temple. The present troubles,' Amerotke continued, 'break out. Imothep does not seem so interested in the Arites as in old maps charting the Sobeck roads out of Nubia. We do not know,' he emphasised with his fingers, 'whether the Arites sent Imothep a warning. It's possible; after all, he was their sworn enemy. Imothep, however, maintains his routine. The day he dies, he moves into this small fortress. Nevertheless, an assassin gets in, strangles your master, plunders his treasure and disappears. You try to rouse Imothep,' Amerotke got to his feet, 'but that fails. You use the outside bar to break in, but when you do, you find Imothep strangled and his treasure gone. No sign of any disturbance, nor did anyone hear anything untoward.'

Rahmel agreed loudly.

'All three of you were outside,' Amerotke continued. 'The servants also witnessed what happened?'

'Yes, they did,' Parmen agreed.

'Except me.' Sihera spoke up. 'Remember, I was ill of a stomach complaint. I very rarely have them, my lord,' she smiled thinly at Amerotke, 'but that evening I lay sick in my chamber. Parmen will confirm that.'

'But something else happened, didn't it?' Amerotke

snapped his fingers and gestured at them to follow him out on to the portico.

The afternoon was dying, the sun beginning to set. Streaks of red scored the sky. A stronger, cooler breeze was blowing through the lush vegetation surrounding the Mansion of Silence. Amerotke sat down on a small stool just beside the double doors and squinted up at them.

'A naked corpse was found here, its hands severed, the red cloth of the Arites tight about its throat. The victim had been garrotted in this garden. Can you show me?'

Parmen pulled a face and walked down the ramp. The rest followed; Amerotke trailed behind. He looked back at the Mansion of Silence. He was determined to reflect on what he'd found there, but for the time being, he would act the student, the scholar with many questions and very few answers. They walked deeper into the garden to an even more desolate part, where the grass rose almost waist high under the trees. Flies buzzed, crickets chirped noisily, birds and monkeys chattered in the branches. Parmen and the rest were beating a path before them. They reached a small clump of terebinth trees. Parmen stopped just at the edge, where the long grass sprouted lush and thick, and gestured down.

'The corpse was found here.'

'Who found him?'

'Our master, Imothep. He was out on one of his morning walks; his saluki hounds were with him, they discovered the corpse.'

'Did you, did he recognise the dead man?'

'No,' Parmen replied. 'Imothep was as astonished as

any of us. He was deeply intrigued. I mean, a stranger, naked, garrotted in his garden.'

'And?' Amerotke asked.

'And what, my lord?'

'From the little I know,' Amerotke declared, 'the Arites strangle their quarry; it is part of their sacred, savage rite. I've never heard of them severing a victim's hand.'

'True!' Sihera's voice carried.

Amerotke turned. 'You seem certain of that.'

'Of course I am.' She wafted flies away from her face. 'The Arites never dismember their victim; that's against what you call their savage ritual. They sacrifice body and soul to the Nema.'

'So why were the hands removed?'

'I don't know,' Rahmel muttered. 'My master's Saluki hounds discovered the body and raised the alarm. Imothep inspected the corpse, then told me to organise its removal to the House of the Dead at the Temple of Nubia.'

'My lord,' Parmen protested, 'what more can we say? We have told you all we know.'

'Yes, indeed.' Amerotke fingered the braided lock of hair hanging down the side of his face and brushed away a bead of sweat. He felt tired and slightly confused, still worried about his family. He looked up at the sky, which was flushed red as the sun began to set, then turned his face to catch the breeze, cool and inviting.

'I'll go back to the house,' he declared. 'I'll meet my escort there.'

Spinning on his heel, he strode back through the grass. Parmen hastened ahead to show him the way. Once back on the portico of the main house, Amerotke had a quiet word with his officer, who'd been busy talking to the servants. What the officer told Amerotke agreed with what the judge had learnt from Imothep's kin. He heard the man out, nodded, then walked back to his hosts.

'Parmen, Rahmel, you have wax?'

Parmen nodded. Amerotke opened the pouch on his sash, took out his cartouche and handed it to the officer.

'I want the Mansion of Silence sealed immediately. The doors must be secured as well as they can be and my seal placed there. No one is to enter that building without me being present.'

The officer hurried off to obey. Amerotke clicked his fingers at Parmen. 'He will need wax. You'd best do that.'

The steward looked as if he was going to object.

'I want it done now, and quickly,' Amerotke snapped. 'There's one more thing I wish to do.' He went and sat on the portico. Neferen offered him a drink of fresh fruit juice, but he shook his head, staring out across the overgrown wild garden. A short while later the officer and Parmen returned. The door to the Mansion of Silence had been barred and closed, three films of wax, sealed with Amerotke's cartouche, placed across both doors.

'Very well.' Amerotke took the fan out of his sash and wafted his face. 'I want to return to where that corpse was found. A thought has occurred to me.'

Parmen sighed noisily but led the way. When they reached the place, Amerotke asked them to show him exactly where the body had been found. Parmen pointed it out. Amerotke told him to go and stand in the shade of the terebinth trees with the rest whilst he, on hands and knees, began to scrutinise the ground. The officer came over to help. Amerotke just shook his head. The corpse had, according to Parmen, been discovered just on the edge of the trees. Amerotke moved along and found the spot, where dried blood, now swarming with ants and other insects, still stained the grass.

'So,' he whispered to himself, 'whoever he was, he was killed here and his hands removed. Parmen?' he called.

'Yes, my lord?'

'Were the man's hands ever found? The grounds searched for them?'

'I don't think so. No, no, they weren't,' Parmen declared. 'My master did not seem interested in that.'

'He should have been,' Amerotke whispered. 'He truly should have been, but enough for the moment.' He rose to his feet, rubbing his fingers. 'Parmen, I am finished here, but I shall return ...'

The shining eye of Horus comes.
In peace it blazes through the darkness.
Ra rejoices on the horizon to see his flames consume all
    evil.
Against the power of the Seth Creatures, I kindle
Fire to shine with Ra and follow adoring in his train
    for ever,
Upon the hands of the Twin Sisters ...

Amerotke sprinkled incense over the small bowl of fire placed on the table before him and watched the scented smoke rise against the darkening sky. He'd returned home from the House of the Forest to find Shufoy ordering the military escort, all three of them, around the garden. Norfret had became agitated about the soldiers, speculating loudly on the whereabouts of her husband. Amerotke had hardly made his ablutions after entering the house before Norfret presented him with a litany of questions. He just shook his head, smiled and kissed her full on the lips.

'In time,' he murmured.

Norfret glared at him and, standing on tiptoe, whispered. 'It will be good to hear what your lips have to speak.'

Amerotke quietly decided that discretion was the best path to follow. He went out into the garden and talked to the escort. Secretly he wished there were more of them, but with the Nubian regiment consigned to its barracks, the other regiments massing south of Thebes and the city garrison ever vigilant against fresh attacks, any request for more men would take days. Amerotke hid his own unease as he played Senet with his sons, roaring with laughter when they caught him cheating. He then joined them in the garden to track down what Ahmase thought was a colony of jerboas that had invaded the orchards. Curfay dismissed them as mere gerbils and declared he'd seen a genet hunting amongst the trees. Amerotke followed the boys around the garden, past the beautiful pools of purity, the green lawns, and the pergolas and walks covered with creeping vines. The elegant flowerbeds and herb patches, delicately painted small pavilions, needle-thin irrigation canals and well-pruned orchards were a sharp contrast to the sombre, tangled garden that surrounded the Mansion of Silence.

The judge wondered quietly what other secrets that desolate place might still hold.

At last he called a halt to the hunt. He and the boys sat under the shade of an ancient holm oak, Amerotke's favourite, to eat delicious semolina cake and sip crushed fruit juice, before both sons raced away to practise their skills as scribes with Shufoy. The little man, all distracted, was wandering the gardens, reciting poetry that Ahmase described as love lines written by 'the Grand Master himself', as they liked to call Shufoy. Amerotke decided to leave his lovelorn friend alone. He'd washed and come up to the roof terrace, where he'd eaten his evening meal of rice and broad beans in coriander by himself. Now finished, he wanted to watch the sky turn its bewildering shade of colours, feel the cool breeze of Amun on his face and offer a prayer for all those he loved. For a long while he sat alone. The spacious roof terrace with its cushions, small tables, flowerpots and incense boats was his favourite place at both dawn and dusk. Nevertheless, the troubles and problems of the day pressed in. The judge drew comfort from one fact he'd learnt. On his return home, Shufoy had whispered the name of the Great House's spy in the Temple of Nubia. Lady Busiris! Amerotke was not too surprised. Hatusu could seduce most people through her flirtatious charm, not to mention the occasional costly gift. Pharaoh's arrangement with Busiris would be courteous, just the gossip of the temple, which Senenmut would immediately pass on to the scribes of the Secret Cabinet for their scrutiny.

Amerotke was eventually aroused from his meditation by Norfret, lovely in a white linen robe, coming up on to the terrace with a doleful Shufoy trailing behind. Norfret brought a jug of cool charou wine, three goblets and a bowl of red cherries. They sat enjoying the evening, though Amerotke realised that Norfret wanted to know what had happened. Those dark eyes in her sensitive face were wary, and she puckered her lips and kept rubbing her brow, the usual signs of agitation. Amerotke eventually told her exactly what had happened, including the attack on himself and Valu. She heard him out with more rubbing of her brow.

'And now?' she asked.

Amerotke rocked himself gently backwards and forwards on the cushions.

'Nubia always looks to challenge Egyptian rule. Tuthmosis delivered a crushing blow, but apparently the Arites now feel strong enough to leave their fortress at Bekhna to spread their poison. They are certainly causing confusion in the city.'

'Not to mention the disappearance of imperial messengers,' declared Shufoy, breaking from his brooding.

'Oh yes.' Amerotke winked at Norfret. 'You know I visited the Oasis of Sinjar, a lonely place a day's journey from Thebes, on the route to the First Cataract.'

'The messengers disappear there?' Norfret asked.

'Yes and no,' Amerotke replied. 'Couriers and envoys have been seen going south on their barges after they have visited the oasis, only to disappear, as if they and their craft were swallowed up by the great snake Apep.'

'So there's no mystery at the oasis?'

'Not that I can prove,' Amerotke replied. 'It's used by desert-wanderers and sand-dwellers, merchants and messengers; it provides shade and a delicious well of water. The oasis chaplain, Nebher, seems competent enough, though he's distraught over the disappearance of his own daughter. I discovered nothing suspicious. There's the nearby fortress of Timsah, a massive ruin, the haunt of scavengers both human and animal.' Amerotke spread his hands. 'Whatever the cause, the disappearance of those messengers is deepening the confusion.'

'The work of the Arites?' Norfret asked.

'I expect so, but I have no hard evidence for that; only a suspicion.'

'Then there is the poisoning of the Medjay scouts,' Shufoy added.

Amerotke smiled, leaned over, plucked a cherry and popped it into his mouth. 'Now that is the work of the Arites. I don't think we will ever find the actual assassin – well, not now – but I know how to stop it. The other mysteries, however, grow more tangled. First, what truly happened at the Temple of Nubia today? Why did that Arites prisoner confess, offer to cooperate, but then . . .' Amerotke paused, listening to the chatter of the birds in the garden below, 'so mysteriously die in the House of Chains? Did those Arites attack me and Valu to kill us, to free him or to do both? And how did he die? How can an assassin enter a locked cell, closely guarded, with no other entrance?'

'Could he have strangled himself?' Shufoy asked.

'A very rare possibility,' Amerotke conceded. 'I don't think so. Then there's the business at the Mansion of Silence: the murder of Imothep, very similar to that of the Arites prisoner, a man locked in a chamber, secure and guarded, yet an assassin got in, strangled him and plundered his treasure. And why was Imothep not openly concerned about the Arites? If they had warned him they were coming, surely he would have asked for protection or taken greater precautions? Or did he just not care and dismissed their warnings for what he saw them, empty boasting? Why was he so concerned about studying maps and plans of the routes south? Did he think he'd be re-employed as chief scout? Then there is the other corpse.' He glanced at Norfret. 'Sickening,' he declared. 'A man found naked in Imothep's garden except for a red cloth tied tightly around his throat, both his hands lopped off.'

Norfret's fingers flew to her lips.

'Why? Who killed him?' Amerotke mused loudly. 'What was he doing there? Why would the Arites follow this name-less man into Imothep's garden, murder him, then leave?'

'How will you end all this?' Norfret asked.

'There is only one way, my lily of the valley.' Amerotke tried to stifle his own frustration at what was happening. 'We must find the Sgeru, capture him, expose him and humiliate him. The disaffection in the Nubia regiment would collapse, and—' Amerotke broke off at the sound of running feet up the outside steps. Ahmase almost threw himself on to the terrace.

'Father, Father, you must come! You must come! There are armed men, many of them, at the gate. The porter is very concerned.'

CHAPTER 5

Netcha: ravenous

Amerotke told Shufoy to guard Norfret. He hurried down, pausing to summon one of the escort. He took the man's sword and hastened along to the gate. This was thrown open, the Medjay scouts thronging in. They looked fearsome with their crimped hair, tortoiseshell ornaments, silver bangles and tawdry jewellery, their fringed kilts hanging down over dusty legs and feet. The leather belts around their waists carried daggers and clubs; each bore a spear and a shield and, slung across their backs, a bow and quiver of arrows.

'My lord Amerotke.' The Medjay commander approached, knelt before Amerotke, bowed, then glanced up. 'I am sorry for the late hour. My name is Hennam: you sent for me?'

Amerotke grasped him by the hand and raised him up. 'So I did.' He smiled and gestured at the men thronging around the gate. 'I invited you to eat and drink with me. I didn't expect your entire company.'

Hennam's rugged-lined face creased into a smile.

'My lord, that is not my doing but General Omendap's. Shufoy also brought news about what was happening to the city. My orders are most explicit. I am to visit you here, listen to what you have to say, then move back into Thebes to help the Divine One. I am to report to the commander of the palace guard.'

'How many men have you brought?' Amerotke peered over the man's shoulder.

'About seventy in all. I assure you they will be no burden.'

'Oh, they are not a burden.' Amerotke smiled. He gestured Hennam forward and put an arm around the man's shoulder. 'You are most welcome. I wish to discuss certain matters with you, but look . . .' He called over one of his escort, who stood looking completely bewildered at the turn of events. 'Take the Medjay,' Amerotke ordered the officer, 'deep into the garden. Call the servants; feed the men wine, beer, dried meat, fruit and bread. Make them as comfortable as possible. The evening is calm and cool; they'll enjoy it there.'

Hennam excused himself and went back to his men. Amerotke's invitation was immediately greeted with exclamations of joy; hands were raised, heads bowed. They needed no second bidding but followed the officer deep into the garden. Amerotke stood and watched them go. Hennam had brought the best; the Medjay looked like what they were: veteran warriors, skilled in fighting, most of them wearing the bees of valour, the collar of gold or bracelets of silver, personal gifts from the Pharaoh and her generals for bravery and stamina in battle. A servant brought a bowl of water and a napkin. Hennam courteously but quickly washed his hands and face, drying himself briskly.

'My lord, I am your honoured guest. I brought no gift.'

'You, yourself are the gift.' Amerotke smiled. 'Come.'

They reached the roof terrace where introductions were made, courtesies exchanged. Servants brought up meat and bread, a fresh bowl of cherries and another jug of charou wine. Hennam was hungry and ate lustily, now and again stopping to stare at Norfret, apparently much taken by her beauty. He kept smiling at her, complimenting both her and the food, apologising for intruding. Once he'd satisfied his appetite, Amerotke leaned forward and touched the man's gold collar of valour which sparkled in the lamplight, then the two bracelets of silver.

'How long have you served the Great House?'

The man squinted up at the sky.

'Seventeen Inundations in all, my lord.' He stretched out his arms. 'These are only some of the tokens conferred on me.'

'So you are a warrior,' Amerotke praised him, 'and a brave one.'

Hennam gazed shyly at Norfret, who clapped her hands softly. She leaned over and filled his jug. The Medjay was clearly enjoying himself.

'You wish to speak to me, lord?'

'I do. How many men have you lost? I mean dying suddenly in camp or out in the Redlands?'

Again Hennam squinted up at the sky.

'The last one was Kaemas, so that makes eight in all.'

'And their corpses?'

'I am no physician, but they were apparently poisoned. Some died outright, others suffered a fit or trance. They could see visions, hideous sights, as if the earth had scrolled back to spit out a legion of demons.'

'You know,' Amerotke declared, 'that in the shops, booths and bazaars of Thebes, you may buy potions and philtres that can make you feel like a god and see dark visions in the dead of night.'

'Of course, my lord, but why these men?'

'Because they were Medjay,' Amerotke replied. He smiled at Hennam's confusion. 'The killer,' he insisted, 'didn't really care who died, as long as it was a Medjay. What is your regiment famous for, Hennam? Scouting, spying, the Eyes and Ears of Pharaoh's army when it goes to war. Now your courage, vigilance and loyalty are tinged by distrust, fear, even terror. Who will die next?'

Hennam studied this secretive-faced judge closely. He'd heard about Amerotke's reputation: wily as a serpent, one man had described him, so where was he leading him?

'You think there is a traitor in our midst?' Hennam asked.

'No, I don't,' Amerotke replied. 'The murder of your men is the work of the Arites.' He paused as the Medjay made the sign against evil with his finger and thumb. 'They are malevolent, malignant creatures of the night. They do not fight out in the open under the eye of the

124

sun, but secretly. They sow chaos and confusion. They don't care which Medjay dies as long as one of you does.'

'But the water stocks, our food supplies have all been checked.'

'And the natron pellets?' Amerotke asked. 'You have baskets full of them?'

'Oh yes.'

Amerotke leaned over and picked up the empty cherry bowl. 'Norfret, how many cherries were in this bowl when you first brought it up?'

She shrugged prettily. 'About thirty.'

'And in the fresh bowl perhaps the same number. So,' Amerotke smiled, 'since you came up here, sixty cherries have been served. What happens if one of them was poisoned? We might not eat it tonight, but someone will eventually eat the tainted fruit and die.'

Hennam stared at him open-mouthed.

'Natron pellets?' he asked.

'Think, Hennam,' Amerotke insisted. 'What do your scouts take out into the desert? What do they look for when they come back? Water is precious. I have fought out in the Redlands. The physicians tell us to drink sparsely, never gulp. No, your water is untainted, but some of the natron pellets aren't. Let me explain. A scout returns from an expedition. He may take a sip of water, then he'll go to the common supply and fill his pouch with natron pellets: they are cheap, given away by the handful. He pops a poisoned one into his mouth, he sucks, chews, whatever, and dies. The same applies to those killed out in the desert. In the end it doesn't really matter where they are, it doesn't matter who they are, they've just been unfortunate. God knows what the potion is. Some poison that disturbs the heart before death stops it. Can you see the sheer wickedness of it, Hennam, the real evil? No individual Medjay is marked down for death; all that matters is that some of you die. It must be the natron pellets,' Amerotke insisted. 'Tell me, Hennam, how are they stored?'

'In great baskets under the quartermaster's care. They are taken by the handful and replaced quite often; it would be impossible to find the murderer.'

'The real murderer is the Sgeru, the leader of the Arites,' Amerotke declared. 'How he perpetrates his evil design is simple. One of his followers, either in the quartermaster's store in Thebes, out at the camp or amongst those who bring in the supplies, is responsible. He is given a handful of poisoned pellets and sprinkles them in with the rest.'

Hennam sat, eyes closed, muttering quietly to himself.

'It's true, my lord, they are brought in by drovers, porters.' He opened his eyes. 'Sometimes in carts or in baskets slung either side of a donkey. If I remember correctly, some of those couriers were Nubians. Indeed, until recently, such people were common in our camp. Then there are the whores, the tinkers, the pedlars . . .'

'So easy,' Amerotke agreed. 'Now, this is what I propose. Select two runners from the men below. Send one straight into Thebes with a message to my Lord Senenmut about what I have told you, and the other to General Omendap. All natron pellets reserved for the Medjay scouts are to be destroyed; they are to be replaced with fresh ones directly from the imperial stores. These are to be brought out and stored under the protection of the Medjay alone. Do you understand?'

Hennam sprang to his feet and hastened down the outside steps.

'So simple,' Norfret murmured. 'So very, very simple. Are you sure, Amerotke?'

'I'm certain.' Amerotke grinned, popping another cherry into his mouth. 'It is logical. An assassin has to get close to someone's food bowl or water cup, a difficult enough task in camp, but out in the desert? Veterans don't gulp water; they drink as little and as slowly as possible to avoid being sick. In fact a natron pellet is the best way to cleanse your mouth: it keeps the throat wet and comfortable. You'll see many a scout chewing in the camp or out in the desert. Ah well,' he sighed. 'Omendap, together with Lord Senenmut, will radically reorganise the supply of the camp. Porters will be dismissed, along with the whores, tinkers and chapmen. Omendap will test my theory: pellets will be given to the scavenger dogs that plague the camp. Undoubtedly before dawn at least three or four of those dogs will be found dead.' Amerotke paused as Hennam came back up the steps. The Medjay squatted on the cushions and took a deep gulp of wine.

'Such a swift death,' Hennam murmured, wiping his mouth on the back of his hand. 'A lesson to us all, my lord.' He grinned down at his cup. 'To be careful what we eat and drink.'

'Tell me.' Amerotke leaned forward. 'These imperial

messengers who've disappeared? You have searched for them?'

'Of course, my lord. Messengers travel south from Thebes to the Viceroy of Nubia either along the Sobeck roads or the river.'

'And they always stop at the Oasis of Sinjar?'

Hennam spread his hands and pulled a face. 'Invariably. Perhaps if they are in a hurry they do not.'

'But you have found no trace of the missing couriers?'

'My lord, we've interrogated the oasis chaplain. He can tell us nothing. We've gone further south and talked to the villagers . . . nothing!'

Amerotke nodded. He and Hennam had reached the same conclusion.

'According to what they told us,' the Medjay explained, 'some of the imperial messengers were seen on their barges or punts passing the villages. Nevertheless, they never reached the Viceroy. They've never been traced: their bodies, belongings, the boats they were in. As if,' Hennam snapped his fingers, 'some magician had made them disappear into the darkness of the night.'

'And you find that strange?' Amerotke asked.

'Of course, my lord. People disappear on the Nile or in the desert, but traces are always found.'

'But there are mysteries,' Shufoy interrupted. 'I've heard of chariot squadrons disappearing.'

'Ah,' Hennam raised a finger, 'very true! Squadrons have gone out deep into the desert to be covered by a sandstorm. However, these messengers are travelling along the river or through the oases, and not just one or two of them but, according to my calculations, six or seven. Some of them escorted by veteran soldiers. Most mysterious!'

'And the nearby fortress of Timsah?'

'A formidable ruin, walls and defences that can be easily manned though we found nothing except for desert-wanderers, sand-dwellers and scavengers.'

'Have you discovered anything out of place?' Amerotke queried, trying to hide his own despair. 'Anything in the desert that strikes you as peculiar?'

Hennam stared down at his wine cup, swirling the dregs. Amerotke glanced up at the sky. The sun was now setting, a beautiful red glow spreading out. Darkness was about to swoop in like some great bird. Already the blossoms of the sky were appearing. It promised to be a beautiful night. Perhaps he and Norfret could sleep up here.

'One thing,' Hennam declared, 'just one. Some hunters, wandering scavengers, arrived in General Omendap's camp. They were hungry. They complained of a shortage of game in the area around Sinjar. They hunt the ibex, whatever can be found, but they claimed that either the game had been driven off or that someone or something else was hunting it.' He shrugged. 'It could be a seasonal occurrence, but apart from that . . .' He lifted his cup in toast. 'What do you propose?' he asked.

'I don't know, not yet.' Amerotke picked up the wine jug. 'In the meantime, we can drink a little more . . .'

Lord Valu sat alone on his roof terrace. He'd bathed, clothed himself in fresh perfumed robes, carefully oiled his hands and face and come up to sit with a goblet of wine and a dish of sesame rings. In the soft glow from an alabaster lamp stand, carved in the form of a lotus, he watched the sunset. Afterwards he recited the poem he'd recently composed for his tomb in the Necropolis, a splendid affair that boasted its own courtyard, entrance, annexes and imposing tomb chamber. He wanted to make sure the poem's lines were correct so that the stone-carver would copy them correctly. When he had done that, he would go down and kiss his beloved daughter good night. The prosecutor drew a deep breath; he would recite the poem once more. He quickly wafted his face with an ebony fan. All was ready. The gods of the night air would welcome and praise his tongue, which was more nimble than a scribe's pen. Valu picked up his curved sceptre, his symbol of authority, fashioned out of wood and sheathed in gold. He laid this across his lap and closed his eyes. The words of the poem tripped easily from his tongue:

> I am true of heart, impartial, trusted.
> One who has walked along the way of the god.
> I was praised in the City of the Sceptre,
> Magnificent to all, gracious to everyone.
> I was well disposed, popular, widely loved, and
>   cheerful.
> I was self-controlled in the year of distress.
> Sweet-natured, well-spoken.
> I was a good shelter for the needy . . .

Valu paused abruptly in his hymn of self-glorification.

The mansion had fallen strangely silent. Had he heard a muted scream? Some servant girl being chased by her friends? He walked to the edge of the roof terrace, grasped the rail and glanced down at his beautiful gardens, now cloaked in darkness. Only here and there a glow of lamplight broke the blackness. Perhaps it would be best if he went down. Valu looked longingly back at the writing table littered with scraps of his poetry, his fan and sceptre glinting in the lamplight. He sighed and went down the outside stairs, so lost in his thoughts that he forgot the escort who should have been on guard at the foot of the steps. He walked through a narrow side door leading into the main hall, normally a place of serene tranquillity. Not so now! Valu stopped. He could not believe his eyes. He must be in some nightmare from the blackest depths of the Am-duat. The hall was lit by the fire in the centre and bathed in the soft allure of lamplight, but all was different. His daughter should have been kneeling on the cushions playing a game of counters; instead, she was naked and half-gagged, a red cloth tied tightly around her throat, her popping eyes staring in terror at him. Valu, mouth opening and shutting like some gasping fish, heart pounding, staggered forward. A masked man stood behind his daughter, grasping that tight red garrotte. Valu glanced around. Corpses littered the hall. Men and women, his servants, the escort included, limbs all twisted, faces grotesque, mouths opened in a last snarl for breath before the cloths tightened around their throats. Valu paused, hands beating the air, staring in shocked terror at the masked figures crowding around him. He tried to protest, but his throat was too dry. This could not be happening! He was Pharaoh's favourite, Royal Prosecutor in the Great Courts of Thebes! He turned to run, but a red cloth snaked tightly around his throat, and he was forced to his knees. He stared in terror at his daughter, who gazed pitifully back as the garrottes tightened to choke off their breath.

Once Valu and his daughter were dead, their limbs no longer jerking, the assassins crept out from the darkness, and clustered around the small group of Arites, undoubtedly Nubians, sinewy black bodies glistening with sweat, faces hidden behind blood-coloured masks.

'It is done,' the Breaker of Bones grated. 'All are dead. The mansion is ours. No sound, no alarm, not one of us was lost.'

'Good.' The leader of the Arites gestured round. 'You and the others collect what plunder you want, a short while, then we'll be gone.'

'And we'll fire the mansion?' the Devourer of Hearts demanded.

The Arites' leader swung around, his serrated dagger grazing the Devourer's neck.

'No fire,' he whispered, 'no sign of what we have done or what we intend. Our time is precious. Collect what you want, then we'll be gone.'

He lowered the knife and led the other Arites out to squat in the gardens whilst the assassins looted Valu's mansion, stripping the dead, breaking into coffers and chests, plucking precious items from their stands; anything small and precious was taken and thrust into leather sacks. As the Arites waited, their leader glanced up at the sky. Darkness was complete. His instructions were clear and precise: Valu and Amerotke must die that night, they and all who were with them. It was time to be gone. He rose and whistled through the darkness before giving orders to his companions, who hastened into the mansion, driving out the assassins with their sacks. One of these, clutching a wine flagon, came staggering drunk.

'By what name are you called?' the Arites' leader whispered.

'The Eater of Shit!' the fellow bellowed drunkenly then roared with laughter. A sound that ended in a choking gargle as the Arites' leader plunged his dagger directly into the man's throat. The other assassins muttered, sacks were dropped, hands going for knives and cudgels.

'Sober until this is done,' the Arites hissed. 'He was a danger to us all!' He leaned down and plucked out his dagger. 'Bring his corpse to the nearest crocodile pool.' He kicked the sack the dead man had dropped. 'Share this amongst you. Now come!'

The host of assassins opened the double gates of the mansion and slipped out, dark shapes flitting through the night. They hurried along the deserted path that skirted the walls of the wealthy mansions to their right, on their left a broad strip of greenery, the trees now darkened in the night. Beyond that stretched the Nile, the torches and lanterns of fishing boats pricking the darkness. If anyone approached, the assassins simply melted off the path and let them pass. On one occasion they delayed a little longer so that the Breaker of Bones and three others could take the corpse down to a crocodile pool. They swung the body into the darkness to splash in the thick reeds fringing the river, then hurried silently back, joining the rest, a flock of malevolent bats flitting under the starlit sky. They reached Amerotke's mansion, mustering silently off the pathway opposite the main gate. The Arites' leader peered through the night. He glimpsed the glitter of lamps on the roof terrace and heard the sound of a man's laugh. He turned to the Breaker of Bones.

'Go now!' he urged.

The Breaker of Bones, who'd also drunk deeply of looted wine, rose, lifting his mace.

'And remember,' the leader hissed, 'Amerotke and his family are to be saved for us.'

The Breaker of Bones led his men in a silent trot towards the wall. They quickly scaled this, dropping down into the garden beyond. The Breaker of Bones whistled softly. The line of men gathered amongst the bushes and trees, paused, then sloped through the darkness like hyaenas. The Breaker of Bones, so intent on reaching the house, screamed in terror as men seemed to rise from the ground before him, dark shapes, bodies glistening with oil. Arrow and spear came whirling through the night. The Breaker of Bones stepped back; his men were equally taken by surprise. The garden erupted into a bloody, vicious hand-to-hand fight as the assassins met unexpected resistance. The Breaker of Bones glanced round. Torches were appearing further down the garden. He and his company had been ambushed! He whistled shrilly three times and turned to flee, but a Medjay caught his outline against the white wall and let slip an arrow. The shaft whirred through the darkness, striking the Breaker of Bones so violently in the back it pierced through flesh and bone to the other side. The attack was over. The assassins, expecting little resistance, were now fighting veteran Medjay in a carefully laid ambush: their courage soon cooled and they joined their leader's flight to the wall. Some reached it safely; others were cut down by arrow, club, mace or dagger. The night air was riven by screams, yells and blood-curdling shouts. The Devourer of Hearts, sobbing and gasping for breath, scaled the wall, jumped down and ran to where he'd left the Arites, but he found only the sacks of plunder taken from Valu's house. He grasped one of these and, without looking back, fled through the darkness.

Amerotke sat beneath the outstretched branches of the sycamore tree and watched the Flocks of the God graze serenely on the succulent meadow grass of the Temple of Nubia. He had walked to the temple, down corridors and alleyways of shifting light, across courtyards that trapped the sun, the only relief from the sweaty heat being a fountain gurgling water over a holy stela. He felt he'd wandered through a forest of stone: soaring statues of the gods, obelisks, their sandstone glowing red, their peaks flashing brilliantly above the silver-embossed cornices of the temple buildings. Incense, blood-soaked sacrifice smoke and gusts of myrrh flowed through the air, mixing with the smell of dung from the animal pens and the sweat of pilgrims and visitors thronging to this shrine or that chapel. Amerotke had walked because he wished to ease the tension in his own heart. He felt deeply worried. He tried to steel himself against the hustle and bustle of the crowd, pinpricks to his own agitation. He'd come here to wait for Lord Khufu. Shufoy had gone courting the lady Mataia, who had greeted them in the Sycamore Courtyard all coy and flirtatious until the dwarf had told her the grim news. The heset's jaw had dropped as she listened in speechless horror. She was about to say something but instead waved her hand, murmuring that Lord Khufu was the best person to speak to before leaving to find him.

Amerotke, eyes half closed, drew a deep breath to ease his troubled heart. He had visited Valu's house but there was nothing to be done. The Eyes and Ears of Pharaoh, Amerotke's sometime inveterate opponent, was no more. That quick brain, that nimble tongue, the darting eyes all silenced for ever. Nothing but a swollen lump of flesh with that ghastly red cloth squeezing his throat. Nearby sprawled Valu's daughter, servants and escort, all brutally murdered. Amerotke closed his eyes. The Seth creatures had plotted a similar death for himself and his family; only the presence of Hennam and his scouts had prevented that. The Medjay had become suspicious. Keen hunters, one of them nicknamed 'Dog', most skilled in detecting scents, had hastened to the rooftop to alert Amerotke. Dog reported how he was sure a hostile force was gathering beyond the walls. Shufoy had laughed but Dog, crouching like a saluki hound, had tapped his nose and explained how the breeze wafting in from the river brought new smells, a sweaty perfume and the stench of the slums. Amerotke, used to the cunning of these scouts, became alarmed. Hennam was certain that danger threatened. He'd quickly deployed his men in the gardens and they closed on the filth that came swirling over the wall with the vice-like grip of a crocodile's jaws. Few of the attackers had escaped. Those who'd survived simply bubbled on their bloody froth and could tell them nothing, so their throats were cut. Amerotke was sure that the Arites had been involved, though not in the actual assault. Sacks of valuables had also been found and recognised. Amerotke had immediately dispatched a runner to Valu's house who came hastening back with the dire news. Shufoy, who'd taken no part in the battle, searched the dead, kicking each corpse. Norfret remained icy cold whilst the two boys had been beside themselves with excitement.

Amerotke had surveyed the dead, given orders for the corpses of the assailants to be thrown into a nearby crocodile pool, then summoned Hennam. The Medjay scouts were paraded in front of him. Amerotke gave each half a deben of silver, congratulating them on their bravery. He solemnly promised that the three scouts who had died would receive the full burial rites of Osiris, whilst the wounded would be tended in the best House of Myrrh at the Temple of Isis. Dog, who had raised the alarm, was rewarded with a costly carnelian bracelet. Afterwards, couriers were dispatched to the Great House, whilst Amerotke had a swift heated discussion with Norfret. He could give her no assurances for their safety. He was chief judge. Sometimes the filth he dealt with came lapping about his own house, though he would do his best to protect them. On this occasion he brooked no argument. His entire family and household would be moved to the security of the Malkata Palace, whilst he and Shufoy would reside at the Temple of Nubia.

Everything was completed before dawn. Messengers arrived from Lord Senenmut promising guards for Amerotke's deserted mansion. The judge then took his family into Thebes before moving to the Temple of Nubia. Lord Khufu had been busy with the dawn sacrifices, but Mataia, still agitated by the news about Valu, had provided them with comfortable lodgings in the guest house. Amerotke had slept fretfully, waking late in the morning ruthlessly determined to resolve these murderous mysteries. Captain Asural and his cohort from Amerotke's court at the Temple of Ma'at had been summoned to serve as his personal bodyguard. Amerotke was burning with fury; anger clouded his emotions, though he realised he had to remain cold and objective. He must collect and sift all the evidence here in the heart of Nubia, this temple with its narrow walks, pillars a smoky red as if a fire burnt within, delicate white walls, soaring black gateways and pebble-dashed paths that glowed like amber. A pleasant enough place, honeycombed with rooms, chambers and passageways, its courtyards a forest of statues, but was it also the heart of a hideous web of conspiracy and murder? The entire Isis regiment now ringed the temple. Nubians, frightened of the dark looks and muttered threats in the street markets, were flocking here, a move secretly encouraged by the Great House, which wanted to contain the problem. Nubian refugees thronged the temple courtyards and public gardens. They unpacked their wooden bowls to cook meals of millet and ground beef or baked cakes of flour, water and a little salt kneaded into dough, tossed from hand to hand until flattened, then pushed under the spent embers of a fire.

All kinds of bizarre figures came flocking into the temple. Wizard men garbed in their stinking dried camel hides; heavy-breasted prostitutes, their wide hips swaying to the clink of horn bracelets; beggars licensed by the priests, the backs of their hands tattooed with the temple insignia, all returning to cast themselves on the charity of the sanctuary. Amerotke suspected some of this influx might include Arites, but there was no hard proof. The chaos was certainly deepening. The news of Valu's murder and the total destruction of his household had chilled the court, Amerotke's escape was viewed as a stroke of good fortune. The chief judge thought otherwise. He had been saved because he was confronting evil, which could be negated through luck perhaps, but ultimately through scrutiny, logic and evidence. He would do that. He would avenge Valu's death. Couriers from Omendap's army had already arrived to inform him how the supplies of natron pellets for the Medjay had been thrown out for the pi-dogs, the yellow-coated mongrels that plagued the encampment. A few had died violently, so all provisions for the Medjay were being burnt. Hennam and his scouts would now be responsible for buying, collecting, transporting and guarding all future stores. More importantly, the Medjay now knew the source of their comrades' mysterious deaths. These were the work not of some hidden demon but of the evil Arites, against whom they had already scored a bloody victory the previous evening at Amerotke's house.

'My lord judge?'

Amerotke glanced up, so lost in his thoughts he hadn't even heard Khufu and the others approach. The high priest's aristocratic face was worried and lined, lips puckered, fingers playing with the bracelet around his wrist. Lady Busiris was no better, lower lip trembling as she sat down, Mataia beside her. Shufoy, lost in admiration for the beautiful Nubian, slipped beside Amerotke like a shadow, eyes still on the new love of his life. Servants hurried up to offer platters of food and drink. Khufu shook his head impatiently, gesturing at them to withdraw.

'My lord judge, I've heard the news.' He wetted his lips. 'An abomination! Dreadful murder! You've seen what is happening here? Nubians flocking in for sanctuary and protection.'

'What can be done?' Busiris wailed, wafting her face. Amerotke glanced at this high priestess who also served as Lord Senenmut's spy. Did she recognise herself as that? Conveying information to Pharaoh's grand vizier in the hope of reward? Mataia seemed calmer; now and again she'd glance at Shufoy, and smile or wink quickly.

'I don't know what to say.' Khufu shook his head. He leaned forward. 'But you and your family are safe.'

'The Lords of Light be thanked! And you?'

'Agitated,' Khufu confessed. 'At the dawn sacrifice, I forgot the words, I spilt incense, the cut I made was not clean.'

'And the reason for this?' Amerotke asked gently.

Khufu took the beautifully embroidered pouch from the sash around his waist and shook out its contents, handing over the three scarabs for Amerotke to inspect.

'The Arites!' Amerotke exclaimed. 'These were sent to you?'

'Two were found outside my chamber,' Khufu replied. 'The third outside Mataia's. The Arites have apparently singled us out for death. My lord, what can we do?'

'Nothing,' Amerotke replied. 'Go about your ordinary business. Take precautions, be prudent. I would strongly advise you not to go into the city. Here at least there will be some security.' He glanced at Mataia. 'I need to visit your House of Books. I wish to look at the records Imothep studied. Is that possible?'

She smiled in agreement.

'And tonight, my lord,' Khufu declared, 'you must be our guest at a special supper. Imothep's corpse has been prepared for his journey into the Far West. I have invited his household – Parmen, Neferen, Rahmel and Sihera – to a funeral banquet here. I think it's appropriate.' He laughed nervously. 'It will keep our minds off these other matters.'

The high priest clambered to his feet, whispering to his wife to follow. Amerotke watched them go. Was their agitation genuine? Yet he could almost smell their fear, and why should they support the Arites? A high priest of a Theban temple?

'My lord, the House of Books?'

Amerotke turned. 'Yes, my lady.'

141

They followed the chief heset across squares and gardens. A few mercenaries thronged about. Mataia explained how Lord Khufu had brought them into the temple for protection: burly, thickset men, dressed in kilted leather aprons and padded jerkins sewn with pieces of metal. Armed with clubs and sticks, the mercenaries were imposing order on the flow of visitors. Mataia eventually led Amerotke and Shufoy away from the main concourse. The House of Books stood in its own sheltered courtyard, a pleasant one-storey building under the supervision of two scribes who looked as ancient as some of the manuscripts they guarded. The temple documents were stored in leather tubes, reed baskets and carved chests in a cavernous annexe with a cellar beneath. The library itself was a long, high-ceilinged hall well served by windows that allowed in light and air for the scholars and scribes who squatted beneath, hunched over their writing tables.

Mataia consulted the book of records, showing it to Amerotke before beckoning him over to a table furnished with a cushion and a scribe's pallet. According to the records, Imothep had studied charts and maps of the area south of Thebes, stretching down to the Oasis of Sinjar and beyond that to the First Cataract.

'Why would he need these?' Amerotke asked. 'Why now?'

'He said he wished to plot the way the Arites might come. Look.' Mataia, in a gust of fragrant perfume, bent over Amerotke's shoulder, one slender finger tracing the Sobeck roads; such desert routes ran parallel to the Nile, connected by small oases or villages where messengers and couriers could stop for rest and refreshment.

'Imothep believed the Arites would use these to thread men—'

'Thread?' Shufoy asked.

'Thread,' Mataia repeated. 'Like beads on a string into Thebes.'

'Did he ever talk to you?' Amerotke asked. 'About his own fears, any threats or danger to him?'

Mataia knelt down on the opposite side of the table, glanced quickly at Shufoy then shook her head. 'Imothep was like a man obsessed. He never referred to any menace, just a deep desire to study the maps and charts.'

Amerotke thanked her and turned to the documents. Mataia and Shufoy withdrew as the judge became immersed in scrutinising papyrus rolls, scraps of parchment, old charts and maps that described the forays and invasions of past rulers. Time passed. Amerotke finished and made notes. He then called for any manuscript the library might hold on the Arites. The lector priest looked surprised. He scratched his wrinkled cheek and rounded his bloodshot eyes but rose and staggered noisily around the library, much to the annoyance of the other scholars. He eventually brought back a basket full of documents, letters and reports. Amerotke sifted through these, writing down what he learnt. First, the Sgeru never revealed himself. A shadowy, menacing figure, a member of the so-called royal line of Nubia, he held the Sesher, the golden cord, the Arites symbol of ultimate power. Second, successive pharaohs had failed to trap and capture him or to destroy the Arites stronghold at Bekhna. Third, no Arites ever broke, confessed or turned traitor. Amerotke ruefully wished that he and Lord Valu had realised this out at the Place of the Skull. Fourth, if an Arites was captured or one of his sacred objects taken, they were regarded by other Arites as polluted, no longer worthy of their religion. Fifth, the strangulation of their victims was the most important part of the Arites' rite, often carried out in a display of audacious ingenuity and cunning. Sixth, the Arites ruled through fear. Once the candidate had taken the blood oath, he and all his kin were held responsible. Amerotke smiled grimly at that. The Sgeru could control Nubians in Thebes whilst his followers hundred of miles to the south could visit his wrath on the kin of any man who failed or even questioned his superiors. Seventh, if caught in battle and expecting death, the Arites always tied their sacred red cloth around their own throats. Amerotke fleetingly thought of the prisoner in the House of Chains. He'd considered the possibility that the prisoner had strangled himself but dismissed this as nigh impossible. Finally, and Amerotke was surprised at this, the military forays of Hatusu's father had been utterly ruthless. According to reports, the Arites, in the main, had been destroyed root and branch. Only those who fled to Bekhna had survived.

'Coming of age!' Amerotke exclaimed. Startled scholars and scribes looked up. Amerotke smiled in apology. Coming of age, he reflected. Most of the adult Arites had been killed in Tuthmosis' time, but now their children had reached maturity; that was why it was happening now! A new harvest of sedition come to fruition. Amerotke glanced around. The day was drawing on; time was passing. He rose, thanked the lector priest and left the House of Books. He entered the blazing sunlight and crossed the crowded temple grounds to the porter's lodge near a postern gate. Once there he borrowed a striped robe from the surprised keeper, as well as a stout walking cane. He dressed, pulled the hood over his head and slipped through the gate, making his way towards the House of the Forest. Shufoy, he reflected wryly, could be left to his courting.

Swinging his cane, the judge made his way through the seething mass of men and animals thronging the thoroughfare. Billowing clouds of dust floated by, rich with all the smells of the tawdry markets lining the route. Tinkers, peasants and craftsmen squatted in rows behind baskets filled with everything from precious stones to flowers and fruit. Onion-sellers, their produce glinting rosily like a heap of copper before them, were haggling with a group of women carrying a basket of sandals, demanding on what basis they would trade. Next to these, the proud owner of a white ox was having it weighed to the tune of pipe and lyre before he offered it for sale. Scorpion men slipped through the crowd. An acolyte from the Temple of Ptah bawled for room as three priests of his temple carried a small naos containing the image of the Man God down to the riverside. Every so often Amerotke would stop to stand on a plinth and stare around as if looking for a particular stall or trader. In truth, he was ensuring that he was not being followed. Once satisfied, he hurried on to confront the murderous mystery surrounding Imothep's death.

CHAPTER 6

Fetqu: destruction

The House of the Forest lay silent as Amerotke approached its great double gates. The porter allowed him in, then led him up through that tangled garden not to the main house but, as Amerotke directed, to the Mansion of Silence. The porter immediately scurried off to fetch Parmen and the rest whilst Amerotke examined the seals. He grunted in approval: nothing had been disturbed. He heard a sound and turned. Parmen, Rahmel and Neferen, with Sihera following behind, came hastening up.

'I am sorry,' the steward spluttered, 'but we were busy elsewhere. I . . .' His words trailed away.

Amerotke studied them critically: Parmen all anxious, fingers fluttering; Rahmel at a half-crouch as if expecting some attack; Neferen standing stock-still like a statue, whilst behind her Sihera studied the judge cynically.

Were they all killers? Amerotke wondered, or perhaps only one of them? Even if they were, the mystery still remained. How had they passed through locked doors and solid walls, murdered Imothep, then escaped? Their victim was a veteran soldier: he would have fought back, surely? The servants outside would have heard the clamour. Had Imothep been drugged? Yet according to the priest physician in the House of the Dead, he had betrayed only the symptoms of a man who'd been strangled, but how?

'My lord?'

Amerotke blinked. He was tired; he had to be careful.

'I was wondering,' Amerotke walked towards them, 'just how your master was murdered. Do you have any theories?'

'We probably made a mistake.' Parmen licked his lips, gesturing around. 'We've talked about it. The assassin may have been waiting within, well hidden. We didn't even look, we thought of that . . .' His voice trailed away.

Amerotke nodded sympathetically. Sihera still stood a little apart from the others, that calculating smile on her face.

'I must study your master's manuscripts,' Amerotke demanded. 'I would be grateful if you could arrange a reading table with lamps.'

Parmen and the rest hastened to obey as Amerotke snapped the seals and pulled open the great double doors. The inside smelt slightly musty, Parmen arranged what Amerotke had asked for whilst the judge wandered around. He noticed the shadowy enclaves near the door. Parmen could be right, he concluded: an assassin might have lurked, struck and hidden again with the treasures he'd looted.

'My lord.'

Amerotke went to the table Parmen had moved to beneath one of the windows.

'My lord, we have been invited to the Temple of Nubia tonight.'

'I know, I know,' Amerotke replied. 'I will also be there. However, in the meantime . . .' He moved to inspect the pigeonholed shelves, coffers and baskets in the second part of the hall, crouching down to read the tags.

'My master was very much the soldier,' Parmen declared sorrowfully. 'Everything always had to be neat and tidy.'

Amerotke nodded his agreement, then paused at the furious barking that carried across the gardens, echoing through the Mansion of Silence.

'What is that?' he asked.

'The master's saluki hounds,' Parmen declared. 'Their pens are on the other side of the house; they demand feeding.'

'The ones,' Amerotke murmured, 'that found the corpse.'

'Ah yes, they did.'

'But not the hands?'

Parmen's brows drew together.

'Well,' Amerotke shrugged, 'salukis are keen hunters: the smell of blood would attract them. They discovered the corpse but not the severed hands.'

Parmen merely pulled a face. Amerotke glimpsed a swift movement out of the corner of his eye as Sihera

149

moved deeper into the shadows. He let it pass. Undoubtedly there was a mystery here, but for the moment, that would have to wait. He picked up a small reed basket. The tag on the side proclaimed what it held: 'Maps and charts of the southern Redlands'. His hosts drifted away, murmuring excuses about how they must prepare for the grand supper later that evening. The Mansion of Silence fell quiet as a tomb, ghostly, brooding, eerily still. Amerotke became aware of the juddering shadows and petty sounds that echoed through that long hall. He also felt uneasy, slightly tense. It was nothing to do with the brutal attack the previous evening; more due to this mansion, a watching malignancy, a sense of threatening danger. He rose to his feet and walked the length and breadth of the hall. From outside trailed a muffled chorus of sounds and the pervasive smell of rotting vegetation. The latter evoked memories of his days as a young officer in the Horus regiment, campaigning in the jungles of the south, a time of terror, utter boredom and profound physical discomfort. Amerotke paused before a recess just near the main door. Had Imothep's killer lurked there both before and after his victim's brutal murder? Yet surely Imothep, a veteran warrior, would have sensed his presence, whilst a lack of disturbance demonstrated the absence of any struggle.

Amerotke went back and sat down. He sifted through the documents even as he was distracted by the thought of Norfret and his two sons. He recalled a question his wife had asked him: *Why? Why all this?* Amerotke's immediate response had been obvious: he was Chief Judge in the Hall of Two Truths; such danger always threatened. But the real answer? Amerotke tightened his lips – that was the problem. He'd always been drawn to the solution of a riddle, the solving of a puzzle, the answer to a question; it was almost an obsession. In truth, when evil and mystery confronted him directly, it held an alluring attraction that he could not shrug off. He had to see it through.

The judge settled down, pulling out the sheaf of papyri. Imothep had been studying the routes south: various scraps and pieces indicated that he had been looking at how a hostile force could move north out of Nubia into Thebes. However, Amerotke also concluded that Imothep had been concentrating on the Oasis of Sinjar and the nearby fortress of Timsah. The old scout had drawn rough but detailed maps of both, and Amerotke realised that though he himself had visited the area, he'd not truly inspected the fortress, with its high crenellated walls, war towers, storehouses, grain pits, caverns, cellars, tunnels and wells. He quietly cursed his own ineptitude. He should have studied everything about that abandoned fortress. And the oasis? Perhaps he should have camped there, rather than at that outlying village. He returned to the sketches. Imothep had made careful notes about Timsah's water supply as well as its deep pits, caverns and cellars for storing goods. His comment to Mataia also implied that if the Arites attacked, they would send a force north, to cut off the imperial forces from their base in Thebes. Amerotke glanced up. Was this the reason Imothep had died? Had he somehow sensed what the Arites were planning? Something was also wrong with these records. Imothep had been an old soldier, neat and precise. The scraps Amerotke was studying were drafts and sketches – where was the finished version? The judge rose and searched but could discover nothing. A doubt nagged him. It was one thing for Imothep to draw and sketch, but for what result? Was he handing information over to someone else?

Amerotke went back to studying the maps, calculating the distance between the deserted fortress and the oasis. He recalled what the chief scout Hennam had told him about the poor hunting around there. How Mataia had mentioned Imothep voicing the possibility of the Arites secretly threading men up into Thebes. Were they already on the move? Amerotke concentrated on the sketches of Timsah. Should he return there? It was a day's journey from Thebes. 'Yes, yes,' he whispered. 'Sinjar and Timsah hold secrets that must be resolved.'

'Master?'

Amerotke jumped and turned. A dark shadow stood just within the doorway.

'Master,' Shufoy walked forward, 'you disappeared. You didn't ask for me or Asural.'

'No, no, I didn't.' Amerotke apologised, then rose to his feet and beckoned the little man forward. 'Shufoy, tomorrow, and keep this confidential, I must return to the Oasis of Sinjar. No. No!' He stifled his friend's protest. 'I'll be safe.' He tugged at the striped robe he was wearing. 'We'll now go back to the temple and change, but then you must hurry to General Omendap. I want a war barge prepared, with an escort of at least thirty Medjay, including the one who alerted us to the attack on my mansion.'

'You mean Dog?' Shufoy replied sulkily. 'That's what they call him. Will I accompany you, master?'

'No.' Amerotke knelt down and tapped the little man on his brow. 'You must stay in Thebes. Look after the Lady Norfret and my two sons, and,' Amerotke smiled, 'pay court to the gorgeous Mataia. But listen.' He gripped Shufoy's hands. 'You must tell no one, and I repeat no one, not even Lady Norfret, about where I am going. Just say I am visiting General Omendap's camp.'

Shufoy solemnly promised.

Amerotke rose to his feet and extended his hands. 'We are finished here.'

They left the Mansion of Silence. Amerotke sent Shufoy to tell Parmen that they were going, then both of them slipped through a postern gate on to the thoroughfare back to the city. Amerotke walked quickly, clutching Shufoy's hand. They reached the Temple of Nubia without incident. Amerotke felt safe within its high walls. The day was drawing on, and servants and acolytes were preparing for the evening sacrifice. The animal and fowl pens were noisy. Smoke and incense carried on the breeze. Chants and songs resonated. Flashes of colour caught the eye as sunlight glinted off carnelian, silver and gold as well as gilded cornices and the sparkling malachite in the lintels and doorways of the temple buildings. Donkeys brayed. Dogs barked.

Heset girls wandered by with flashing smiles and gorgeous wigs, a flurry of linen and sweet clouds of perfume. Amerotke strolled across the gardens. He was going through a gateway when his cloak was grasped. He turned and gazed down at the beggar, eyes pleading, toothless mouth gaping. Shufoy went to free the judge's robe and Amerotke noticed the temple tattoos on the back of the beggar's vein-streaked, spotted hands, the official licence for him to solicit for alms on holy ground. He grasped the mendicant's hands and recalled the corpse found in the wild garden at the House of the Forest. Was that victim a beggar? Was that why his hands had been removed? But why? And why didn't the prowling saluki dogs discover such grisly, blood-reeking morsels?

'Master?'

Amerotke let go of the beggar. 'Give him a deben of copper, Shufoy.' He walked on through the garden, into his lodgings at the guest house and up to his chamber. Shufoy joined him. Amerotke stripped and stretched out on the palliasse over the cot bed, staring up at the raftered ceiling, shifting his head so his neck lay comfortably on the rest. Thoughts and images came and went as Shufoy laid out his robes, court sandals, sash and jewellery. Amerotke slept for a while. When he woke, he bathed and changed, glancing through the window to glimpse the fiery glow of the setting sun. It was time he left. Across the temple grounds reverberated the music of the orchestra; between each burst of playing, the voices of the temple choir rang out:

All praise and glory to you Lord of Light.
All honour to he who conquers the night.
All heads bow, all knees bend to the east.
All souls drift to the splendid feast . . .

Amerotke put on his collar, bracelets and rings of office
and wrapped the richly embroidered sash around his waist.
In its folds he concealed a knife, thin, sharp and pointed
as a bodkin. He anointed himself with scented perfume
and did the same for Shufoy. The little man, impatient to
interrogate the judge on what solutions there might be to
the mysteries, gave vent to a torrent of questions inter-
spersed with curses against the Arites and their bloody
attack the night before. Amerotke just listened. Once the
dwarf was breathless, he led him outside. They secured
their chamber and walked down the outside steps to the
Hall of Jubilees, the temple's great banqueting hall with
its red and yellow lotus pillars, floor of deep blue tiles and
cedar-beamed ceiling. The walls, celebrating beautiful
pastoral scenes, were painted in a range of delicate colours.
A poet, a blind harpist beside him, sat just within the
doorway reciting sweet love stories to the heart-plucking
sound of strings. Hesets, slim and scantily clothed, fluttered across like butterflies, their lips painted, eyes lined
with kohl, finger- and toenails carmined and gleaming.
These handmaids of the gods offered trays of sweet-smelling
lotus and cones of perfumes to fragrance the heads of
guests, as well as strips of luscious melon to quench their
thirst. Khufu, Busiris and Mataia, resplendent in their

finest robes and precious jewels, welcomed Amerotke and Shufoy. More iced drinks were served, with sesame cakes. Hesets danced and music played, as if Khufu was desperate to create an atmosphere of harmony and peace, to repel the terrors haunting them all.

Amerotke led a reluctant Shufoy away.

'Go now,' he urged, and smiled. 'Mataia will wait. Alert Asural and his guards, then visit General Omendap. I want those Medjay and the war barge ready at first light. No, no, don't worry, I'll be safe.' He stooped, kissed Shufoy on the brow and pushed his little friend towards the doorway.

Amerotke watched Shufoy go, then returned to the dining area. Servants brought in platters heaped with delicious-smelling food: fish, lamb, bowls of vegetables and bread fresh from the bakery. The guests from the House of the Forest took their seats, all dressed in fine linen robes, pleated and adorned with strips of precious stone. Amerotke watched them closely. They had, in deference to Khufu, removed all signs of mourning, though they remained solemn-faced, at least until the wine circulated. Sihera seemed more distracted than the rest. She'd stare quizzically at Amerotke, those old but clever eyes assessing him, weighing him in the balance. The first course drew to a close. Khufu clapped his hands for silence and formally welcomed his guests. He alluded to the present troubles, but assured Imothep's household that their master's going into the Far West would be most honourable. He discussed the funeral arrangements, but also made direct references to Imothep's bequest of the

House of the Forest, and all within it, as a god-offering to the Temple of Nubia. Parmen, along with the others, quietly agreed, adding that once the house was sold they would all go their separate ways. Amerotke watched intently, thoughts, images, memories and scraps of information fluttering like a blizzard of sand through his mind. He felt like a hunting cat, sure that his quarry must be close, yet profoundly uneasy. Tensions ran deep here. The apparent peace and harmony were an illusion waiting to be swept away. He studied the aristocratic Khufu, courteous and elegant in all his gestures. Busiris, so friendly. Mataia, the perfect heset, trained in the exquisite etiquette of court and temple. Then Parmen, like a shield to the rest of his household, bluff and protective. The only exception to this was Sihera, silent and watching. The heat in the dining chamber increased. Temple hesets brought in large perfumed flabella to waft the guests as servants refilled goblets and served tajines of lamb and chicken followed by silver dishes heaped with glazed walnuts. Khufu rose, beckoned Amerotke and took him into an enclosure overlooking the Garden of Perfumes.

'My lord,' the high priest dabbed his face with a scented cloth, 'you've drunk little. This present crisis?'

Amerotke stared hard at this man trying so desperately to hide his own fears. He decided to trust him – or was it to test him?

'My lord Khufu,' he leaned closer, 'I leave Thebes early tomorrow. I must visit the Oasis of Sinjar.'

'Why?' The priest looked startled.

'There must be a solution to all this evil mystery,'

Amerotke whispered. 'The oasis may be part of it. But, my lord,' he stepped closer, 'I must have your word, your sacred word, that no one, and I mean no one, be told of my going. Do you understand?'

Khufu held up his right hand. 'I swear by our holy of holies,' he whispered. 'But,' his face creased into a smile, 'why tell me?'

'I need to take a leather-scrolled tube from your House of Books. It contains maps and charts of the Oasis of Sinjar and the routes around it.' Amerotke gestured at the garden. 'It is cool. No one will mind if we walk in the gardens; the House of Books is not far.'

Khufu agreed. Busiris and Mataia were now entertaining Parmen and the other guests with riddles and puzzles. The high priest and Amerotke left, going out across the scented gardens, which were beautifully lit by alabaster oil jars and coloured lanterns. They reached the House of Books. Khufu whispered to the guard outside. The door bars were lifted, lamps were lit and, with Amerotke's help, the leather document tube with its papyrus tag was found. Amerotke clutched this, thanked the high priest and returned to his own lodgings to hide it away. He then decided that courtesy demanded he rejoin the rest of the party in the Hall of Jubilees. By the time he returned, Parmen and the others had left, loudly wondering what had become of Lord Amerotke. The judge simply smiled at that as he sat down on the cushions. Polite conversation ensued, then paused as a faint scream rang across the temple grounds. Mataia shrugged and returned to what Parmen had told her about selling the

House of the Forest before travelling north to Memphis. Khufu was about to reply, even as Amerotke prepared to leave, when the warning bray of conch horns stilled all conversation. The doors to the hall were thrown open, and a wide-eyed acolyte staggered towards the dining area.

'My lord Khufu,' he wailed, 'we are under attack! The Arites.'

Amerotke followed Khufu out into the temple grounds. Torches had been lit, trumpets bellowed, gongs clashed, guards were running, strapping on belts, as officers shouted orders. The harmony of the temple had been truly violated. Asural and his men gathered, sweaty faces gleaming in the breeze-whipped torchlight.

'Go,' Amerotke whispered, 'find out what is happening!' He withdrew into the portico.

The clamour eventually subsided. Asural returned. 'Nothing but corpses,' he gasped, 'temple people caught and strangled by the Arites. A guard stumbled over one of these and raised the alarm. The attackers seem to have disappeared.'

'How many were killed?' Amerotke asked.

'Four in all!' Khufu, his exquisite robes all dust-stained, came out of the darkness. He sat down on a stone plinth, mopping his brow. 'The keeper of the House of Chains,' he declared, 'a lector priest from the House of Powders, a servant girl and a guard. There may be more. I don't really know.' His voice rose. 'Nor can we establish how the Arites got in or how they escaped.'

Amerotke asked the high priest to repeat the list of

dead. The judge stared into the dark, his mind teeming. Had the Sgeru made a mistake?

Amerotke squatted in the shade of the date-palm trees that fringed the Oasis of Sinjar. He peered across the undulating sand at the dark mass of the fortress of Timsah. All around, Asural and his guards, together with the Medjay, were preparing camp. Amerotke glanced up at the sky. The sun was setting, bathing the desert in a bewildering array of colours. They had left the chaos and upset at the Temple of Nubia in the late watches of the night. The war barge, manned by marines from the imperial corps, was in midstream long before Amerotke, sitting in the shadow of the great mast, had glimpsed the first reddish tinge of dawn. *The Vengeance of Horus* swiftly left the quaysides of Thebes behind as it made its way south. The crew, seasoned veterans, sensed that this journey was both important and probably very dangerous. A full armament had been taken aboard; food supplies had been restocked, water casks and skins freshly filled. There would be no stopping, not even to escape the full blast of the demon heat at midday. The *Vengeance* had quickly passed the villages on the outskirts of Thebes, with their prominent brick-lined storage bins for grain, longhorn cattle, wandering goats and pigs, and stockades of woven grass peeping above the high banks overlooking the Nile. It was a pleasant enough journey. The Inundation was still fresh. Mounds of black earth were being eagerly raked back from the riverside, disturbing the bird-haunted papyrus groves where hippopotami, crocodiles and other beasts nosed in the shallows. Villagers came down, shouting how they had radishes and succulent lettuces for sale. Perhaps a red beaker of ale or beer? Or even wine sweetened with honey or the juice of the pomegranate? Fishermen brought their narrow skiffs in to offer the fresh catch. The crew simply shouted friendly greetings and shook their heads. They passed sandbanks, gruesome places of execution, where river pirates had been impaled alive on stakes then left for the river beasts to finish off. Barges and pleasure boats drifted by, their crews and passengers curious about the royal war barge under its broad blue and gold Horus pennant. Some of these drew closer, only to be warned off.

In the end, the *Vengeance* made good progress, moving alongside the makeshift quayside beneath Sinjar as the sun began to dip. A group of sand-dwellers and desert-wanderers immediately fled at their approach, provoking Amerotke's suspicions, but for the moment, there was little he could do. Now he sat in the fringe of trees and stared across at Timsah. Merentpath, his beloved brother, had been killed in a place like this. Merentpath, whose death had broken the hearts of Amerotke's parents. The judge closed his eyes and whispered, as he did every night, the lament for his dead brother:

> *The glory of Egypt has been shattered.*
> *How did the Heroes of Horus fail?*
> *Merentpath, loved and most lovely,*
> *Swift as an eagle, courageous as a lion.*

Amerotke opened his eyes. He was on the edge of the great desert, the gateway to the House of Fire. An evil place, surely? The abode of malevolent beings such as the Hunter of Hearts, that ghastly figure who wandered the sands hungry for souls, a Seth creature who lulled his victims before he bit out their hearts and gathered their souls into his dark sack. He broke from his reverie as Dog, the Medjay scout, flanked by his companions, came and knelt to Amerotke's right, chests heaving, faces gleaming with sweat.

'So?' Amerotke asked. 'You've been across to Timsah?'

'My lord,' Dog replied, 'you must judge for yourself. The place reeks of blood and carrion.'

'Is it deserted?' Amerotke asked.

'Haunted by ghosts,' Dog replied, 'and more importantly, by hyaenas . . .' The scout made to say more, but thought otherwise.

'You are sure of that?'

'Certainly, my lord. Sniffers of blood have come in from the desert. Strange: they rarely hunt where man goes.'

Amerotke nodded. 'Take your rest. We will return there tomorrow. You studied the maps I brought?'

'Yes, my lord.'

'You also searched for the oasis priest?'

'Nebher,' Dog replied, 'appears to have vanished.' The scout picked up a waterskin and squirted a gulp into his mouth. 'You sent me as a scout.' Dog wetted his lips. 'I am to report what I observe, but . . .'

'Go on.'

'Timsah,' Dog replied in a rush, 'is a mixture of smells: dead flesh, dried blood . . .'

'And?'

'Sweat, my lord. Many men have been there. They may still be hiding there.'

'You followed my orders?'

'Yes, we stayed in the forecourts, but . . .' Dog shrugged. 'I don't want to be mocked as a garrulous old man chomping on his gums.'

'Speak directly.'

'Corpses are buried there, not the long-dead, but fresh. On the breeze I smelt their salty tang, as well as sweat, food and burning.'

'Yet we saw nothing,' one of Dog's companions broke in.

'Nothing at all?' Amerotke rose to his feet. 'You're sure the place is deserted?'

'Except for a group of sand-dwellers, desert-wanderers,' one of the scouts murmured. 'They fled at our approach.'

'So what is worrying you, Dog?' Amerotke helped the sweaty Medjay to his feet. 'Speak your suspicions, however vague they may be – not just your observations.'

'I felt . . .' Dog bared his teeth, scratched his crinkled hair and played with the tortoiseshell amulet around his neck. 'Timsah is not deserted,' he replied in a rush. 'In fact, not at all.'

Amerotke held up a hand to still the protests of the other Medjay.

'I will now say it, my lord. We may not have seen them, whoever they are, but they definitely saw us. They know we came from the river. We are not just Medjay scouts wandering south; even that would be surprising. I suspect that if an enemy lurks there, they will not allow us to leave. I mean,' Dog stared up the darkening sky, 'they must know why we came.'

Amerotke startled at the strident cry of a night bird nestling in the trees behind him. The sweat on his body prickled with cold; a stab of fear provoked a belly-wrenching spurt of agitation. Dog was right! He stared across at the sinister outline of Timsah. He had to be sure himself. He must set aside all doubts and enter that fortress.

'We will return now!' he declared. 'I want to go there quickly, before nightfall.'

The Medjay could not refuse. Amerotke took off his robe and, dressed only in a loincloth, stepped out of the line of trees. He broke into a trot, a slow but steady run as he had practised so many times on the searing-hot parade grounds of the military camps around Thebes. It was a strange experience, the hot sand beneath his bare feet clinging and cloying as if it wished to drag him down, then on to a stretch of hard gravel and up the occasional rocky outcrop, where the evening breeze chilled his sweaty body. He was aware of the light changing rapidly as they approached the entrance to Timsah, a towering sculpture of ruined yet soaring battlements, jagged fortifications, gaping windows, gateways and porches. A grim, grey but mighty fortress rising from an ancient bed of rock. A yawning, hollow-sounding place full of shadows, battered statues, ruined plinths and chipped stelae. Built of dried mud-bricks and blocks of granite, Timsah's defences comprised high enclosures, ramparts, ditches and heavily fortified gateways approached by derelict drawbridges.

Inside lay administrative complexes, barracks, workshops and small temples. It was a haunt of dappled, eerie light, where an oppressive silence hung like some dark cloud.

Amerotke stopped. Had he glimpsed figures flitting along the ramparts? Surely that was a trick of the dying light, the sinister games of twilight? Buzzards soared and circled. Bats in small, darting black clouds squealed and turned. Amerotke and his escort walked into the centre of the courtyard. Dog sniffed the air like a saluki hound. Amerotke closed his eyes, willing himself to relax. He was right. This fortress could conceal an army, and they had yet to probe and explore what he knew lay beneath: an elaborate labyrinth of corridors, storerooms, dungeons and chambers. He twisted his face to catch the breeze. Dog's sniffing grew more agitated. The judge felt a prickle of fear. This was dangerous! He quietly prayed that Omendap would act on his second message. He was now convinced. He had no real evidence, just Dog's agitation and his own gathering suspicions, whilst the other Medjay were also becoming increasingly nervous. He marvelled silently at the Arites' cunning: a huge, deserted fortress, yet self-sufficient enough to hide an army.

'We must be gone,' he whispered, and swiftly led his escort back through the gateway, offering a prayer for protection to Horus of the Red Eye.

Amerotke was relieved to reach Sinjar, and immediately called for Asural and the Medjay commander. All around them the soldiers were singing softly or talking as they prepared to camp for the night.

'Listen now.' Amerotke crouched by the oasis pool, indicating that they do the same. 'I have been across to Timsah. I believe we will be attacked tonight.'

'What?' The Medjay officer almost sprang back to his feet. 'My lord, attacked? Here in a deserted oasis? By whom? Desert-wanderers?' He forced a laugh.

'No,' Amerotke replied flatly. 'By a cohort of Arites who are hiding out at Timsah. Please listen,' he insisted. 'Timsah is built on bedrock. Beneath those towers and walls run a honeycomb of caverns and passageways, a veritable maze of tunnels and chambers. I have studied the maps and plans of Imothep, who once commanded the Spies of Sobeck. He wondered how the Arites could move north. Did he suspect Timsah could be a staging post? I think he did,' Amerotke asserted. 'The Arites have moved into Timsah; they hide in its underground chambers. They recruit the local sand-dwellers and desert-wanderers as their allies and spies. Timsah has underground wells and springs, whilst the Arites go deeper into the desert to hunt for fresh meat. Little wonder stocks have fallen low. From Timsah they can control the movement of the Arites out of Nubia, and are well positioned to attack all couriers and messengers from Thebes. More importantly,' Amerotke gestured with his hand, 'General Omendap will march. He must pass Timsah on his journey south . . . '

'And if the Arites are hiding in Timsah,' Asural intervened, 'they can attack any scouts or messengers he sends back to Thebes, harass his rearguard, create more chaos behind the imperial army.'

'But Nebher, the oasis chaplain?' the Medjay spluttered. 'He must know . . .'

'Probably dead by now,' Amerotke replied. 'I have considered that. The Arites kidnapped his daughter and forced him to work for them. Now they no longer need him.'

'And the others?' Asural asked. 'Those who also disappeared? All of Thebes has been talking about them.'

'The same way.' Amerotke chewed on the corner of his lip. 'It must be.'

'Merchants, yes,' Asural declared, 'but imperial messengers with an armed escort? They've disappeared without any trace.'

'Precisely,' Amerotke agreed. 'They would come here and shelter for the night. They would drink water from the pool. Nebher, the oasis priest, was their host. He would, according to his duties, serve them wine. The men would be tired, exhausted. A sleeping potion mingled with the wine would render them as vulnerable as children when the Arites emerged. In turn, that explains their complete disappearance. Bury people in the desert sand and the scavengers will soon detect them. The same is true of throwing a corpse into the river: sooner or later some trace will be found. But if you kill people, transport their corpses to the deep chambers under Timsah, then return to remove all traces of any conflict, not to mention weapons and personal effects . . .'

'And the boats?' Asural asked.

'The same way,' Amerotke declared. 'They can be dragged ashore and easily dismantled. The Arites would need wood to cook, to light fires. If any smoke was detected, any sign of life provoked suspicion, the Arites would simply melt into the shadows, let the desert-wanderers explain it all away.' Amerotke shrugged. 'It would not be difficult. This is a lonely, deserted place. The Arites would soon be alerted about any approach to either Sinjar or Timsah by Nebher or the sand-dwellers. If anyone did wander into that fortress to search thoroughly . . .' he suppressed a shiver, 'the Arites would strike.'

'But they went hunting?'

'Out in the desert,' Amerotke replied, 'a vast emptiness – they'd also pay the sand-dwellers to assist them.'

'But sometimes the messengers who disappeared were seen journeying further south.'

'Of course they were.' Amerotke smiled through the darkness. 'It's easy to garb yourself in dead men's clothes, wear the cartouche of a messenger around your wrist, use the boat to travel a few miles south only to cross the river and journey back. Who would suspect? Villagers, simple people, were asked about movements south; an imperial boat returning north would hardly be commented on. A clever trick, to confuse and confound. It must be here,' Amerotke insisted. 'This is where the messengers disappeared. Imagine it as we are now. The courier and his escort drag their boat ashore to be welcomed by Nebher. They light a fire, drink, then fall asleep. Perhaps they set a guard, perhaps they don't. Darkness falls. The fire burns low. The Arites emerge from their fortress to massacre them. They later remove all corpses and weapons, any sign of a struggle, if there was one.' The judge rubbed his arms. 'Last time I came here, we camped in one of the villages. If we had stayed here, Asural, we'd certainly have died.'

'And Nebher was party to such treachery?' Asural asked.

'Of course, they kidnapped his daughter.'

'But now he too has disappeared . . .'

'Too dangerous to leave,' Amerotke murmured. 'They've been warned.'

'A traitor?' Asural asked.

'The Sgeru,' Amerotke declared, 'learnt that I have been studying Imothep's maps and charts as well as those at the Temple of Nubia. Undoubtedly a courier was dispatched to warn the Arites lurking here.'

'Why don't they just retreat?' Asural asked.

'Too late,' Amerotke replied. 'When Omendap marches, the Arites will seize their opportunity. They will break out from their hiding place, inflict chaos and mayhem, drive a wedge between the Divine One and her commander. Imagine the effect that will have in Thebes. A hostile force only a day's journey to the south.'

'We could leave now,' the Medjay muttered.

'By night? By river?' Amerotke countered. 'Highly dangerous! We would have to light torches. The Arites would track us along the bank. We dare not go midstream: one mishap on the river could make us truly vulnerable.'

'If they attack . . .' The Medjay gestured at the gathering dark. 'It won't be now. They'll wait until just before dawn, when we are at our weakest, and the light is strange, shifting and blurred. That haze that gathers over the desert just before sunrise makes it worse.'

Asural grunted in agreement. 'They'll not use their red cloths,' he murmured, 'not at first; this will be spear and shield.'

'They'll attack from the front,' the Medjay continued, 'but that will be just a ploy. Their real assault will come from both flanks at the same time. They'll slip out of Timsah in the dark, divide, then close in.'

Amerotke agreed, and for a while they discussed tactics. They decided to mislead any watchers by acting as if expecting nothing out of the ordinary. The campfires were built higher with dry bracken and the animal dung found in and around the oasis. Beer, bread and onions were distributed. The soldiers were encouraged to sing and shout as if they were relaxing before a night's sleep. Secretly the oasis was prepared for attack. Nebher's house was raided. Nothing remarkable was found, but its jars and pots were collected and smashed. The sharpened pieces, along with dried thorns smeared with human dung, were strewn along the narrow paths that wound into the oasis from either side. Weapons were brought up out of the war barge, together with oilskins. These latter were emptied on to the dried grass and gorse along the flanks of the oasis. Amerotke divided his force: two contingents in an arc on either flank. A token force was deployed directly facing Timsah, whilst the principal officers would stay by the pool.

After the orders were carried out, Amerotke sat down with his back to a palm tree. He could not sleep as his mind drifted through the fog of murky mysteries threatening him. He divided the problems neatly, each with its own list of unanswered questions. The Arites were lurking in Thebes, but who and where was the Sgeru? How could they launch their murderous attacks on the Divine One, himself and Valu in the very heart of Thebes? The Nubian regiment was confined in their barracks, surely? The Temple of Nubia was surrounded by imperial troops. Yet the Arites seemed to slip through the city like shape-shifters. Amerotke took a sip of water. Undoubtedly the attacks on Hatusu, Valu and himself were led by a few Arites; the rest were hired killers. The Arites must have bought the allegiance of one or more of the gangs of assassins that swarmed like rats through the slums of both the city and the Necropolis. Yet how did they penetrate the Temple of Nubia that night to carry out those attacks? To create consternation, strike chaos at the heart of Pharaoh and her royal circle? To show they could not be contained? And their victims at the Temple of Nubia? This nagged at Amerotke. Were they randomly selected? The keeper of the House of Chains, a priest from the House of Powders, a guard? Amerotke shifted uneasily. He wondered if the murder of these individuals was connected in some way to the death of that Arites prisoner. And how could a man locked in a stone box, the door barred and closely guarded, be strangled so quickly, so quietly, without provoking any alarm?

Amerotke rose, stretched and stared around. This was the hour of deep blackness. The Medjay had now ceased all pretence. The precious fires had been doused. The men lay on the ground, weapons at the ready. They, like him, were wondering when the arrows would fall, the spears come whirling, the crack of the mace, the slithering knife. Would their lives end here, in a frenetic blood-splattered struggle in this lonely oasis deep in the desert? The coughing bark of a hyaena was echoed by the dull, deep-throated roar of a hunting lion. Amerotke breathed in and sat down. He returned to the tangle of mysteries at the House of the Forest. Imothep strangled in a securely barred chamber, a man who'd locked himself in only to meet his assassin. No alarm had been raised, there had been no sign of disturbance; nevertheless, that veteran scout had been killed, his treasure plundered. And that strange corpse with its severed hands? A beggar from the Temple of Nubia, strangled and mutilated, but why? Where were the hands? Why didn't the saluki hounds find them?

Amerotke startled as the undergrowth crackled around him. He glanced at a wineskin lying near the pool. And this place of murder? He thought of those who had been silently massacred amongst these trees, their corpses dragged away without any chance of honourable burial. He was certain the victims must have been drugged, a potion mixed with their water or wine. It would be easy to lull men exhausted after a day's journey along the heat of the river. He picked up the wineskin. A thought occurred to him and he smiled thinly recalling the Lady of the Dark in Thebes, that mistress of poisons. On his return to the city he must have a word with her, but for the moment . . . Amerotke rubbed his stomach. He felt queasy, and the back of his throat was dry. He thought of Norfret and the two boys, Shufoy wooing Mataia, and whispered a prayer for their protection to Ma'at. He glanced around and recalled from his own soldiering days the advice of a veteran standard-bearer:

'Do not reflect too much: imagination is the soil where fear takes root.'

CHAPTER 7

Nemm-t: slaughterhouse

Amerotke was roughly shaken awake by Dog, who pushed his face close in a gust of beer and raw onion.

'My lord!'

Amerotke rubbed his eyes, then stood up. It was cold. The sky was not so dark now.

'They are coming,' Dog whispered. 'I can smell them on the breeze. Their scent comes in over the desert. Cooked meat.' He turned and spat. 'Dung and urine. They are as filthy as a pack of hyaenas.'

Amerotke peered through the poor light. He could hear and see nothing untoward, but Dog had already alerted the others. Shapes moved, hissed orders came from the standard-bearers, weapons were being quietly collected. Amerotke joined Asural and the Medjay commander by the pool.

'Dog says they are coming,' the Medjay warned. 'I trust him.'

The silence grew oppressive. Amerotke stood like a hunting hound. He was sure he heard a sound. He glanced to his right and jumped as the Medjay war cry rang out from the men gathered on the fringe of the oasis in front of them. The attack had been launched. The Medjay commander ordered more fuel to be tossed on to the fire even as the night air was broken by screams, shouts, war cries and the heart-chilling sound of wood and metal clashing in deadly combat. Amerotke peered through the darkness, which was now illuminated by the leaping flames. He could make out shapes, bobbing heads and long oval shields. A mass of men were trying to break through the fringe of trees. Surprise was now over. Asural, commanding the right, and the Medjay officer on the left shouted their orders as the attack spread. The Arites intended to outflank them. Fire arrows were loosed into the dry gorse. Sheets of flame shot up to burn the Arites, even as others were caught by the sharp shards of pottery and the dung-smeared thorns, which pierced their calloused naked feet. Some of the Arites broke through the wall of fire, only to be clubbed, stabbed or hacked to death. One warrior, naked except for a loincloth, armed with spear and shield, escaped the deadly gauntlet and charged Amerotke. The judge stepped back, moving to the attacker's right whilst driving his mace at the man's head. He missed, but hit his assailant's arm. The man staggered. Again Amerotke swung the mace, shattering bone and flesh as he smashed his opponent's face. Dog raced forward, grabbed the Arites by the hair, jerked his head back and slit the man's throat. The attack broke off abruptly, only to resume almost immediately. Deceit and cunning were now replaced by brutal, bloody hand-to-hand fighting. Rank upon rank of enemy warriors swept towards them, determined to break through and put everyone to the sword. The Medjay commander breathlessly informed Amerotke that the enemy must be at least a hundred strong, supported by sand-dwellers and desert-wanderers.

The attacks were beaten off, to be replaced by a hail of shafts loosed from powerful Nubian bows. Amerotke and his company sought whatever shelter they could. Night was now passing, the sky brightening, the darkness thinning. The morning breeze thickened with the stench of sweat and blood. The cries of the wounded were soon stifled by mercy cuts, and the attacks began again. The Arites stayed away from the still-smouldering flanks of the oasis, and concentrated on breaking in from the front, directly facing the fortress. Desperate to inflict damage, they surged in, shields out, spears jabbing. The Medjay, reinforced by Asural's guards, held the line. Nevertheless, Amerotke sensed a growing desperation amongst his men. They must hold at least until full light, when they could try to evacuate the oasis. This would mean a long, bloody fight down to the war barge unless the gods or General Omendap intervened.

Amerotke was conferring with Asural and Medjay when the strident wail of conch horns rang out from the direction of the river. A scout was sent racing back. He'd hardly gone a few paces when Amerotke heard a full-throated roar and ran to the edge of the oasis. The Arites, a dark mass of men, had now broken, fleeing across the sand, whilst from both flanks raced lines of pursuing imperial troops. They must have landed on either side of Sinjar, clambered up the banks and attacked immediately. Their abrupt appearance shocked the Arites, who must have expected any reinforcements to land immediately below the oasis and thread through it. Omendap's troops used such surprise to their advantage. Fresh and eager for battle, they streamed across the desert like a pack of hunting dogs. They soon caught up with the stragglers and the wounded to deal out swift and brutal death. The defenders of the oasis, still furious with battle lust, needed no encouragement: they too poured out to join the deadly hunt against their former tormentors.

Amerotke went and collapsed by the pool. He cupped his hands, wetting his mouth, splashing water all over himself. Omendap's officers, resplendent in their white kilts, leather breastplates adorned with silver and golden bees, necks and arms decorated with collars and bracelets of valour, swaggered into the oasis. Their commander was a chief scribe of the army, an officer from the Anubis regiment, a gruff old man with sharp, darting eyes, a clipped voice and an abrupt manner. He questioned Amerotke roughly until he realised he was speaking to Pharaoh's chief judge; then he quickly apologised and described how he'd left Omendap's camp just after noon the previous day.

'We've been here some time.' He grinned. 'We thought it best to deploy. I am sorry if you thought you'd been deserted. General Omendap's orders were most explicit.'

The scribe got to his feet. 'To save you, trap the enemy and kill them. That is what I am going to do.'

The rest of that day was spent in a bloodthirsty hunt through the ruins of Timsah. One officer nicknamed the fortress 'the Beehive' because of the honeycomb of passageways and tunnels that ran deep beneath it. A gruesome sequel to the battle ensued as pockets of Arites were found, isolated and destroyed. The enemy did not ask for pardon; none was shown them. They were killed where they stood or burnt out of caverns and chambers. The imperial commander ringed the fortress so that no one could escape. It was late afternoon before the blood-letting ended. A few Arites, wounded and beaten, were taken alive. Amerotke tried to question them, but they just mocked and spat at him. The commander had them impaled high on the fortifications, using their own spears as weapons of torture. The sand-dwellers, about eleven in number, proved more amenable. After five of them had joined the Arites on the battlements to scream out their lives in gushes of blood, the survivors bargained for their lives: some water, a little bread and the right to leave unmolested. The commander, at Amerotke's insistence, agreed.

The sand-dwellers told a tale that only confirmed Amerotke's suspicions. How the Arites, some hundred and fifty in number, had arrived weeks earlier, very know-ledgeable about Timsah. They had hired the sand-dwellers and desert-wanderers through a mixture of bribes and terror, then set up camp in Timsah using them as spies. They'd immediately kidnapped Nebher's daughter, threatening the oasis priest, who quickly complied. Nebher would inform them about anyone who arrived, and a sand-dweller would leave the oasis just as the visitors came. He would report to the Arites whilst Nebher drugged the new arrivals. In the cold watches of the night, the Arites would swarm in, strangle their victims, then remove all traces of them ever having been there.

'And the boats and barges?'

'Valuable firewood.' The sand-dweller grinned, blackened teeth bared. 'We were not given any plunder from the dead but paid with small ingots of silver. Everything else was removed.'

'But some of these merchants and messengers were seen further south?'

'Not far,' the sand-dweller retorted. 'The same barge, the same pennant, but usually manned by us. People would watch it, then we'd run the craft ashore in some deserted place to be destroyed. We'd carry the wood and cloth on our backs to Timsah.' He shrugged. 'Or use our dromedaries.'

Amerotke nodded. The mention of dromedaries recalled memories of Omendap's army and its horde of camp-followers, desert people with their swift-racing dromedaries, an ideal way to send messengers south. Amerotke knew enough about the Arites to realise that they would enforce their discipline with the utmost cruelty. The sand-dwellers and desert-wanderers were easy prey: they moved in families. The Arites undoubtedly took hostages or issued threats about what would happen if their orders were not carried out.

'And the dead?' Amerotke asked.

The sand-dweller shrugged and rose to his feet. He led Amerotke and the principal officers to the far side of the fort, through a ruined gateway to the foot of a soaring tower. Narrow, steep steps stretched down into the blackness. Amerotke, fearing an ambush, ordered more torches to be lit, and a company of Medjay went before them. They continued their descent, plunging into the grimy murk of Timsah's underworld. Despite the heat, it was a cold, spectral place. Shadows juddered against the walls. The faint screams of those recently impaled along the battlements followed like some ghastly chant. A soul-chilling journey, made even more so by the sickly stench of corruption that wafted about them. They reached a small antechamber with two tunnels leading off it. The sand-dweller indicated the one to the right. They walked down a narrow passageway. Amerotke pinched his nose: the stench was now offensive. They entered a gaping cavern. The Medjay trotted forward, raising their torches to reveal the horrors of that gruesome chamber. At least thirty corpses were neatly laid out in rows. The rank smell made some of the escort gag and they left to retch as Amerotke and the commander examined the cadavers. All the victims had been strangled, their bellies slit open to diminish the foul effects of corruption before being covered in sand. Some had decomposed beyond recognition. Amerotke recognised the lean-featured Nebher; beside him was the pathetic corpse of a young woman, probably his daughter, her bruised face almost hidden by long black hair. Amerotke closed his eyes and breathed a prayer.

'Those who can be identified,' he got to his feet, 'should be cleaned and taken back to Thebes for honourable burial. The House of Silver will see to that. The rest must be burnt, quickly.' He stepped back and stared around that hideous chamber of the dead, an evil place, the work of wicked hearts. 'The lady Ma'at,' he murmured, 'the Goddess of Truth, will bring this malice to an end.'

On the same afternoon the battle of Timsah drew to an end, Shufoy, personal equerry as he styled himself, to Amerotke, Pharaoh's Chief Judge in the Hall of Two Truths, was revelling in his own well of happiness. Never had he been so content, as he stretched out on the soft linen sheets of Mataia's stately court bed with its feather-stuffed palliasse, blue and gold headrest and plump, richly embroidered cushions. He stared up at the silver-lined cedar-beamed roof of the bedchamber. He had just made love to Mataia, a frenetic yet sensuous experience of soft touches, tender kisses and the most fragrant of perfumes. Mataia, her beautiful face framed by a wig decorated with small gold and silver roses, had smiled down at him, her rich, warm body, naked except for collars and clasps of the most exquisite jewellery, nestling against his. Afterwards they had feasted on crushed fresh fruit, soft figs in honey and goblets of the best wine from Buto. Shufoy thought fleetingly of his master out in the scorching Redlands, then pulled himself up to watch Mataia, who was sitting beyond the screen of curtains.

A simple loincloth around her, Mataia was gazing into a hand mirror of polished bronze, plucking at her eyebrows, stopping now and again to search her lovely face for any imperfection. The curtains served almost as an eyelet or spyhole through which Shufoy could watch his beloved, lost in her delicate toiletry. Mataia was humming softly to herself. Shufoy recognised the tune and recalled the exquisite yet provocative dance she'd performed before their lovemaking. His heart glowed with pleasure. Mataia did not care about appearances. She laughingly described how other men strutted and posed wherever she went and mockingly dismissed them as empty-heads. Instead she'd been fascinated by Shufoy's various schemes and plans while sharing her own with him. She told him how she was tired of the Temple of Nubia, frightened about what was happening and deeply alarmed at the threat the Arites posed. She explained that she was trying to persuade Lady Busiris to empty the hospital of the walking sick and keep a stricter watch on the high priest's residence. She even hinted that she might seek Amerotke's protection at some other temple or even the Malkata Palace.

'Would you go?' Shufoy asked.

'Of course,' she murmured, pressing herself against him. 'Do you think I want to stay here? Yes, I am an orphan, the daughter of a peasant, a temple girl. I dance and sing before the statues. I praise the gods. I carry out my administrative duties. I was happy here until now. It's ended, Shufoy. The Divine One has turned her face against all things Nubian. Hesets from our province work in other temples; I will do the same. I will lose myself, let the Arites forget me.'

'Are you sure?' Shufoy had asked.

Mataia had repeated that that was what she wanted, wishing that the evil that threatened would disappear. Shufoy caught her tension, a desire to be protected. During his master's absence, he and the temple heset had grown closer. Shufoy had also used Amerotke's journey south to learn all he could, making his own secret enquiries of temple servants, acolytes and visitors. The more he questioned, the more he became concerned about the secrecy of Lord Khufu, who in calmer days had argued that Nubia should be given more freedom under Pharaoh's rule. Lady Busiris was no different. In all, an enigmatic couple! Perhaps they were estranged from each other? Servants certainly gossiped about tension between them. Yet this was just chatter; the same could be found in any of the Mansions of a Million Years throughout Thebes. Mataia spoke highly of Lord Khufu and his wife, whom she regarded as generous and loving patrons. Shufoy concluded that Lord Khufu and Lady Busiris, indeed the entire temple hierarchy, were caught between two camps. On the one hand was their allegiance to Pharaoh and the royal circle; on the other, loyalty to their own people, the folk memory and history of Nubia.

'Ah well,' Shufoy whispered to himself. 'I can only collect, let my master sift.' He turned to grasp the goblet on the bedside table, only to jump at a piercing scream from deep within the high priest's quarters. He sprang out of bed and dressed hastily, searching for his knife.

The sound of running footsteps in the gallery outside was followed by a furious pounding at the door. Mataia hurried across and slipped back the bolts. Khufu and Lady Busiris almost burst into the chamber. Lady Busiris was crying, a red cloth clutched in her hand.

'We found them,' Khufu exclaimed.

'Draped over the headrest of our bed,' Busiris cried.

Shufoy guiltily recalled his love tryst with Mataia, the frenzied excitement, pillows, bolsters, sheets and headrests tumbling off the bed. He stared bleakly at Mataia, who gazed coolly back. Like a dream-walker, she stepped by him, and went through the curtains to the head of the bed. She pulled back the heavy palliasse and searched the gap between that and the wall. She paused, head down, and Shufoy watched in horror as she slowly pulled up the ghastly red cloth, a death warning from the Arites . . .

Amerotke stood in the Garden of a Hundred Fragrances in the Temple of Nubia. He'd arrived back in Thebes the previous evening, the ghastly memories of Timsah and its macabre secrets still fresh in his mind. He'd left the fortress, gazing back at the impaled enemy corpses, black and stark against the light blue sky, as if mocking the glory of the day, whilst from the courtyard streamed plumes of smoke from the funeral pyres. He'd been only too eager to leave that filthy place and return to the city.

He made to walk on, then decided he'd sit in one of the brightly coloured garden pavilions. Inside, it was cool and sweet-smelling from the small baskets of flowers pushed under the cushioned seat that ran around the wall. Amerotke made himself comfortable and stared out at the carving of the dwarf god Bes, with his popping eyes, protuberant belly and grotesque mask of a face. In a nearby chapel a beautiful voice practised a hymn: 'Magnificent as the dawn. Lovely is your presence to all creatures . . .' Amerotke whispered his own prayer of thanks for his safe return and for the security of his family, whom he had visited at the Malkata. All was well, though Norfret sorely missed both him and home. They'd sat for a while in the imperial gardens sharing the same goblet of charou wine, whilst the boys played noisily around a fountain. Shufoy had also been present, tight-lipped and frowning. Only when Norfret kissed her husband and left did the little man tell Amerotke about what he'd learnt, as well as the warnings delivered at the Temple of Nubia. Amerokte heard him out. He recalled Valu's cynicism about all things Nubian, and once they'd left the Malkata, dispatched Shufoy with a sealed letter to the House of Secrets demanding that all of the prosecutor's reports and papers on the present crisis be handed over to him. Before he left, Shufoy had also asked that Mataia be taken into the judge's protection. Amerotke had solemnly promised to consider it, but in the meantime . . .

Amerotke stared at the statue of the dwarf god. So many questions, so few answers! How did the Arites know about the caverns and tunnels at Timsah? The fortress was firmly in Egyptian territory. Why had they chosen that one? True, it was near the Oasis of Sinjar, but there were other oases and riverside resting places. On reflection, Timsah was an ideal place for the Arites to plot their mischief, but how did they know so much about it? The archives at the Temple of Nubia had maps and charts, but to Amerotke's best recollection, the detailed plans of that fortress had been the work of Imothep. Had that loyal servant of Pharaoh turned traitor? Had he really handed over his own maps of Timsah? The judge had pondered such questions during his swift return by imperial barge to Thebes. Other suspicions about Imothep had surfaced. The real trouble in Nubia had begun over a month ago, followed by the crisis here in Thebes, yet Imothep had been studying the maps of Timsah long before that. Why? One further problem. Imothep, according to all appearances, had been the veteran opponent of the Arites. He definitely saw them as a threat, surely? Whilst that coven of malignants would certainly mark Imothep down for death, a vow they'd eventually carried out. Yet if the evidence was to be believed, Imothep had not been threatened, nor had he taken special precautions to protect himself, even after that dismembered corpse, an apparent victim of the Arites, had been discovered in his garden. That was strange! Moreover, Imothep had been assassinated, but had he been warned? If he had, surely such a threat would have alerted him to the impending danger. Yet if he had not been warned, why had the Arites broken with their murderous custom of taunting their prospective victim? Had that nameless, mutilated corpse been their threat? And Khufu? He'd acted very swiftly in preventing the assassination of the Divine One – why hadn't he been attacked on that same morning, or since? After all, the Arites had assassinated one of their own kind in that locked cell beneath the Temple of Nubia. A short while later they'd infiltrated the temple gardens and murdered whoever they wanted, yet so far they had launched no assault on a high priest they must regard as a collaborator, a traitor to their cause. Shufoy had told his master about the red cloths, another warning to Khufu, Busiris and Mataia, but were the Arites really hunting them or just playing with their victims like a cat with a trapped bird? Were they waiting for some public occasion to strike terror into the Temple of Nubia?

Amerotke squinted through the doorway at the fountain gushing up in the far distance. He, too, must take greater care. News of the recent victory over the Arites at Timsah had swept the city, a stunning blow against the cunning of the enemy. This had followed fast on the revelation of how the Medjay scouts had been murdered and the threat to them removed. The aura of invincibility the Arites had created was crumbling. Pharaoh's power was not to be doubted. The Arites must know of Amerotke's part in this. They would surely be waiting for him: a prize victim in their deadly war against the Great House.

The clash of weapons startled the judge. He caught the glint of armour in the trees beyond the fountain. He sprang to his feet, then relaxed as the Silver Shields, an elite corps of Maryannou, emerged from the greenery. Shields glittering, spears at the ready, the escort moved in a tightly disciplined way, protecting the two hooded figures in the centre. Amerotke sighed. Hatusu had come to see him! He went out and knelt on the grass. As the Silver Shields approached, their ranks opened and Hatusu emerged in a swirl of fragrance, leaning on the arm of Senenmut. Amerotke went to nose the ground before her.

'Not now, not now!' she snapped. 'Out of the sun, my lord judge, out of the sun!' She tapped him on the shoulder as she swept by him into the pavilion. Amerotke grimaced, clambered to his feet and followed her inside. Hatusu, pulling back her linen hood, gestured at the judge to sit opposite. As he did so, he caught Senenmut's warning glance. The harsh-faced grand vizier certainly looked worried. Little wonder. Pharaoh was beside herself with rage. Amerokte recognised all the signs. Hatusu was not wearing a single item of jewellery, and her lovely face was unpainted, those strange bluish eyes large and watchful, the sensuous lips twisted in a grimace. She chewed the inside of her mouth, one hand beat against her thigh, whilst a silver-sandalled foot tapped the floor as if she was listening to some invisible music. In truth she was: the anger seething in her own heart.

'Divine One, it is good to look upon your face.'

Hatusu's cat-like eyes remained unblinking

'You have heard about Timsah?' Amerotke remarked tactfully.

'Congratulations.' Senenmut intervened swiftly. 'That nest of vipers has been burnt and destroyed.'

'They killed my messengers,' Hatusu declared, 'they butchered imperial couriers, broke the seals on our message pouches, read the plans and designs we sent to our Viceroy of Nubia. They planned to harass our troops.

For weeks they've lurked like a pack of hyaenas around our oasis, a mere day's journey from Thebes!'

'And their wicked plans have been brought to nothing!' Amerotke intervened. 'They are all dead, some of them cruelly so.'

'Yet nothing,' Hatusu raised a clenched hand, 'nothing found, no documents, no papyri.'

'The imperial commander,' Amerotke declared, 'carefully searched for such evidence . . .'

'And found nothing,' Hatusu retorted, glaring at Amerotke, 'nothing but feathery ash. The prisoners should have been tortured.'

'Divine One, if they had confessed it would only have been a litany of lies and deceit to confuse.'

'Time is passing.' Hatusu let her hand fall. 'In five days the army marches. I must have an end to this bloody conspiracy. Do you understand me, Amerotke?' She leaned forward. 'I want this Sgeru taken alive. I want to expose him to my troops.'

Amerotke glanced at Senenmut, who just closed his eyes.

'Imothep,' Amerotke tried to remain calm, 'the former chief scout, did he ever inform you, the House of Secrets or Lord Valu about his maps of Timsah?'

'No,' Senenmut replied, plucking his lower lip. 'Why should he?'

'Yet his searches alerted you, did they not?' Hatusu asked.

Amerotke nodded. 'And what is more curious,' he confessed, 'is that Imothep began his search before this evil manifested itself. Puzzling.' He shook his head. 'Imothep was not of the Arites, yet how did he suspect what was being planned?' Amerotke kept his face impassive. 'More importantly,' he continued, 'even though a corpse, its hands severed, was found in his garden, apparently strangled by the Arites, Imothep was not unduly alarmed by the emergence of his former enemies in Thebes.'

'Which means what?' Hatusu snapped.

'I don't really know,' Amerotke replied. 'The same goes for Lord Khufu. He miraculously saved Your Excellency from assassination. I know his wife tells you all of what happens here, yet though Khufu is threatened, he is not—'

'Not harmed.' Senenmut finished the sentence. Pharaoh's grand vizier and lover paused, head slightly turned. Amerotke suspected he knew more than he was saying. Senenmut looked under his eyebrows at Amerotke. 'You asked for Lord Valu's papers at the House of Secrets? I've personally delivered them to your lodgings.'

'But have you been through them?' the judge asked.

'Yes, though only cursorily. They tell us very little. Lord Valu was suspicious of Khufu. He felt that our high priest's intervention, though it saved the Divine One,' Senenmut's hand went out to clutch Hatusu's, 'was too fortuitous, rather swift. In other words,' he gently released Hatusu's hand and faced Amerotke squarely, 'you are following the same path Valu did. He suspected that the Temple of Nubia was involved in this crisis, but he had no proof, and neither did we, until very recently. Something

189

happened whilst you were gone.' Senenmut rose, went to the door and spoke softly to his guards.

A short while later, an old priest in a linen kilt, a leopard skin around his shoulders, stepped into the pavilion. He immediately made full obeisance in the direction of Hatusu, who courteously told him to rise, then threw a cushion so he could make himself comfortable squatting on the floor. He was a venerable old man with deep-set eyes and sunken cheeks, the Ankh and Sa, hieroglyphs for 'Peace' and 'Protection', tattooed on his right arm. He sat on the cushions fingering the small amulet on a silver chain around his neck, totally unabashed by the august company.

'This is Maneso,' Senenmut explained. 'Chief Priest of the Chapel of the Ear in the Temple of Nubia.'

Amerotke held Maneso's gaze. The chief priest was an exalted person, a mystic, an exorcist skilled in the casting-out of demons. A man who'd undergone the great fast to prepare himself to listen to the sins of those who entered the Chapel of the Ear. Such penitents would press their lips against the wooden grille, confess their secret sins and so purify themselves before making sacrifice.

'We have brought him to you,' Senenmut murmured, 'because of what he told us.'

Amerotke startled in surprise.

'But the confessions of sinners are strictly for the god.'

'Not so, not so.' Maneso's voice was clear and strong. 'If the peace and harmony of the god is threatened, the seal can be broken, and it has been, my lord judge.' The priest pronounced each word as if with divine approval.

'Blasphemy has occurred here.' He glared fiercely at Amerotke. 'Murder and mayhem! Innocent blood spilt on holy ground! The abomination of the desolation in the sanctuary of the holy place.'

Amerotke nodded understandingly.

'The peace of the god,' Maneso murmured, 'transcends the petty confessions of sinners.'

'Tell him,' Hatusu soothed. 'Maneso, tell him what you told me.'

'I hear the Divine One's words. I have looked on your face and marvelled at its beauty.' Maneso intoned the ritual greeting.

'Then tell him!' she snapped.

'I am Chief Priest of the Chapel of the Ear. I was visited many times by the murdered scout Imothep.'

'How do you know it was he?' Amerotke asked.

'My lord, if a man comes long enough to talk about his past, about the men he has killed in Nubia, his alienation from his own kind, if he describes his domestic situation . . .' Maneso spread his hands. 'You recognise voices and situations. Imothep was like an old friend. A quiet, secretive man, though under the influence of a certain woman.'

'He was a widower.'

'So, my lord?'

Amerotke smiled. 'Did he ever name this woman?'

'No, and even if he did, I could not, would not tell you; that was a matter of the heart.'

'Continue.'

'Yes, Divine One.' Maneso suddenly winked at Amerotke

as if amused by Hatusu's self-importance. Amerotke warmed to this little priest, who must have decided to break his vow of silence for very grave reason.

'Just before the last full moon,' Maneso continued, 'Imothep came again. He confessed that he had done something to compromise his loyalty to the Great House. He did not say what, but he confessed that he'd done it to protect those he loved.'

'His family? His kinsfolk at the House of the Forest?' Amerotke asked.

'Undoubtedly!'

Amerotke wondered about the woman who'd influenced Imothep. Neferen, or Sihera? Certainly the steward's daughter was comely enough. More importantly, why did such a woman, not to mention the rest, need protection, and against whom? The Arites, or someone else?

'I also know,' Maneso resumed his story, staring hard at Amerotke, 'that Imothep was a regular but quite secretive visitor to this temple. He would slip in through a postern gate to meet someone other than Lord Khufu.'

'A woman?' Amerotke asked. 'A heset? Lady Busiris, perhaps, or her principal handmaid Mataia?'

'Perhaps,' Maneso replied, 'yet they were never seen with him. On quite a few occasions Imothep visited the House of Books. The lector priests claimed he did not seem concerned about Mataia or she with him. It could have been someone else.' Maneso raised his eyebrows. 'Of course I was intrigued, hence my enquiries.' He grinned. 'We priests are known for our curiosity.' His face became grave. 'The revolt occurred in Nubia, followed by the assault on the Divine One, Imothep's murder, the death of the Arites prisoner, that night attack on our temple and the hideous news from Timsah about what had happened to the imperial couriers.' The old priest paused, his eyes filling with tears. 'I knew one of them, Amtef, a young man, my lord, fleet as a gazelle and as graceful, full of pride at wearing the Divine One's cartouche. Amtef was strangled, I understand, or so rumour has it, his corpse dragged away by those hyaena-hearts. Do you believe in ghosts, my lord judge?' Maneso didn't wait for an answer. 'I've dreamed of Amtef on a number of occasions. When I heard the news about Timsah, I wondered if Imothep's confession had been the source of all this bloodshed and death. So,' he rose wearily to his feet, 'I sought an audience with the Divine One and she kindly agreed.' He made as if to make full prostration before Hatusu, but she rose, a singular gesture, and from beneath her cloak brought out a pair of red gloves, a mark of exceptional favour. Maneso took these and bowed.

'I have made my confession, Divine One. My sacrifice to Amtef's ka.' The old priest smiled, put on the gloves and shuffled out into the sunshine.

'Well?' Hatusu took her seat, indicating that Senenmut and Amerotke should do likewise.

'I don't know what all this means.' Amerotke spoke quickly to anticipate Hatusu and Senenmut. 'Did Imothep know about the uprising? Was he party to it? Why did he work so earnestly drawing up those detailed plans of Timsah? Did he send them to the Sgeru or to Nubia? And why? Because he was a traitor? Or to protect his kin, but from what?'

Hatusu rose to her feet. 'Find out.' She stepped closer, eyes glittering fiercely. 'Bring me the Sgeru, Amerotke! On this don't fail me!' And beckoning at Senenmut, she swept from the garden pavilion.

Amerotke sat for a while listening to them go. A horn of sacrifice sounded, followed by the summons to prayer. Amerotke got up wearily and walked out towards the guest house. Two Silver Shields were waiting outside with sealed pouches containing Valu's papers. They handed these over, saluted the judge and left. Amerotke went up to his own chamber and made himself comfortable. He broke the seals but paused at the sound of footsteps outside. The door was pushed open, and Shufoy led Mataia into the chamber. She was dressed in a dark blue travelling cloak, her head and face unadorned, a leather bag in one hand, Shufoy's walking stick in the other. As she knelt on the cushions before the writing table, she seemed frightened, uneasy. She gathered the cloak closer about her, and Amerotke caught the glint of the exquisite silver cord around her waist.

'What is the matter?' Amerotke bit back his own impatience at being interrupted. He was tired, desperate to sift Valu's papers and discover some clue to the evils confronting him.

'I am sorry, my lord,' Mataia began. 'I know you have just returned. Many problems must vex your heart. However, I have come to ask for your protection. I am fearful here. I have petitioned Lord Khufu and Lady Busiris and they have given me permission to leave the Temple of Nubia for a while and seek sanctuary elsewhere.' She indicated the leather sack. 'I have packed a few possessions, those precious to me.' Before Amerotke could reply, Mataia took the sack and emptied its contents on to the table between them. They amounted to very little: rolled-up linen robes, a pair of sandals, small leather purses of jewellery and some miniature coffers. She sifted amongst these, opened a bejewelled casket and showed Amerotke the beautiful carnelian bracelet within. 'My lord, I humbly seek protection, as your family did, at the Malkata Palace. I offer this as a gift to your lady wife.'

'No, no.' Amerotke smiled and gently pushed the casket away. He noticed that Mataia's hands were trembling, her lovely eyes on the verge of tears. 'You may join the lady Norfret at the Malkata. Shufoy will accompany you there.' He indicated the possessions. 'Are you sure this is all you want to take?'

'Shufoy,' Mataia was now all smiles, 'says he will use my chamber and look after what is there. If I need anything he will bring it.'

'What are you frightened of?' Amerotke asked. 'The Arites?'

'And more.' Mataia chose her words carefully. 'A great rift has appeared between the Divine House and Nubia, and despite appearances, that includes this temple. My lord judge, whom can I trust? I need to be away, to think.'

'Tell me.' Amerotke helped Mataia put her belongings back into the sack. 'Chief Scout Imothep? He came to your House of Books to study maps. Rumour alleges he was a fairly regular visitor, sometimes secretive.'

'Perhaps.' Mataia seemed distracted. 'My lord, I have

already shown you what Imothep did here. He was probably going back over his old fighting days in Nubia. Ask the lector-priest. However, where he went before or afterwards or whom he visited on other occasions I truly don't know. I mean,' Mataia lifted her head and looked directly at Amerotke, 'ask Lord Khufu. Surely all visitors to the temple would be reported to him?'

Amerotke considered this. He glanced at the window, recalling his own searches at both the House of Books and the Mansion of Silence. He decided to leave. He wanted to walk off the tension, which sapped his strength.

'Mataia,' he declared, 'you may join the Lady Norfret at the Malkata Palace, but first,' he got to his feet, 'I need to revisit the House of the Forest. Shufoy, you and Mataia must accompany me.'

CHAPTER 8

Sept-ab: protector of the dead

Amerotke summoned Asural and his guards and they left the Temple of Nubia. The main gates were guarded by officers from the Isis regiment; these allowed Amerotke and his party through on to the thoroughfare that ran between the city walls and the river. It was late in the afternoon. Most of the day's trading was done, so farmers and peasants, their carts and donkeys loaded with family and goods, were wearily making their way home to the outlying villages. It was a busy, noisy thoroughfare. The dust floated like a haze. Flies buzzed in black hordes over the dung and waste that littered the road. The smell of dried fish and the rich stench of mud floated in from the river. Envoys from the Halls of the Dead, or Heralds of the Far Horizon, as the traders from the Necropolis liked to call themselves, had set up makeshift stalls advertising all the furniture of the tomb. Some of these enterprising hawkers tried to inveigle passers-by into ordering items or even crossing the Nile on a specially prepared punt to view a possible tomb. Scorpion men bellowed the beneficial effects of potions and philtres.

Amerotke recalled those silent, ghastly murders at the Oasis of Sinjar and quietly promised that he would pursue a suspicion that kept pricking his mind. For the moment, however, he remained vigilant against any threat. He glanced up and flinched at a dark shadow in a date-palm tree, but it was only a boy searching for fruit. Amerotke glanced at the Shardana mercenaries who, instead of Nubian and Kushite troops, patrolled the roads: these fair-faced mercenaries with their tawdry armour and colourful insignia seemed out of place. They were being taunted and mocked by a group of monkey-priests, drunk and sottish, carrying the grotesque statue of their god to some deserted oasis outside the city. The inebriated priests were accompanied by heavily painted whores whom they had purchased for the night. The scent of cooked food thickened the air. Amerotke glimpsed Nadif, standard-bearer in the Theban police, busy with his awkward nephew and other members of the city corps. They were using the cadaver hounds, saluki dogs specially trained to sniff out corpses along the riverbank, a favourite place for murderers to bury the remains of their victims. Amerotke was tempted to go and greet Nadif, but thought otherwise. Shufoy plucked at the sleeve of his robe and asked why he and Mataia had to accompany Amerotke to the House of the Forest.

'For company,' Amerotke replied. 'Loneliness can be a

help, it can also be a hindrance.' The judge glanced quickly at Mataia, who was walking elegantly in delicate sandals, her travelling cloak, despite the heat, wrapped tightly around her, probably to hide the costly cord and other jewellery.

They eventually reached the House of the Forest, and its gates swung open to greet them. Amerotke immediately went to the Mansion of Silence, asking a disconsolate Shufoy and Mataia to stay outside. He broke the seals on the double doors, lifted the bar and went in with Asural and some of his guards. Lanterns and lamps were lit. Amerotke immediately selected the basket of documents he'd inspected before.

'My lord?' Asural stood sweat-soaked, moving nervously from foot to foot, wary of this long, dark chamber. 'What else are we to do?'

Amerotke didn't lift his head. 'Search those wild gardens, Asural, and I mean everything.' He paused. 'Especially the stagnant pools and derelict fountains. You'll know why when you find it.'

Mystified, Asural left Shufoy on guard. Amerotke stared around the Mansion of Silence, then emptied the basket on to a writing table. He quickly sifted amongst the contents and found the maps of Timsah. They were roughly drawn but much more detailed and precise than he'd first imagined. He stared at them, drumming his fingers against the tabletop, then glanced towards the door. Shufoy and Mataia sat on cushions in the cool of the portico, heads together, deep in conversation. Amerotke went back to the plans. What was wrong here? Imothep had drawn these plans up before the revolt in Nubia had broken out or the Arites emerged in Thebes, so what was missing? The sound of voices made him pause. Parmen, Neferen, Rahmel and Sihera came into the Mansion of Silence. The steward bustled across.

'My lord judge,' he gasped, 'your men are searching the grounds! What are you looking for?'

Amerotke ignored him and stared at Neferen. She was certainly comely and nubile, pleasant-faced, though now she looked distinctly nervous. Sihera, as usual, stood slightly apart from the rest, staring at the judge.

'My lord?' Parmen went to repeat his question.

'I heard you,' Amerotke retorted. 'My men will search until they find something, as I will here.' He indicated that they should join him in the dining area. Amerotke chose a small stool. Shufoy and Mataia also came in. The heset had now taken off her cloak, fanning herself with her hand.

'Your master,' Amerotke began slowly, 'Imothep, he hated the Arites. Yes?'

They all agreed.

'He came here to work,' Amerotke declared. 'He drew up plans of the fortress of Timsah long before the revolt in Nubia or the present crisis in Thebes. Was your master threatened?'

'Not that I know of,' Parmen blustered. 'Nobody came here.'

'No one from the Temple of Nubia?' Amerotke asked. 'Lord Khufu, Lady Busiris or even Chief Heset Mataia?'

Parmen looked Mataia full in the face and shook his head.

'Did Imothep,' Amerotke persisted, 'ever say whom he visited at the Temple of Nubia?'

'The House of Books,' Neferen declared.

'I appreciate your master was a widower,' Amerotke continued. 'Was he particularly friendly with any woman?'

'The only person I heard him praise or talk warmly about,' Parmen replied, 'was the Lady Busiris. He may have visited the House of Courtesans, but . . .' His voice trailed off.

'Let me be blunt.' Amerotke tried to control his temper. 'I believe Imothep knew about the revolt in Nubia long before it occurred. He may even have been in alliance with the Arites.' He ignored the short, sharp laugh from Sihera. 'He was definitely meeting somebody at the Temple of Nubia. I also think he was frightened. He was protecting you all from some mysterious threat, probably the Arites. I ask you again. Do you know anything that can assist me?'

'My lord,' Parmen pleaded, 'our master Imothep was secretive. He was a veteran, he kept his own counsel. He was courteous and kind. As for where he went and whom he met, why should he discuss that with us? Yes, he cared for us, he may have been protecting us, but we don't know.'

'And yet the riddle remains.' Sihera spoke up. 'That corpse found in our garden, the hands severed, a red cloth wrapped tightly around his throat. No explanation has ever been found.'

Amerotke closed his eyes and breathed in deeply. Where, he wondered had Imothep gone? Whom did he meet at the

Temple of Nubia? That lay at the heart of this mystery! Khufu must surely know. Amerotke opened his eyes, rose and walked towards the doorway. Was he chasing shadows? Moonbeams across the desert? In the far distance he heard the saluki hounds barking raucously.

'What's the matter?' He turned.

'That will be your men,' Parmen replied. 'The dogs are locked in.'

Amerotke walked back. 'It's strange,' he mused.

'What is, my lord?'

'That the saluki hounds found the corpse but never the severed hands. I wonder why? Was he a beggar from the Temple of Nubia? Mataia, the temple acolytes tattoo a mark on the back of a beggar's hands, a sign that he is permitted to beg in the temple precincts.'

She nodded. 'True, my lord, but why should someone remove a beggar's hands?'

Amerotke was about to answer that he didn't know when he heard shouting and hurried towards the door. One of Asural's guards stood outside, hands on his knees, gasping for breath.

'My lord, Asural has found something; you must come now.'

Amerotke hastened down the steps and followed the guard along a winding path through thick, lush vegetation. The heat was cloying; flies and insects swarmed. They made their way around overgrown flowerbeds and herb plots, decaying fountains and rectangular pools that must once have been graced with lotus blossoms. They went deeper into the garden, through a clump of gnarled, twisted trees, so ancient they must have been there for ever. Amerotke realised they were now approaching the curtain wall around the estate. Asural and his guards were waiting close to this, near a stagnant pool. A myriad of insects buzzed over its dirt-slimed surface; thick green sedge circled its rim. Amerotke noticed that the steps leading down were overgrown with weeds. Asural stood precariously on the first step, sifting the filthy water with a stick. At first Amerotke could see nothing, then he glimpsed something move, a flash of red. At the judge's instruction, two of the guards splashed into the filthy pool and drew out the decomposing mud-caked corpse; it looked like a bundle of decaying vegetation or disused clothing until an arm flopped, the blackened, severed stump of a wrist making it all the more grotesque. Asural shouted for clean water. Parmen hurried away as the corpse was moved to a nearby stone bench. Amerotke knelt beside it, cleaning the mud from the face and upper chest to reveal the red cloth tied tightly around the scrawny throat. The judge stood back as the water, brought in large pitchers, was poured over the corpse. The thick coating of ooze and slime was cleared, though the noisome stench from the remains grew even more rank. Amerotke, pinching his nostrils, examined the bloated, wrinkled face, the shaven skull, the spindly legs, the old scars healed into slightly protuberant welts along the bony back.

'An old soldier,' Asural murmured. 'One often beaten by his officers.'

Amerotke nodded in agreement. He turned his attention to the arms, which had been neatly severed at the wrists as if by a flesher's cleaver. An old man, Amerotke concluded, well past his prime. He stared hard at the face. The old soldier, he reflected, had died a heinous death. His temper welled within him, a clammy sweat of fury. He asked for a dagger and sawed at the ghastly red garrotte around the throat. Eventually he cut it, examined the two pieces carefully then threw them to the ground. He went to get up but slipped, and his hand slid along the mud-splattered face, brushing the protuberant lips, hooked nose and deep, slime-choked eye sockets. Amerotke's patience snapped. He sprang to his feet and glared around.

'On your oath,' he yelled at Parmen and the rest, 'do you know who this is? Why he was murdered?'

They gazed blankly back. Amerotke could tolerate no more.

'See to the corpse,' he ordered Asural. 'Shufoy, take Mataia to the Malkata. As for the rest . . .' He did not finish the sentence, but strode away lost in his own furious storm of thoughts.

A few hours later, just after sunset, Amerotke, bathed, changed and feeling less angry with the world, squatted before the writing desk in his chamber at the guesthouse. He'd eaten and drunk and was now sifting amongst Valu's papers. From outside drifted the last sounds of the evening sacrifice: the call of horns, the clash of cymbals and the faint strains of the temple choir. Shufoy had returned from the Malkata looking desolate at being separated from his beloved. Amerotke tried to curb his impatience and act as understandingly as possible. Shufoy, however, simply sat on a stool like some lost soul and swiftly downed a large goblet of wine. Now he lay sleeping on the floor, his head comfortably cushioned. Occasionally he'd move and mutter, 'Mataia.' Amerotke glanced at the snoring Shufoy, smiled then returned to the collection of papyri. Some of them were of the finest quality, the work of Valu's chancery; others were dirty grey scraps from informants. Valu's temple was that of the Lady of Hathor: on the steps leading up to it, he had constructed a statue of Nekhbet the vulture goddess with stretching neck and gaping beak, and had persuaded what he termed 'worried' or 'anxious' citizens to place petitions into the back of the carved bird. In truth, the dead prosecutor had invited denunciations, gossip and rumour. Amerotke had encountered such scurrilous evidence in his court and given it little heed. None of this information was worth reading, yet for Valu, it provided a path into the seedy, dirty politics of the city. His most recent collection included a number of denunciations about the Temple of Nubia. Khufu in particular was singled out for vile comment and invective: his intervention to save the Divine One was bitterly scorned and portrayed as part of some mysterious, malevolent design against Hatusu.

Two items quickened Amerotke's interest. The first, scrawled on a piece of papyrus, maintained that Lord Khufu could not be trusted: he was a member of the Arites and should be arrested. More importantly, the high priest nourished and cherished a nest of traitors in his temple and enticed even the most loyal into treason. The second piece was written on a fine stretch of papyrus. Its writer warned Lord Valu that to break the power of the Arites, he must call on the help of the Churat, who, with his pet mongoose, could, for certain rewards, provide vital information about the Arites. Valu had scrawled a dismissive line beneath this. Amerotke, however, tapped the piece of papyrus and breathed a sigh of relief. He had found a door! The Churat of the Am-duat was well known to him. He styled himself Eater of Foul Things in the Underworld, and was the leader of one of the most powerful gangs in the Necropolis. He sheltered in the Abode of Darkness, the very heart of the filthy, seedy underbelly of Thebes. The Churat was an outlaw who'd managed to successfully evade both capture and prosecution, a highly dangerous man with whom Amerotke had done business before. So, what was he offering Lord Valu? And why the reference to the mongoose? Amerotke pushed himself away from the table. Why had the Churat approached Valu? Why hadn't he sent a message to Amerotke? He heard Shufoy groan and glanced towards the little man, who was now struggling to sit up. Amerotke went and crouched beside him.

'Shufoy.' He grasped the dwarf's shoulder and shook him awake. Shufoy blinked, licking his lips, one hand going out as if searching for a wine goblet. 'No, no,' Amerotke warned. 'Listen, Shufoy, you know the Churat?'

'Of course I do, master, we've done . . .' The words faded.

'Shufoy,' Amerotke warned, 'did the Churat send a message to me?'

Shufoy's fingers flew to his lips.

'He did, didn't he?'

Shufoy nodded. 'Master,' he protested, 'I forgot! While you were away, one of his lieutenants, the Monkey, was waiting for me outside the Temple of Nubia. He said his master wanted to show you his pet mongoose, that you should visit him. Master, I forgot, I didn't think it was connected with this business.'

'Well it is,' Amerotke declared. 'Look, Shufoy. Get up, wash and be out of the temple before dusk. Go across to the Necropolis, tell the Churat . . .' He paused at a knock on the door. Asural came in.

'My lord, we've finished our search of Imothep's garden. We found nothing else.'

'You are sure of that?' the judge asked.

'Certain, my lord, nothing else.'

'Then tomorrow,' Amerotke said, 'I need you again, Asural. We are going to visit an old acquaintance in the City of the Dead . . .'

Early the next morning, Amerotke, Shufoy and Asural, together with a heavily armed escort, landed at the Great Mooring Place of Osiris, the principal quayside of the Necropolis. Along its wharfs a group of itinerant priests, surrounded by their acolytes, tended a makeshift altar and sang the dawn hymn:

He is like the lotus,
Springing up in splendour,
Fed by the breath of Ra.
Rising up in sunlight,
Out of the soil of darkness.
He blossoms full above the Eternal Green Fields of
Yalou.

The incense sprinkled over their offerings mingled with

the smell of dried fish, the cheap perfume of wandering whores, the ever-pervasive odour of sweaty, oiled bodies and the heavy stench of Nile mud. Apes caged in huge crates screeched and scrambled about, banging the bars at two tame baby giraffes being led away. Further along, a troupe of dancers, sacred to Hathor, the Lady of Drunkenness, stamped and whirled to the noisy crescendo of drum, cymbals and castanets. Fishermen, sailors and marines gathered around the cookshop fires, the charcoal spluttering noisily under fatty chunks of antelope meat roasting on the makeshift grills. Next to these, cross-legged scribes prepared their writing trays, whilst bakers leaned over their kneading troughs pounding the dough for the ovens being fired in the nearby bakeries. A Danga dwarf, his elongated head balanced by two enormous ears, his foolish face streaked with various colours, slit eyes ringed with kohl, bawled the attractions of two courtesans waiting for custom in the Moon of Memphis. Scorpion and lizard men lurked in the shadows, watching the keepers of the sepulchres assemble for the day's entombments. A priest of Anubis, resplendent in his black and gold jackal mask and kilt of the same colours, went down the Steps of Osiris to meet the first funeral barge of the day. Around him swarmed flunkeys carrying smoking incense boats and black-and-red-dyed flabella to drive away the flies. Bringing up the rear were acolytes bearing the insignias of various gods fixed on poles as well as trays of dried cakes and wine cups for the expected mourners. A snake man, one of the Guild of Filchers, skilled in cutting bags, purses and pouches from the unwary, had been caught red-handed. The quayside officials had thrown him over a wooden trestle to be scourged with splintered rods until the skin on his back burst and the blood splattered out. A blind beggar, paid to dance and sing, almost drowned out the prisoner's screams with his raucous din. Professional mourners gathered in groups of six to rehearse their wailing chants, only to be mocked by a drunken mercenary from a nearby guard post.

The clamour subsided as Amerotke, under a resplendent blue and gold imperial pennant borne by Shufoy, processed across the quayside and up into the winding streets of the City of the Dead. They passed through the various trading quarters: scarab-makers, coffin-carvers, enamellists, silver- and coppersmiths, whose workshops, booths and stores fronted streets as narrow as a dagger blade, dark tunnels hidden from the light, filled with leaping shadows, uncanny noises and pungent smells. On to these streets debouched needle-thin alleys and runnels stinking of all sorts of filth, the hunting ground of yellow pi-dogs and amber-coloured cats. Naked children, eyes red-rimmed, bellies swollen, fought over the strips of dried dung so necessary for fuel. Now and again this maze of horror would abruptly end and they'd enter a dusty, sun-filled square where market people prepared for a day's trade. Under palm and sycamore trees, barbers, hawkers, tinkers and cooks set up shop, whilst wandering scribes chose shaded corners to welcome their pupils. Whores, their faces all smeared, oil-caked wigs askew, helped their inebriated customers towards the water-carriers, who were eager to sell what they described as 'the purest of the pure, to slake a thirst as hot and dry as the desert wind'. In one of these squares a wandering preacher, his skin burnt almost black by the fierce sun, stood on an overturned barrel, one hand combing his tangled beard, the other holding a flickering torch.

'Listen!' The preacher's grating voice rang out across the square. 'In Nubia, the Kingdom of Kush, a fierce torrent of flame and smoke flows. The final days are upon us. The bolts of heaven have been drawn. The gates of the Underworld forced. Signs and portents first! The sun will turn black as the deepest night. The stars will glint with ice. The moon will drip with blood. Men will quake, die in fear at what is to come. Listen now ...'

Amerotke paused even as the preacher fell silent as he glimpsed the royal standard.

'Shall we arrest him?' Asural murmured. 'He is gabbling treason.'

'No,' Amerotke replied, 'he is talking sense and dressing it up as prophecy. Soon General Omendap marches. The gods only know what will happen in Thebes. Let's move on and help the gods.'

They left the square. A labyrinth of twisting, stinking alleyways snaked towards the Abode of Darkness, a huddle of decaying buildings and fetid rat-runnels reeking of wickedness. They passed through a ruined porch, the Gate of the Unclean, into the Abode itself. The streets were seemingly empty, though Amerotke glimpsed a legion of flitting shapes. Voices echoed ghostly chants: 'Here is the Lord Amerotke': 'Pharaoh's man': 'Soldiers bringing death':

'Welcome, welcome to the Halls of Impurity, so easy to enter, so difficult to leave.' The chants continued, an attempt to unnerve Amerotke and his escort. Screams, catcalls and the ominous beating of a drum grew louder. Occasionally shutters flew open. A horn suddenly brayed. Amerotke glanced up. A warlock, festooned with black and red feathers, stood on the flat roof of a house, his ugly painted face glaring down at them. In one hand he held a sistra, in the other a smoking pot of herbs. Next to this grotesque crouched a dwarf-woman shrouded in a filthy camel skin, her blood-encrusted greying hair framing an evil, narrow face. Amerotke curbed his fear. He recognised the Churat's war against his soul. Everything here was shadow and no substance, masks to fright the nervous. The taunting continued. Amerotke glanced at Asural's men. Fear pinched their faces; soon it might freeze their hearts. Amerotke drew a deep breath and, in a powerful voice, intoned a favourite hymn of veteran soldiers, a song of praise to the ever-victorious Horus.

I am yesterday, today and tomorrow.
The divine hidden soul who created the world.
And who nourishes the breath of men . . .

Shufoy joined in the next lines.

I am the Lord of those who rise from the dead,
Whose souls glow like lamps in the House of the
   Dead,
Whose shrine is the earth.

Asural came next.

> When the sky is illuminated with crystal.
> These gladden my soul and broaden my path.

Amerotke grinned as the entire corps took up the final verse, a defiant chant against the evil around them.

> Keep me safe from the Sleeper in Darkness . . .

The resounding hymn of praise rang out like a trumpet, driving back the gathering terrors. They reached a sunlit square dominated at the far end by an ancient temple. At first glance the concourse stretching before the steps leading up to the gloomy portico seemed deserted, then Amerotke glimpsed the garishly garbed killers camped in the entrances to alleyways and crumbling doorways. A gong sounded from the temple, and a figure garbed in white linen robes walked out from the portico. He was escorted by two attendants carrying huge golden-coloured flabella. Even from where he stood, Amerotke could smell the heavy perfume they wafted.

'Come.' The white-garbed man's voice resounded across the square. 'The Churat welcomes Lord Amerotke, Chief Judge in the Hall of Two Truths . . .'

A short while later, Amerotke was making himself comfortable deep in the Churat's audience chamber. It was an elegant room, its walls painted in eye-catching colours, the floor of polished tile, the furniture fashioned from gleaming acacia wood. The Churat looked like some benevolent priest with his shaven head, kindly eyes and constant smile. He personally served Amerotke slices of delicious fruit bread and cups of crushed juice whilst servants took care of the judge's escort in an adjoining room. Amerotke smiled. The Churat apparently considered himself his equal, though Amerotke also suspected that the outlaw's assassins were present, hiding deep in the shadows of that long chamber.

After the courtesies had been exchanged, the Churat dabbed his mouth with a napkin and spread his hands.

'Interesting times, my lord judge. The Divine One faces danger from both within and without.'

'The Arites,' Amerotke replied. 'You sent a letter to Lord Valu saying you could help. He has now gone into the Far West, and his assassins have been punished. Pharaoh's justice will be done.'

'I hope so.' The Churat smiled. 'I sincerely hope so, though rumour has it that when General Omendap leaves, there'll be unrest in Thebes.'

'Tell me what you know,' Amerotke demanded.

'Why should I?' the Churat whispered. 'My lord judge, what do you offer me?'

'Life,' Amerotke declared. 'I could arrest you.'

The Churat laughed, rocking backwards and forwards on his cushions.

'Really, my lord judge, are we here to bait each other? Let me tell you what I know, then we will do business. Nubia is in revolt; its viceroy has withdrawn to the great fortress of Buhen. You did great work in cleaning out those vipers at Timsah, very good, very good! I could have helped you there! Nothing is ever stolen, my lord judge, that does not eventually appear in Thebes. Yet merchants and envoys, men with costly bracelets and weapons, disappeared along with their boats and parcels, whatever they carried—'

'As you say,' Amerotke interrupted, 'that danger has been removed.'

'But not the one in Thebes.' The Churat's smile faded. 'Let me tell you this. The Sgeru, whoever he is, lurks in Thebes, I am sure of that. He directs his minions, his assassins around the imperial city.'

'Where?' Amerotke asked.

'My lord judge, it's a matter of logic! Where better than the Temple of Nubia, but who he is and how he does it?' The Churat shook his head.

'And what do you think will happen when Omendap moves?' Amerotke asked, biting into the soft bread.

'There will be riots.' The Churat narrowed his eyes. 'A time of harvest for people like myself. You can have squadrons of chariots and regiments loyal to the Divine One, but how can they hunt an enemy they cannot truly see?'

'You mean assassins will strike?'

'Precisely!' the Churat replied.

'I suspect the same,' Amerotke declared, 'but you did not bring me here to explain the obvious?'

The Churat turned and whistled into the darkness. There was a patter of feet and a man emerged from the gloom, a Nubian of middle years, light-skinned, sharp-faced, a scar on his right cheek, another twisting his upper lip. He was dressed in a white kilt, and the war belt strapped across his chest did not disguise the purple welts of ancient wounds. He sat down on the cushion next to the Churat and gazed mournfully at the judge.

'This is the Mongoose,' the Churat introduced the newcomer, 'once a master bowman in the company of Nekhbet, a native of Nubia, a former soldier in the imperial army and, more importantly, an Arites.'

'Impossible!' Amerotke shook his head. 'The Arites do not break their blood oath; none can be turned.'

'Not by the likes of you,' the Mongoose grated.

The Churat struck him on the arm with his fan.

'Speak respectfully,' he hissed, 'to the lord judge.'

The Mongoose's head went back, and he peered at Amerotke from half-closed heavy-lidded eyes.

'Tell him!' the Churat whispered.

'Two seasons ago, when the Sgeru was plotting in Thebes, suborning the likes of me—'

'Who is he?' Amerotke interrupted.

'No one knows. His orders are relayed by messengers. All we are told is that he is a descendant of our ancient rulers. He holds the Sesher, the sacred golden cord of the Arites.'

'Where does he lurk?'

'Anywhere, my lord. Rumour has it that it might be someone in the Temple of Nubia, but that is only a rumour.'

'And a name?'

'Lord Khufu, perhaps.'

'But the high priest is not a descendant of the royal line.'

'My lord,' the Mongoose smiled, 'the Arites do not advertise who carries the sacred blood. They disguise it well. If anybody was proclaimed as a member of the royal line, surely the Divine One would seize them?'

Amerotke nodded. That made sense, a fact he'd overlooked.

'The Arites,' the Mongoose continued, 'work under the cover of darkness. No one really knows who is a member, as not every Nubian wishes to break his oath to the Divine One. I was one of those, so they threatened my family in Nubia.'

'How?'

'Messengers travel constantly backwards and forwards between Thebes and Nubia. My kin lived in a village just south of the Second Cataract. I wavered; they threatened, so I took their oath.'

'And?'

The Mongoose put his face in his hands; when he took them away, tears brimmed in his eyes.

'I'll never know whether it was deliberate or a mistake. I suspect I wavered too long. I joined the Arites. Weeks passed, then the news came from Nubia. My father, mother, brother, his wife and my sister had all died in a fire.'

'Murder!'

'Of course, my lord. Naturally I was summoned to the Arites circle. I met them.'

'Where?'

'In the Necropolis, at a beer shop; that is the way they act. You go into a brothel with comrades for a drink, your arm will be plucked, you'll be led away, down a maze of alleyways into a darkened chamber. I was summoned in such a way. I was grieving, but the Arites still taunted me. They pointed out that I had other kin, that they too were vulnerable: was I sure of my oath? I said I was, but I lied. I couldn't control my rage. I was taken out of the meeting by two masked guards. They gave me back my knife.' The Mongoose pointed at his lip, and cheek, the scars on his chest. 'I am a warrior. Twice given the silver bracelet of bravery, once the gold collar of valour. That night it was cold, and bleak. I stared up at the sky. I regretted breaking my oath to the Divine One. They had turned me into a traitor and still murdered my kin. My rage boiled over. I drew my dagger and killed both of them. I never even stopped to strip off their masks. I just fled deep into the Necropolis.'

'I hear what you say,' Amerotke replied slowly, 'but how do I know that you are still not a traitor? A spy sent here for some secret, nefarious purpose?'

'Oh, he speaks with a true heart,' the Churat murmured, wafting himself with his fan. 'The Arites pursued him. They offered gold, silver and jewels for his return.'

'And?'

'I am a man of honour, my lord judge. When I give my word, I keep it. My men picked up this warrior. I marvelled at his courage and cunning, hence his name, Mongoose. I always need men like him. The Arites can offer whatever they wish; they shall not have him back.'

217

'And yet you can tell us nothing?' Amerotke asked.

'Probably nothing you don't already know,' the Mongoose conceded. 'Just suspicions, straws in the wind.'

The Churat held up a hand. 'My lord, what we've already told you may be of interest. But we have something else. However, everything in Thebes has a price; I have certainly mine. You have children, my lord?'

'Two sons,' Amerotke replied. 'You know that.'

The Churat smiled. 'I have a son, eight summers old, and a daughter two years younger. One day, my lord judge,' the Churat wafted his face gently with the fan, 'one day I will travel into the Far West. The Divine One has already guaranteed that I will be given an honourable burial, my own tomb, undisturbed, so that I can journey to meet the gods.'

'An interesting meeting,' Amerotke declared.

'My son and daughter?' the Churat continued blithely. 'I do not wish them to live in the Necropolis, near the Abode of Darkness, for the rest of their lives. They must not follow my path. I want your oath, my lord judge, speaking on behalf of the Divine One, that my son and daughter will enter the House of Life in the Temple of Isis,' He chuckled at the surprise on Amerotke's face. 'My son is to be trained as a scribe, to enter the royal service, to become like you, Lord Amerotke.'

'And your daughter?'

'A temple heset like the graceful Lady Mataia, with whom your friend Shufoy is so enamoured. Do I ask much, my lord? Do I not ask what you yourself want for your own children? Is it against the law or righteousness?'

Amerotke hid his surprise. Here was the Churat, one of the greatest villains in Thebes, a man responsible for many a wickedness, yet he followed his path as Amerotke did his, and in this they were no different. They wanted the best for their children.

'My lord judge, I will not lie. I speak with true heart and clear tongue. My lips are not sordid. I sent that information to Lord Valu and the invitation to your servant Shufoy.' The Churat shrugged. 'I was surprised that you did not respond, but there again,' his eyes crinkled with amusement, 'Shufoy has other matters on his mind, or should I say on his heart? My lord,' he spread his hands, 'I await your response. If you wish, you may go back to confer with the Divine One and Lord Senenmut, but in the end, what you promise, the Divine One will guarantee. All I am asking for is a door to be opened. My children must be taken in, not as hostages to be used against me but treated as if they were children of great nobles. They must be given every dignity, allowed to progress, to use their talents and become true servants of the Great House.'

Amerotke held up his right hand.

'I swear by Ma'at, the Goddess of Truth,' he declared, 'that your children will be given the same treatment as mine. I will keep them close to my heart; the promise will be fulfilled.'

The Churat leaned across, hand outstretched. Amerotke clasped it.

'I have your oath, my lord judge.'

'No, my lord.' Amerotke smiled. 'You have my word; that is more sacred.'

The Churat gripped Amerotke's hand and released it.

'Our friend here,' he turned to the Mongoose, who was watching Amerotke intently, 'has something to ask as well.'

'Which is?' Amerotke replied.

'When this is over,' the Mongoose spoke up, 'and it will be, my lord Amerotke, if the Divine One agrees, full pardon, restoration to my regiment, my record purged, a mark of honour given to me for the services I have rendered.'

Amerotke agreed, stretched out his hand and the Nubian clasped it.

CHAPTER 9

Tchar: Book of Breathings

'This is what I know.' The Mongoose paused, choosing his words. 'I speak now as if I am on sacred oath: I swear by the blood of my kin. I talk of rumour and gossip, of secret whispers, my lord, but listen well. First, when General Omendap marches south, the Sgeru will foment dissension and revolt in Thebes. Perhaps it will begin in the Temple of Nubia, but he has also hired gangs from the Necropolis, assassins and plunderers, every outlaw crawling under the sun. Is that not correct, my lord?'

'I have been approached,' the Churat agreed. 'But I refused.'

'It is something we expected,' Amerotke declared. 'Continue!'

'We, the Arites, only met in the dark. We always wore masks. No one ever used their own name. Instead we assumed the identities of animals: one would be the Cat, another the Fox, or the Wolf, the Polecat. It was very easy to meet, particularly in the barracks, well away from spies and informers. One thing was made very clear to us. There was a list of those singled out for death: the Divine One, Lord Senenmut, Lord Valu and, of course, you.'

'Who else?' Amerotke controlled his excitement. Unlike the Arites killed in the House of Chains, this man struck him as truthful.

The Mongoose provided a few more names of notables at court, including General Omendap and certain leading officers.

'Other names were mentioned?' Amerotke asked.

'Yes, the names of those who were not to be harmed in any way, whatever the appearances. Two of these I do remember. One was the old chief scout, Imothep. We were surprised, because he had fought against the Arites in Nubia, and had plundered their sacred possessions. Nevertheless, the instructions were issued: Imothep was of great service to our cause, and was not to be harmed.'

Amerotke hid his astonishment. 'Are you sure of that?'

'My lord, you may dismiss this as rumour, but it was made very clear. The other name was Lord Khufu. Naturally, we were intrigued by this. Both Imothep and Khufu were regarded as renegades and traitors. Questions were asked, but we were told to obey our orders and ask no more.'

'And yet warnings were sent to Lord Khufu?'

'They may have been, but he had nothing to fear from us. The Arites did not pass sentence of death on him.'

'And Imothep?' Amerotke asked. 'Why him?'

'All I know is that he was not to be harmed.'

'Yet he was strangled? Did the orders change?'

The Mongoose pulled a face. 'I doubt it. Once the Arites have sworn an oath to kill, they'll kill. If they swear an oath not to, then it won't happen.'

'And you know of no other reason why these two were to be protected?'

'They must have been of good service to the Arites.'

'Tell me ...' Amerotke paused, scrutinising the Mongoose intently. 'Tell me about the corpse found in Imothep's garden, its hands severed? Yesterday I found a second corpse, thrown into a stagnant pool, well hidden. Could those murders have been the work of the Arites?'

'I doubt it,' the Mongoose replied. 'If the Arites take an oath not to harm someone, that includes their property and anyone who lives with them. Moreover, the Arites kill for public show. I heard about the corpse being found, and now you mention another. Why the Arites should steal into Imothep's garden and kill such men, I cannot tell you.'

'You say Khufu was protected, hence also his house and retainers, yet the Arites launched an attack on the Temple of Nubia. They killed a number of servants, amongst these the keeper of the House of Chains, a lector priest and a guard. Can you explain that?'

'No, I cannot.'

'And Lady Busiris, how did the Arites regard her?'

'Never mentioned her at all.'

'And the lady Mataia?'

'Dismissed as a heset whore who'd be handed over to our victorious troops for their pleasure.'

'My lord,' the Churat intervened, 'when I heard about

Imothep's death, I made my own enquiries. The Mongoose told me what he has told you. First, Imothep was a widower, an old man but virile. I have a finger in many pots,' he smiled, 'pleasure houses, brothels, yet despite my searches, one thing I discovered was that Imothep never visited any of these. Indeed, from my spies I learnt that there was no woman in his life. Yet Imothep,' the Churat spread his hands, 'was like all of us men. He needed his pleasures, his satisfaction. So where did he go?' He shook his head mournfully. 'Nowhere!'

'And the lord Khufu?' Amerotke asked.

'Ah.' The Churat smiled. 'The lady Busiris may be nubile, fresh-faced, skilled in all forms of art. Lord Khufu, however, likes variety. He has been known to visit certain houses of pleasure and take his rest there, though that is true of many in Thebes. They do not act on what they preach.' He pointed a finger at Amerotke. 'Except for you. You are faithful to your wife and family, and for that I praise you.'

'Is there anything else?' Amerotke turned to the Mongoose.

'Just rumour. Imothep's housekeeper, Sihera? In her youth she may have been married to an Arites. Gossip, chatter.' The Mongoose shrugged. 'One last thing. The Arites found strangled in the cell? You do know that their warriors in battle, when they realise they are going to die, always tie a red cloth around their throats to meet their goddess.' He spread his hands. 'That is all I can say.'

'In which case,' Amerotke rose to his feet and bowed to the Churat, 'I must take my leave. I have business to tend to.'

'I am sure you have,' the Churat replied. 'You'll have safe passage back to the quayside. No one will harm you. Still, I warn you. You've brought a strong guard? I plead with you, keep them close!'

During his journey back, Amerotke reflected on what he had learnt. He could not fathom the mystery around Imothep. He'd been murdered, whatever the Mongoose said. Khufu, though, was a different matter. Once back at the Temple of Nubia, Amerotke quickly wrote a letter, which he sealed and handed to Shufoy to take to the Lady of the Dark, the mistress of poisons in Thebes. He asked her two simple questions, for he believed she could provide the solution to some of the mysteries. Shufoy looked distinctly unhappy at having to return to the Necropolis.

'No, no,' Amerotke reassured him. 'You will be safe. Take two of Asural's guards. Whoever is hunting me will not be stalking you. Give the Lady of the Dark my warmest greetings. Show her the letter. Ask for a written reply, then return immediately to me. Now, Asural,' Amerotke turned to the captain of his guard, 'go and tell Lord Khufu I wish to see him in the pavilion beside the pool of purity in the Garden of Fragrances. Tell him to come immediately. Once he is closeted with me, stay close until I have finished. You understand?'

Asural nodded and hurried off.

Shufoy murmured about his desire to visit the Malkata.

'No, no.' Amerotke crouched down. 'Shufoy, do what I've asked. First justice, then we'll turn to matters of the heart.'

Amerotke left, some of his guards following. He went into the Garden of Fragrances and made himself comfortable in the pavilion. He heard Asural approach and Lord Khufu swept in. The high priest was distinctly agitated, fingers plucking at his lower lip. Amerotke gestured at the cushions and squatted down opposite him.

'My lord, I apologise for taking you away from your other duties, but unless you give me honest answers to direct questions, I shall take you even further away and hand you over to the House of Chains, because you, sir, have told me lies.'

Khufu opened his mouth to protest even as fear flared in his face.

'Don't lie,' Amerotke insisted. 'I am going to put certain matters to you. I demand your honest reply. Lord Khufu, the Arites have apparently warned you, yet they have never carried out that threat against you or yours. You are master of this temple. The former chief scout Imothep often came here. He was secretly visiting you. Correct? Now, I have spoken to someone who has given me information that the Arites solemnly promised that you and your household would be safe. Surely they would only give such a promise in return for a very generous response? What was that response? You can either tell me here or in the torture chambers at the palace. Which path do you wish to follow?'

Khufu plucked at his robe, his fingers running along the embroidered sash around his waist. He turned longingly towards the door, then back to Amerotke.

'To whom have you spoken?'

'An Arites,' Amerotke replied. 'A man who calls himself the Mongoose, a fugitive from that murderous secret society. My lord, to whom I talk is a matter of no consequence. I want the truth from you.'

Khufu rubbed his face. He went to speak, then paused. 'Very well.' He sighed deeply. 'I was approached here in the temple by an envoy from the Arites, who demanded my cooperation.'

'When?'

'Weeks before the revolt in Nubia.'

'You could have warned the Divine One.'

Khufu just swallowed hard.

'Who was it that approached you?' Amerotke asked.

The high priest licked his lips. 'Imothep!'

'What?'

'Imothep,' Khufu repeated, staring hard at Amerotke. 'He said he'd been trapped by the Arites, menaced by them. They'd visited him secretly, threatened him that unless he made a similar approach to me, both our families would die! Imothep's household, Lady Busiris and the lady Mataia: they'd all be strangled, sacrificed to the Arites' gods.'

'But this is nonsense,' Amerotke breathed. 'Was Imothep an Arites? Could he have been the Sgeru?'

'Can't you see?' Khufu pleaded. 'They couldn't have chosen a better envoy. Imothep was their enemy; they forced him to coerce me. He had been instructed in what to say, not only threats but blackmail. The Arites had learnt about my visits to certain courtesans in the city. They threatened to publicly expose me.'

'And you agreed?'

'What else could I do?'

'But Imothep was a veteran warrior. He'd fought the Arites. He could be as ruthless as them.'

'I cannot answer that; only Imothep could, and he is dead. Nevertheless, I tell you this: at the time he was as frightened as I am now. The Arites simply wanted our cooperation. Imothep was to come into the temple. He wanted to study the maps of the eastern desert as far south as the First Cataract. I agreed. Naturally,' Khufu wiped the sweat from his brow with the back of his hand, 'they wanted more. They told me I was not to interfere. To carry on business as normal but to allow Imothep to come and go as he wished. Imothep explained how he had drawn up plans of the fortress at Timsah. He was to bring them into the temple and give them to me.' Khufu breathed out. 'Imothep visited our House of Books whenever he wanted. Every so often he met me to ensure I kept my word to the Arites. From time to time he also gave me packages sealed in pouches. I took these and buried them under a great sycamore tree close to the curtain wall. On one occasion I went back to check: the pouch was gone.'

'Did Imothep tell you how they approached him?'

'No, but he was a regular visitor here. We were both trapped. Once we were drawn in, there was no going back.'

'And the stranger found strangled in Imothep's garden?' Amerotke asked.

'Imothep didn't know. He thought it might be a fresh threat to both of us not to confess to the Divine One.'

'And yet you saved Hatusu from the assassins?'

Khufu glanced away.

'It's true, isn't it?' Amerotke murmured. 'You knew in advance what would happen?'

'I tried to resist,' Khufu confessed. 'I began to wonder if Imothep was a member of the Arites, even the Sgeru himself. I confronted him with this. He may have informed the Arites. They responded that they could strike at whoever they wished, whenever they wanted. Imothep was to tell me to be most vigilant when the Divine One landed in Thebes from her victorious expedition in the north. I was to keep a careful eye on the Nubians who carried her palanquin.'

'Impossible,' Amerotke breathed. 'The Arites were willing to sacrifice their own men?'

'What did they care?' Khufu exclaimed. 'They wanted to convince me of their power, and they did. I don't think it mattered if Hatusu died or not. The Arites wanted to demonstrate that they could strike at Pharaoh in her holy of holies. On the morning the Divine One returned, I was alert, ready for danger. I had already warned the Great House to be wary. As soon as that palanquin-bearer collapsed, I recognised the moment. The assassin darted forward and I intervened, but that is how cunning the Arites are. I was depicted as the saviour of the Divine One, so the Temple of Nubia could not be regarded as a nest of traitors. I suspect Lord Valu had other ideas.'

'Yes, he did,' Amerotke retorted. 'You were denounced!'

'Who by?' Khufu shrugged. 'Ah well, what does it matter now? The Arites will sacrifice me as they did that prisoner in our House of Chains. They planned that.'

Amerotke stared at the lance of light piercing the door of the pavilion. He recalled Lord Valu and himself returning from the Place of the Skull, bringing that Arites with them . . .

'But that's not possible,' he murmured. 'Lord Valu's decision to bring the Arites back here was totally unexpected.'

'I cannot answer that. The attack on you and Valu, the death of the Arites in the House of Chains, both remain a mystery to me.'

'And the warnings the Arites left you? The scarab, the red cloths?'

'Perhaps warnings that they were not far, that they could strike whenever they wanted.'

Amerotke recalled what he'd learnt from the Mongoose.

'But the Arites had given you their word they would not attack you, yet they did! They murdered people here in the temple: that night attack when we were feasting?'

'I cannot answer that either. I thought they had broken their word. Perhaps they wanted to heighten the tension, deepen the fear . . .'

Amerotke stared down at the ground. He recalled his own days in the House of Life in the various temples of Thebes where he'd studied logic and constructed an argument. He wanted a path out of all this. He had to gather all he'd learnt, break it down, form it into a logical pattern, an argument that would lead to the truth.

'My lord Amerotke?'

The judge glanced up.

'Am I a traitor?' Khufu declared. 'Will you denounce me to the Divine One?'

'No,' Amerotke replied. 'The Arites would love that. Your arrest would provoke only more confusion, unrest and unease. Not for the moment. The key to all this is Imothep. Did he ever talk to you about his own household? Someone threatening him?'

Khufu shook his head.

'Did he ever complain or voice his suspicions about his household?'

'Far from it,' Khufu replied. 'He loved his kin. He was deeply devoted to them.'

'Do you know any rumours about Sihera, his housekeeper, formerly married to a member of the Arites?'

'All I can tell you,' Khufu declared, 'is that Imothep, even more when he was being blackmailed, hated the Arites. He told me that if he had the opportunity he would escape from their trap and confess all to the Divine One. My lord judge, I have told you what I know.'

Amerotke let him go without further questioning. Khufu, he reflected, was a weak man, caught out by his own cowardice and sins, inveigled into a conspiracy then trapped deeper in it. A sign of the times? the judge wondered. Or something more sinister? Was the high priest's petty treason the result not just of cowardice, blackmail and threats but of a deeper malignancy? A latent fear that the Arites might succeed? That their conspiracy might provoke a revolt in Thebes and the removal of Hatusu? The latter was not inconceivable. Once the war in the south began, a well-planned uprising in Thebes might shake the Great House to its foundations. There were those in the City of the Sceptre, once Hatusu's most loyal general was gone, who would whisper about the female pharaoh's weakness being the real cause of the present problems. Amerotke smiled grimly. If the crisis deepened, a palace revolt might be staged. He himself could not ignore the damage such a storm could inflict on him. After all, he was Hatusu's principal judge: would he also be removed, placed under house arrest, or even exiled? Khufu, Amerotke concluded, was cunning in his cowardice: he was keeping his choices open. Were Busiris and Mataia privy to such deceit? Did they secretly support Khufu's attitude? If the Arites were annihilated, Khufu could pose as the loyal high priest who intervened to save Hatusu. If the Arites were victorious or brought about a change in power in Thebes, he might follow another path. Amerotke narrowed his eyes. That would have to wait. There was a more frightening possibility: was Khufu the Sgeru, the leader of the Arites? Had Amerotke misread the signs? Was Khufu guilty of greater treasons? If so, it would be better if the high priest was trapped in such a conspiracy with the evidence to dispatch him to a gruesome death at the Place of the Skull.

Amerotke left the pavilion and returned with his guards to the guest house. As he passed through fragrant gardens and sun-washed courtyards, decorated with gorgeous bouquets and large pots brimming with flowers, he found it difficult to accept that such tranquil surroundings concealed the murky swirl of treason and murder. On reflection, though, the Temple of Nubia was the ideal place for such deadly sins to flourish like rank weeds. Visitors from Nubia, rich and poor, flocked here. Undoubtedly many were loyal pilgrims, priests, wandering scholars, sight-seers, beggars, as well as the infirm looking for free treatment in the hospital. Nevertheless, all the Arites needed were a few members of their murderous sect to mingle secretly with the flow of visitors, an easy enough task when Khufu had been blackmailed to look the other way.

Lost in such thoughts, Amerotke returned to his own chamber. He washed, changed and slept until he was roused by Shufoy, who thrust a piece of parchment into his hands, muttering how the Lady of the Dark sent her greetings and hoped that Amerotke would accept a gift of almonds. He added something about visiting the Malkata and left quickly. Amerotke took some time to wake fully. Once he had, he broke the seal and took the Lady of Darkness' reply over to the window. Her message was stark enough. She began with the usual greetings, then added: 'It is possible, but discover that for yourself: consult the temple's book of poisons.' Amerotke walked to the door and asked Asural to go to the House of Powders and bring their book of poisons.

'On my authority,' he ordered, 'and that of Lord Khufu.'

Asural pulled a face and hurried off. Amerotke barred the door behind him, then prepared his writing tray, smoothing out two pieces of papyrus. On each he drew steps, a method of problem-solving the scholar priests had taught him in the House of Life.

'The Arites,' he murmured as he wrote. 'First step: the Arites are a secret society of warrior murderers, the heart of all resistance to Egyptian rule in Nubia. They were almost wiped out by former pharaohs, except for their secret fortress at Bekhna. Second step: devotees of their hyaena goddess, the Arites take the blood oath and strangle their victims with a red cloth as a heinous holocaust to their demon. The coven leader is the Sgeru, all-powerful, a scion of the blood royal, the sacred line of Nubian rulers. Third step: for years the Arites have lain dormant – why? They must have been waiting until a fresh cohort of leaders emerged under a new Sgeru. Once they were ready, they infiltrated the Temple of Nubia as well as the regiment in Thebes, appealing to their sacred past as well as through murder and coercion. Fourth step,' Amerotke murmured to himself: 'the Arites wait for Pharaoh's involvement in a campaign against the Sea People in the north, then raise the banner of revolt in Nubia. Fifth step,' he wrote as he spoke, his reed pen skimming the papyrus from right to left: 'the Arites force both Imothep and Khufu to cooperate with them. They use the former to secure detailed drawings of Timsah, the Oasis of Sinjar and the Sobeck routes south. Imothep obeys and hands over such information to Khufu to pass on to the Arites. Meanwhile, both he and the high priest act as if there is no crisis and hope such treasonable cooperation will not be detected.

'Sixth step: the Arites infiltrate Timsah and use it to ambush and murder imperial messengers and couriers who arrive at nearby Sinjar. The Arites also plan to use that deserted fortress as a base to harass the rear of Omendap's forces, once they've passed into Nubia, as well as disrupt communication between Pharaoh and her power in the south. Seventh step: the attack on Hatusu. The only logical answer,' Amerotke breathed, 'is that the Arites didn't care if Hatusu lived or died. She'd be succeeded by another pharaoh. They simply wanted a public display of their audacious power as well as a warning that Pharaoh could not really trust her Nubian regiment. They were also secretly threatening Khufu, whilst depicting the high priest as Pharaoh's saviour and, even more cunningly, a saviour who might know too much about the plot he frustrated. In the end they created the very effect they wanted: chaos, confusion and deep suspicion. Eighth step: the attacks on himself and Lord Valu. Again to create further instability as well as remove the two men Hatusu would use to investigate and hinder the Arites' conspiracy. An attack on both our mansions was logical, but the ambush perpetrated as we returned from the Place of the Skull? Was that just another display of the Arites' power?' Amerotke shook his head: he could not answer that.

'Ninth step: the Arites who agreed to cooperate with us. Why was he ordered to do that? To mislead the Great House, to sow more lies and errors? The attack in the streets of Thebes was not to free him.' Amerotke paused: he was sure of that. 'Nevertheless, how and why did the Arites mysteriously murder that prisoner only a short while later?' He stared down at the last question: a riddle with no solution. 'Moreover, how did they know he was being taken to the Temple of Nubia?' He recalled the events of that day from the moment the prisoner agreed to talk until his incarceration in the House of Chains: no more than an hour or two? Valu had sent a messenger ahead to inform Khufu. Amerotke remembered what the Mongoose had confirmed: how, if the Arites believed they were about to die in battle, they tied their sacred cloths around their throats, making themselves an offering to their goddess. Had the prisoner done that? But he couldn't have strangled himself! He would have lost consciousness and the strength to totally cut off his breath. So how had that man died? Amerotke felt a tingle of excitement. A mere suspicion! Had the murder of the Arites prisoner been too hasty, a mistake, perhaps? He wrote down his conclusions and moved to the second set of steps on the other papyrus sheet, about the events at the House of the Forest. He chose a sharper reed pen and began the process again, only to pause at a knock on the door. Asural came in with the book of poisons which he placed on a stool. Amerotke absent-mindedly thanked him.

'First step,' he whispered as Asural closed the door behind him: 'Imothep, former Chief Scout in the Spies of Sobeck, a Nubian who hated the Arites, fought against them and plundered treasures from their holy places, was apparently murdered by his enemies in the Mansion of Silence. Second step: by his own admission, despite his opposition to the Arites, Imothep had been coerced into cooperating with the Arites to protect his kin, and in particular, perhaps, that mysterious woman who had such a hold over him. He'd confessed as much to the chapel priest. Third step: despite all this, Imothep was still murdered. And those other two corpses, their hands severed, found in his overgrown garden? Were they beggars from the Temple of Nubia? But why would the Arites murder them so mysteriously?'

Amerotke felt his eyelids grow heavy. He was exhausted. He doused the lamp, put down the pen and went across to his bed. He intended to sleep only a short while, but dawn was breaking when Asural shook him roughly awake.

'My lord.' The captain lowered the lamp he carried. 'My lord, you must come. The Arites have struck again! Hideous murders at the House of the Forest.' He helped the startled but sleep-laden Amerotke get up, then whispered how Parmen and his entire household had been massacred.

'And Shufoy?' Amerotke asked. 'Is he here?'

'Not returned, my lord.'

Amerotke dressed hastily, throwing a thick cloak about him. They left the temple. The morning chill still hung heavy, the light greying as the sky flashed tongues of red. A hurried, breathless march ringed by armed men carrying torches. Amerotke heard the keening and mourning as soon as they entered the House of the Forest, a low, ominous chant cutting through the darkness, preparing him for the macabre scene on the great roof terrace of the mansion. Used for banquets and evening meals, its floor especially plastered and smoothed, the entire roof space was cordoned off by a splendid fence of brightly painted wooden slats, sharpened at the top and reinforced on the inside by two parallel thin beams. Amerotke reached the top of the outside steps and gasped in horror. Lamps and torches had been rekindled to reveal horrid murder. Three corpses lay sprawled across wine-stained tables and cushions. Each had been strangled, the red cloths gripped about their throats as tight as any animal snare. Amerotke leaned against the fence, studying the grisly scene. The corpses must have jerked and thrashed about in their death throes, scattering jugs, cups and platters.

The judge startled as a bird, its great feathered wings wafting the air, swooped over that place of ghastly murder like some envoy from the Halls of Darkness before wheeling away with a raucous cry. Voices sounded from below, and Amerotke heard Sihera issuing instructions. He looked over his shoulder and glimpsed the grey-haired woman talking softly to other servants.

'Keep everyone away,' he whispered to Asural. He walked across the roof terrace, gazing around. Three corpses in all. Parmen, Neferen and Rahmel, all viciously strangled, their faces that strange bluish-black, hideously contorted, eyes bulging, lips slightly bared, dried froth staining the corners of their mouths. Amerotke brushed each with his fingers. Their flesh was cold, the effect of the deep dawn chill, their faces, hands and clothes sticky with the heavy red wine dried on them. Each lay differently. Neferen faced in the direction of the Mansion of Silence. Parmen was sprawled on the cushions in the centre of the tables, which must have been arranged in a U shape for the feast. Rahmel was the nearest, as if he'd been turning to go down the outside steps. Amerotke moved carefully. Beautifully fluted water glasses had been used at the feast; these had slipped off the table and shattered, along with jewel-encrusted wine goblets and dishes. Amerotke picked his way around. All three victims were dressed in their best robes, glittering jewellery and fine wigs. They'd certainly dined well. One wine jug still stood brimming to the top, smelling fragrantly of the full ripe grapes from the best vineyards of Thebes. The dishes held the remains of melokhia cooked in cloves, olives and coriander, garlic croutons, chickpeas in cumin and black pepper, tameya lightly coated in olive oil, along with a range of other delicious dishes. From none of these could Amerotke detect any odour or taint. The judge stood in the half-light, staring around at the destruction. A soul-tearing scene, the work of the Arites? Although he had just arrived, he felt deeply uneasy about what he was observing. What had truly happened here? Why should the Arites kill three ordinary people? He inspected the roof terrace fence but could detect no break or breach; no stain or sign of the assassins scaling the sheer walls to murder their victims.

'They must have come up the outside steps,' he murmured. He glanced back. 'Asural, bring Sihera up here.'

The housekeeper arrived shrouded in a dark brown cloak, its hood pulled across her long grey hair. She stepped delicately on to the terrace, her face even paler, but those clear eyes still calm and watchful. She glanced quickly at the corpses, shuddered, then turned to Amerotke.

'My lord?'

'Asural,' Amerotke ordered. The captain of the guard also came on to the roof terrace. 'Look.' Amerotke gestured around. 'Cut the cloths from their throats, then find a cart. All three corpses must be removed to the House of Death at the Temple of Nubia. Tell the keeper not to begin the funeral rites until I say. Sihera,' Amerotke walked around the remains of that last deadly meal, 'I need to question you, but not here.'

They met in the small hall of columns below. A servant

was building up a fire in the central hearth; others, desolate and frightened, moved about, all eyes on this taciturn judge who'd come to view the savage murder of three of their household. Amerotke made himself comfortable on a stool near the fire. Sihera knelt on the cushions before him. She remained serene, only the slight blink of her eyes or the occasional gesture to move an imaginary hair from her face betraying any nervousness. Amerotke sat, head slightly turned, as if listening to the sounds of the house: servants crying and mourning, the occasional shout, the clamour from outside as his escort hitched oxen to a cart and prepared to remove the corpses.

'What happened here, Sihera?'

'My lord, I don't know.' She gazed back. 'I truly don't. Yesterday evening Parmen decided to break our mourning fast with a banquet; you know that is permitted. He claimed it was to celebrate the life of our master, to wish his ka well on his final journey across the Far Horizon. I joined him and the others on the roof terrace. We ate and drank.' She touched her stomach. 'I felt slightly ill,' she smiled wanly, 'too much rich wine, so I withdrew to my own chamber. When I left, Parmen, Neferen and Rahmel were deep in their cups, but hearty enough. I saw or heard no danger. I went to my own chamber, dressed for bed and fell into a deep sleep. A servant later aroused me. He sleeps near the dog pen and was aroused by the barking of the saluki hounds. He went out but could detect no cause for alarm until he glimpsed the lamps still glowing on the roof terrace. He also found doors opened that should have been barred. He went up the steps, saw what had happened and hurried to wake me. I sent a runner to the Temple of Nubia for you. My lord,' she shrugged, 'that is all I can say.'

'And what do you suspect?'

Sihera sighed noisily and glanced away. 'Only the Lords of Light know. I suspect that the Arites, for their own secret, nefarious purposes, had planned to execute all of us. Perhaps they have a spy in this household.' She pulled a face. 'They must have crept in during the early hours.'

'Yet there is no sign of any resistance?'

'My companions were drunk.' Sihera moved a hand across her face. 'My lord, they were about to start a new jug of wine. They cleansed their mouths with water.' She shook her head. 'I could take no more, so I left. By doing so, I saved my life.'

'And the Arites came?'

'They must have,' Sihera replied wearily. 'The Seth creatures, lurkers in the dark. The house was silent; no one expected such an attack.'

'Did the Arites send their warning? They always do!'

'Perhaps,' Sihera sniffed, 'perhaps they sent one of their damnable scarabs to Parmen. However, if they did, he never told me.'

'But if they didn't, it's strange,' Amerotke continued. 'And if they did, surely Parmen would have been frightened, alarmed, and shown it. He was not a warrior but a steward whose master had already been murdered by the Arites.'

'I don't know,' Sihera whispered. 'I truly don't.'

'So you retired for the night, while Parmen and others continued their celebrations?'

'Yes.'

'Strange,' Amerotke mused, 'that they should celebrate during the time of mourning.'

'I've told you,' Sihera moved on the cushions, 'they had the right to break the funeral fast, to replenish their strength as well as to wish our master well. More importantly, they wanted to discuss leaving Thebes. Our master is dead. This mansion now belongs to the Temple of Nubia. It really was time for us to go.'

'So you retired,' Amerotke continued, 'and the Arites slunk into the gardens and raced up the outside steps to the roof terrace. Parmen and the others were drunk, deeply inebriated, easy victims. The Arites strangled them and left, but the saluki hounds, caged in their pens, caught the scent and barked the alarm. A servant discovered the murderous mayhem; he woke you, and you immediately sent a message to the Temple of Nubia.'

'Yes,' Sihera nodded, 'that's how it was. Look.' She rose quickly to her feet. 'I shall summon that servant so you can question him yourself.' She went to the door and called a name.

Amerotke studied the painting on the far wall. It was executed in green, brown and gold and depicted fowlers hunting on the marshes along the Nile. That's what I am, he reflected, a hunter, and I sense something very wrong here. Why should the Arites kill these three? He broke from his reverie as Sihera returned with a thin-faced young man, the dog-keeper, who slept in an outhouse near the saluki pens. He crouched down and quietly described what had happened, an accurate reflection of everything Sihera had said. Amerotke thanked him, then waited until he had gone.

'Strange.' He stared at this woman who looked old yet whose eyes were bright and, when she smiled, revealed some of her former beauty.

'Strange, my lord?'

'Your master was coerced by the Arites to cooperate with them.'

'Never!' Sihera spat the word out.

'Oh yes, Imothep confessed as much to a chapel priest at the Temple of Nubia. He agreed to supply the Arites with detailed plans of the fortress of Timsah.'

'Impossible,' Sihera whispered. 'Imothep hated the Arites.'

'He was also frightened of them,' Amerotke added.

'Nonsense!'

'Very well.' Amerotke smiled. 'I concede that. No, Imothep did not fear the Arites, but he was frightened for those he loved, his kin and perhaps a woman who, according to a Priest of the Ear, exercised considerable influence over him. Were you that woman, Sihera?'

She laughed girlishly, bringing her hands up to her face.

'Me, an ancient crone? No, my lord, Imothep loved and lusted with young Neferen.'

'You believe that?'

'Yes, I certainly do.'

'And what will you do now, Sihera? Go back to Nubia? Will you be welcome there? After all, many years ago—'

243

'I know,' Sihera interrupted harshly. 'Many years ago I was married to an Arites, but as you've learnt, they keep their allegiance secret. I only found out after he joined the rebels, and by then, what did it matter? Pharaoh's soldiers killed him in a jungle glade. I was forced to flee. Imothep, a distant kinsman, took me into his house.' She half smiled. 'He was a good man.' She glanced coyly at Amerotke. 'My lord, I can tell you no more. All you see in me is a relic of events, lives, loves and hates from so many years ago. Now it is finished, as am I. Do you have more questions for me?'

'Those other two corpses,' Amerotke demanded, 'found in the gardens?'

'I know nothing about them.'

'Then finally, Sihera, a question that truly puzzles me. Imothep was important to the Arites, but why should they kill the likes of Parmen?'

'I do not know the mind of the Arites, but Parmen, indeed all of us, were Imothep's kin. I realise what is happening in Thebes: everything is coming to a head. Perhaps the Arites will deal out punishment to those they think deserve it. My lord, I do have other duties . . .'

Amerotke watched her leave, then rose and followed her out on to the portico. He stood on the steps. The sun was now rising in a burst of glorious gold. He turned his face from the light shooting through the trees. He felt the last cool breath of Amun, the dawn wind, which would soon disappear in the heat of the day. He closed his eyes and intoned a morning prayer:

You are the Lord of Light,
The self-begotten youth.
First born of life,
The First Name from nameless nothing,
Come to me, my Lord—

A screeching cut across his prayer. Amerotke opened his eyes. Asural came around a corner of the house, followed by plodding oxen pulling a cart. On it sprawled the three corpses, now pathetic in their tawdry finery, their uncovered faces still mottled embodiments of horror. Amerotke watched the cart trundle towards the gates. Whatever he prayed, Seth the Red God still prowled the corridors of his soul. The judge turned back to the sun, which was now rising faster and stronger. 'Comfort me,' he whispered.

Master Consoler, Eternal Judge, call me
Into the vineyards of your truth.
For thou art ever youthful.
Prince of all the world,
You and your daughter Ma'at,
Your truth I have lived, your truth I have loved.
Favour me now, my lord,
Light Immortal, Light Divine, reveal to me the truth . . .

CHAPTER 10

Tekhanu: hiding place

Amerotke knelt before the writing table in his chamber at the guest house. He'd washed and purified himself; now he ate strips of delicious duck cooked in pomegranate and encased in soft fruit bread. He chewed absent-mindedly as he stared down at the two papyrus documents illustrating the steps he'd drafted the night before. One brutal fact spanned both sets of steps – the Arites! Amerotke paused in his eating as he recalled the probing mind of his scholar-priest teacher and his perennial question: 'Is that true: prove it!' Indeed, he reflected, there was very little evidence, apart from the manner of their deaths, that the victims at the House of the Forest had been killed by the Arites. He remembered his unease the night before about the murder of that prisoner in the House of Chains. 'What if,' he murmured, 'there is no connection whatsoever?' He quickly moved the dishes aside. He glimpsed the book of poisons Asural had brought from the House of Powders, and recalled how the lector priest there had been one of those murdered by the Arites in their night attack on the temple. He picked up the manuscript, reflecting on Shufoy's message about the Lady of the Dark sending him a gift of almonds. He stared around. No almonds had appeared, so why such a message? Was the Lady of the Dark, that mistress of poisons and powders, teasing him as she always loved to? Amerotke undid the cord and unrolled one sheet after another, all neatly sewn together, describing the appearance, malignancy, symptoms and possible antidotes of a macabre list of powerful poisons. He feverishly searched the scroll until he reached the entry for almonds, cherries and plums. He was astonished at what he read. The fruits themselves were wholesome, but the juice or powders distilled from the seeds and inner pulp were swift and savage in their effects. He moved to the symptoms, and his heart skipped a beat. 'It would seem,' a lector priest had written, 'that the victims of such poison appear to have been strangled from inside as if by some invisible force.' The writer described how the seeds and pulps of such fruit in themselves were harmless enough unless broken up, when the poison distilled from them had no real antidote. He then returned to describing the symptoms in detail. Amerotke caught his breath and reread the entry time and time again. 'So simple.' He lifted his head and whispered into the silence. 'So very, very simple.' He picked up the book of poisons and studied the final entry. The lector priest concluded that the powerful poison from such distillation could not really be detected except for an elusive 'bitter almond odour that can be distinguished in some cases, in others not at all'.

Amerotke sprang to his feet, hurried to the door and called Asural, giving him sharp instructions for the Keeper of Corpses in the House of the Dead. He then went back to his scrolls, drawing up a third set of steps listing the victims at the House of the Forest, though this time with a different cause of death. He then took all the other scraps of information he'd collected, forming them carefully around his theory. Once he was satisfied, he slipped on his sandals, pushed a knife through the sash around his waist, put on his cloak and left the guest house.

The Keeper of Corpses in the House of Death was waiting. He breathlessly explained how they were busy with cadavers from the temple hospital as well as the three victims from the House of the Forest. Amerotke courteously informed him that he must inspect the three corpses from Imothep's residence, so the keeper led him down the steep, narrow steps into what he called his 'kingdom'. The only natural light poured through square ground-level windows; the rest of the murky, smelly gloom was lit by oil lamps and shuttered lanterns. Their flames only made the chamber of death more ghostly, with their shifting shadows and swirling stench through which the priests of the tomb moved with their acolytes to prepare the corpses for their final journey. Amerotke followed the keeper past wooden boards on which corpses sprawled in various stages of mummification. Beside the benches lay the knives, hooks and scrapers used to cleanse the cavities of the bodies. The smell of natron, acacia, cinnamon, cedar oil, henna, juniper and other herbs failed to disguise the foul stench of entrails being slopped into canopic jars and brains drawn through the nose into specially prepared pots. Occasionally the words of a chanting lector priest echoed through the gloom: 'Here are spells for thy body, cool resin for thy skin . . .'

At last they reached the corpses of Parmen, Neferen and Rahmel, stretched out on wooden slabs slightly tilted so the juices from the bodies, together with those of the herbs used, would drain into the waiting jars. Each of the faces was covered with bloodstained cloths, proof that the bone of the noses had already been broken and the brains drained out. The priests had moved swiftly after receiving Amerotke's instructions from Asural. They had used the sacred obsidian knife to cut a slit on the left side of the stomach as well as along the diaphragm, so that the entrails of all three had been plucked out and laid in a great bowl beside each corpse.

'You washed them first?' Amerotke asked.

'Of course, my lord. We stripped their clothes; the wine was sticky on their hands and arms. It must have been there some time.'

'Yes, yes, it must have been,' Amerotke agreed. 'Now, did you detect the odour of bitter almonds on these or any corpse brought from the House of the Forest?'

'My lord,' the keeper chose his words carefully, 'as regards Imothep, no. The same is true of those corpses found with their hands severed. You see, my lord . . .' He noticed Amerotke's impatience and smiled. 'My lord, to put it bluntly, the contents of the stomach, not to mention the stench of the entrails, would mask such an odour, especially,' he gestured at the corpses, 'when they've eaten highly spiced food and gulped rich wine. Moreover, the corpses have been left for some time; the same is true of Imothep and the other two found without their hands. By the time we become busy with them, such a smell may well have evaporated, vanished.'

'These three corpses,' Amerotke asked, 'they've been dead for some time?'

'Well, they were brought here just after dawn, but I would calculate that they were strangled hours earlier.'

'And?' Amerotke asked.

'The two men had gorged and drunk deeply during their last hours. The young woman, as befits a virgin—'

'What?' Amerotke intervened.

'Oh yes, may the gods protect her,' the Keeper of the Dead gabbled on, 'the young woman had no knowledge of man; her virginity is intact. Anyway, as befits such an innocent, she drank very little wine. On her, the smell of bitter almonds was quite pronounced . . .'

Amerotke returned to the House of the Forest later that afternoon. He had left the Keeper of the Corpses and withdrawn to his chamber for hours, developing his case as he would before he entered court to deliver judgement. He demanded that Asural and his full escort accompany him, and also summoned a cohort from the regiment encamped around the Temple of Nubia. At the House of the Forest, the servants were still in shock. Amerotke courteously shooed them away. He then broke the seals on the Mansion of Silence, lifted the bar and, with Asural beside him, swept up into the dining area, where he arranged the cushions as he wanted them. He'd hardly finished when Sihera, still cloaked, was ushered in. Amerotke indicated the seat opposite. She sat down, looking as serene and composed as ever; only the occasional twist of her mouth or the constant moving of her fingers betrayed any agitation.

'My lord?' One hand fluttered to her chest.

'My lady.' Amerotke smiled. 'When I came here this morning and viewed the corpses, I felt uneasy. I could not really understand why the Arites had killed a fat steward, his virginal daughter and an old soldier long past his prime. Why? I ask again.'

'They were Imothep's associates, his kin.'

'But the Arites didn't kill Imothep either, Sihera, you know that. In fact, they had sworn that as long as he did what they asked, he and his household were safe. You were also aware of that.'

Sihera's eyes held Amerotke's, and her enigmatic smile returned.

'Look, I shall tell you a story,' Amerotke declared, 'one you already know, but it's worth retelling. Imothep was Chief Scout in the Spies of Sobeck, a warrior who waged bloody war in Nubia against the Arites. He defeated them in battle and plundered the treasures of one of their holy places. He was a man blessed and patronised by Pharaoh with a young Theban wife, lands and more marks of favour. He was a true soldier, loyal to his Pharaoh and to his kin, whom he also brought to Thebes. Amongst these was you, Sihera, widow of a former Arites. Imothep was your lover, wasn't he? He truly loved you despite being married. Both of you must have hidden your passion well. Perhaps it ended when Imothep married; however, once he became a widower, he was free to return to you, the great love of his life.

'Now, the years passed in relative contentment and security until a fresh revolt occurred in Nubia and the Arites emerged in Thebes. All this shattered your harmony. Imothep had changed over the years. He was an old man, childless, clinging on to the little he had left: memories, his exploits, and above all, you. He was also devout. Like many veteran soldiers who had no real family, he bequeathed his house and possessions to the Temple of Nubia. This caused a serious breach between him and his kin, although they hid it well. Imothep probably made secret plans for you, but as for Parmen, what would happen to him, his daughter and Rahmel after Imothep's death? Why, they must have asked themselves, wasn't Imothep more generous to those who'd served him over the years? They wanted more than just a bequest: probably this mansion and all it contains. Greed and anger, Sihera, corrode the soul, narrow the heart and rot all affection. Parmen began to plot his master's murder, but how? Why not by poison? I have no proof of this, but I will after a thorough search through the city. Parmen began to study potions and powders. Our murderous steward came across a powerful poison, the juice of the almond: its victims suffer the same symptoms as if they've been strangled. What better way for Imothep to die, especially when the Arites emerged? Of course, Parmen knew nothing about Imothep's secret negotiations with that murderous sect, or the passion that existed between you and your master. He was like a saluki hound following a trail, and the others became his accomplices. They bought the poison, but they had to make sure.

'Now, Imothep was Nubian. It was only natural that beggars from the temple would come here looking for bread, anything to help. Parmen as steward would deal with them. He invited two of them into the garden and gave them wine laced with the powerful almond powder. He and his accomplices watched those two poor beggar men die. They noticed the symptoms and calculated the time it took. Of course, to invite beggars in and murder them is one thing; to dispose of their corpses another. So Parmen was brutal. He stripped them of everything. He also severed their hands so that their bodies couldn't be traced, because the backs of their hands carried the temple seal, giving them the status of legitimate beggars. These severed limbs were placed in a sack and probably taken out to the nearest crocodile pool. The corpse of one of the beggars was hidden in the jungle of Imothep's garden, the other more effectively in that stagnant pool. Parmen also added his own macabre touch, tying red cloths around their throats so that if and when they were found, they'd be viewed as two more victims of the terrible Arites. Parmen had what he needed: the potency of the potion, how long the victim would take to die, and the symptoms. The red cloths squeezing their throats made it look as if they had been asphyxiated. A very skilled doctor might detect the bitter almond smell, but that only lingers briefly, whilst sometimes it cannot be detected at all. Parmen must have been very pleased when the Arites attacked the Divine One at Karnak. After all, if such blasphemers were arrogant enough to attack Pharaoh herself, why should they ignore the likes of Imothep, against whom they nursed a grudge?'

'Why didn't Parmen bring me into his conspiracy?'

'Oh, very simple, Sihera. You were never one of them. Because you were Imothep's secret lover, you kept your distance: friend to all, ally to none. Parmen didn't trust you enough. More importantly, they didn't need you. Parmen was going to look after himself, his daughter and, of course, Rahmel, his helper. Imothep suspected nothing about this and neither did you. On the afternoon he was murdered, Imothep, lost in his own schemes, his secret love for you, retreated into his Mansion of Silence. Wine and water were brought in for him. What he did not know was that the almond poison is made even more powerful by distillation in water. He probably drank both water and wine. A seizure followed. He would have lacked the strength even to get to the door to ask for help. It was too late. He died here, not knowing the cause of his death or those behind it. Parmen, Neferen and Rahmel bided their time. On that afternoon, they'd also made sure that you were occupied. You fell ill with a stomach complaint, though you told me that your stomach was strong and you rarely fell sick. The cause was something they had slipped into your food. You were out of the way, whilst the other servants were very much in awe of Parmen.

'Parmen carries out the pretence of knocking on his master's door to try to secure entry. Of course he knows that Imothep is past hearing. The door is eventually broken down. Remember what happened then? Rahmel stayed outside, Parmen went in. He takes out the red cloth and wraps it around his dead master's throat like a noose, trying the knot tightly as if he was a professional assassin, and lowers the body to the ground. He then goes out to announce the dreadful news. Everything is chaos and confusion. Rahmel and Neferen act their parts. Again, the servants are kept out. Parmen does not want them to see their master. A stretcher is taken in. Parmen and Rahmel, assisted by Neferen, place the corpse on the stretcher, then plunder Imothep's treasure, taking that precious statue as well as the small ingots of gold and silver. These are hidden on the stretcher or about their persons, and they take Imothep away. As for the poisoned water or wine?' Amerotke shrugged. 'Who would care? It would be poured away. Imothep had been strangled, so why look for another cause? I certainly didn't.'

Amerotke paused. 'The robbery is now complete. Imothep is dead. True, the House of the Forest will eventually go to the Temple of Nubia, but what does that matter? Parmen and his fellow conspirators have amassed enough wealth to see themselves comfortable over the years, not to mention the treasure they must have plundered in the rest of the house. Naturally Imothep's murder is ascribed to the Arites, part of the great mystery burgeoning in the city. All that Parmen, Neferen and Rahmel have to do is act the mourners, the disconsolate servants grieving over their murdered master. One thing they missed.' Amerotke pointed across at Sihera. 'They never even imagined the real relationship between Imothep and you. More importantly, Imothep had told you exactly what had happened between himself and the Arites, how they were blackmailing and threatening him. He could not accept that, not at his age: he'd lost his first wife, he certainly wasn't going to lose you, so he cooperated but he still informed you.'

'Even if what you say is true,' Sihera lifted her head, 'the Arites could have changed their minds, decided that Imothep be silenced so he could not betray what he'd done for them.'

'No,' Amerotke replied, 'Imothep was truly trapped. If he confessed all to Pharaoh, he might have lost everything, been publicly disgraced, fortunate to escape execution. In turn, the Arites would certainly have carried out their threat and massacred his entire household, including you. No, they had Imothep neatly trapped, as they had Lord Khufu. You knew that too. Imothep must have talked to you about the high priest. In the end, Sihera, think! Why should the Arites devote so much time and energy to the murder of Imothep, an old soldier locked away in his house? What would it profit them? They had the plans for Timsah; their conspiracy at Sinjar was well advanced. They also had a list of other names in Thebes whom they wanted to strike at, myself included.'

'Didn't they murder Imothep to retrieve their treasure?'

'Not true,' Amerotke declared. 'You know, as I do, that the Arites were not interested in treasure taken from a sanctuary many years ago. They would regard it as polluted, no longer worthy of their attention. No, in their eyes, Imothep could keep his baubles, his life, his house; they were hunting more important quarry.'

Sihera leaned back on her heels, pulling back her hair behind her head, revealing a noble face, sharply edged; a strong woman, Amerotke reflected, quite capable of taking vengeance into her own hands.

'Parmen was very cunning,' he continued. 'He'd committed the perfect murder. His poor master, locked away in the Mansion of Silence, strangled by his old enemies, a perfect example of their guile! Who would suspect Parmen, plump as a duck? Everyone knew where he and the others were that afternoon. He had to force the door. He was the one who found his master strangled. Parmen couldn't have done that! Imothep would have resisted, raised the alarm. Moreover, everybody realised that Imothep had been killed hours before that door was forced: his flesh was cold, that red cloth tied tightly around his throat; his treasure had disappeared. How could Parmen have achieved all that? You, however, were distraught but deeply puzzled.' The judge paused. 'In fact, you were in a labyrinth, one riddle after another. You asked yourself questions. Had the Arites changed their minds? If so, why hadn't they sent a warning as is their custom? If they had committed that murder, how did they do it? Stealing into an overgrown garden, securing entry to a fortified room, killing an old soldier plundering his treasure, then leaving without raising the alarm? You must have confronted the logical possibility: had Parmen murdered Imothep as soon as he entered the Mansion of Silence? However, that seemed impossible. Then there was that corpse found with its hands severed, not to mention the one I discovered later. You waited and you reflected. I am sure that here in the secrecy of the House of the Forest, Parmen and his accomplices made little mistakes that you would observe. Eventually, because you could get no answer, you turned the whole matter on its head, as I did. What if Imothep had died of other causes before Parmen had even entered? If those causes were natural, then why the cloth around his throat? That left one other possibility: murder by Parmen and the others. But how? Like me, you stumbled on a possible poison, a potion, almond powder distilled in water, the seeds and pith of a fruit, a malignant concoction that provokes the same symptoms in its victims as if they had been strangled.'

Amerotke smiled. 'We reached the same conclusion, Sihera. Imothep had been murdered in the Mansion of Silence not by the Arites but by the poison he must have drunk during that afternoon. The rest was simply playacting by Parmen and his accomplices. So what could you do about it? Time was passing. Perhaps, you thought, I might reach the same conclusion as you but not swiftly enough. After all, I was distracted: there is a crisis bubbling in Thebes and soon it might come to a head. Moreover, if you were watching them, I am sure Parmen was watching you. You must have felt threatened. Who would care if a lowly housekeeper suffered an accident? So you searched the city for a suitable poison. If I had the time and the energy, I could make a thorough search of the temples in Thebes, amongst those who sell powders and potions. You're an educated woman, Sihera. You can read a book of poisons as accurately as I can, and of course, there are those in Thebes who would sell anything to anyone. You made your decision. Parmen held his feast. It wasn't a memorial, it wasn't a salute for their dead master. What was it, Sihera, a celebration? In your eyes it was blasphemy! They gathered in their finery, their best wigs, their jewellery, to guzzle like pigs. You waited until the rest of the house fell quiet, then struck. An easy task for a housekeeper. Parmen called for more wine. They cleansed their mouths with water, and into that you poured the poison. They drank their death, which came swiftly: the usual symptoms, dizziness, feverishness. They didn't even have time to broach the fresh jug of wine.'

'They could have attacked me, tried to escape.'

'No, no, Sihera how could they do that when they couldn't even draw breath? They found it difficult to move, their limbs racked with pain. The convulsions followed swiftly. You watched all three die. This occurred just after midnight. The servants had retired, knowing nothing about the murderous drama being enacted on the roof terrace. Parmen, his daughter Neferen and Rahmel jerking and shuddering, knocking over bowls, cups and platters, even the water glasses. You had to make sure they were smashed. Beautiful fluted glass drinking cups, they contained the evidence, and what wasn't drunk just drained away on the terrace. The wine, the food and the night breeze would waft away any odour.'

Sihera turned her face away and laughed. Amerotke could see she was fighting to control her breathing.

'My lord.' Sihera licked her lips. 'These are serious charges. What proof?'

'I'll be honest, Sihera, I have not all the proof I need, but after this house is searched – and it is being searched – I'll find all the evidence I require. We will find the treasures. Parmen may have hidden them; you might have them.'

'No, I don't!'

'No, but they'll be hidden somewhere, in Parmen's chamber or out in the garden. We'll certainly find the poison smelling of bitter almonds. Neferen's corpse betrayed that. The smell of poison is very heavy on her. I have visited the House of Death; its keeper will verify my words.'

'But I didn't poison—'

'Then the court will ask who did. Well, Sihera, who did go up on to that roof terrace last night?'

She stared back at him.

'There are other questions. Neferen was a virgin, yet to distract me, you alleged that Imothep was lusting after her. The Keeper of the Corpses will take an oath: Neferen died a virgin. You also made a serious mistake about the barking of the saluki hounds.'

'They raised the alarm.'

'No. Remember the sequence of events? The dog-keeper was roused and went out to see what was wrong. He

261

glimpsed lamps still burning on the roof terrace. He went up, viewed that horrid scene, then woke you. You dispatched a courier to the Temple of Nubia. One event swiftly following the other. However, when I arrived – and the Keeper of the Corpses will verify this – the flesh of your victims was cold: they'd been dead some hours. More importantly, the wine that splashed their hands and clothes had dried. In other words, they must have been murdered long before the saluki hounds raised the alarm.'

'I . . . I don't follow.'

'Yes you do. You delayed too long between the murders and raising the alarm. Perhaps you panicked. You wanted to compose yourself, or just waited to be sure they were all dead. You then slipped out of your own chamber, rattled a stick along the saluki hound cage and fled. The rest followed quickly.'

Amerotke paused at the shouts and exclamations that carried across the garden.

'That must be Asural,' he murmured. 'He is searching. I have told him to brook no opposition or resistance. In conclusion, Sihera, my explanation is the only one that would explain all the deaths here in the House of the Forest. I have enough evidence to present a bill of indictment against you. You are a Nubian. Pharaoh's heart has hardened towards your people. What mercy can you expect? The torturers of the Scribes of the Secret Cabinet will violate and humiliate you. It truly is all over.' Amerotke stretched out his hand. 'Sihera, your life has run its course. You murdered three people; they deserved to die, but at Pharaoh's justice, not yours.'

Sihera rose. She touched his hand lightly, then walked past him towards the door.

'They'll find it,' she called over her shoulder. 'They'll find the poison, certainly in Parmen's chamber as well as that hidden in mine.' She turned and walked slowly back, arms crossed. Then she stopped and looked down at Amerotke. 'What's the use?' she whispered. 'You are right. My life is over. I've done what I wanted.' She half smiled. 'I watched you, Amerotke, I truly did. I wondered if you were following the same snaking path as myself to the gate of truth. Yet even now,' she leaned over and touched him softly on the face, 'you are troubled. Dark shadows ring your eyes, lines furrow your skin. You miss your wife, Lord Amerotke, your children?' Her eyes brimmed with tears. 'I miss Imothep so much. My lord Imothep, my heart and my soul, has gone into the Far West. I wish to follow him. You are troubled, my lord Amerotke, by the crisis in Thebes. I could not wait for you. How did I even know you would survive this evil hour? I loved Imothep. I always have, I always will. Years ago I married a Nubian warrior, an Arites; he was killed. Imothep took me into his household. They say our kas are formed incomplete, unfinished, that our soul only achieves fulfilment when it meets the other that perfects it. Imothep was my perfection, my completion, my whole. After the war in Nubia, we returned victorious to Thebes. Pharaoh offered Imothep a wife, the daughter of a noble Theban merchant. He wanted to refuse. I begged him not to, lest he offend Pharaoh's heart. He might think that Imothep preferred a Nubian peasant to a lady of Thebes.

Imothep married. We agreed to observe his holy vows to Isis. Yet love cannot be curbed, you know that. It springs, flows and bubbles over. How can we trap the sunlight, the air we breathe? However, never once did Imothep's wife or any of his household suspect the truth.

'Imothep's wife eventually died, and our relationship resumed, but again in secret. Everything remained harmonious. Imothep even considered returning to Nubia, so that we might marry and live a new life.' She pulled a face. 'Then the change came. Straws in the wind, like the first drops of rain: the revolt in Nubia and, more chilling, the emergence of the Arites here in Thebes. Imothep used to visit the Temple of Nubia. One night on his way home he was ambushed. The Arites gathered around him in the dark and demanded his plans of the Sobeck roads, the Oasis of Sinjar, and above all, Timsah. You now know, my lord, how that fortress has hidden wells, cisterns, secret pools; caverns to store food, places where meat can be cooked whilst the smoke and smells can be hidden. It holds grain pits, storerooms, a maze of corridors and passageways. Imothep realised why the Arites wanted it. Years ago he had stayed there and, like the scout he was, mapped the entire fortress with the help of desert-wanderers and sand-dwellers who've long gone into the Far West. At first he refused to cooperate with the Arites. The next day I was in the coppersmiths quarter in Thebes. It happened so fast. I was pulled into an alleyway, a red cloth tied around my throat, not tightly, just as a warning. The Arites pushed a scarab into my hand.' She swallowed hard. 'Despite my pleas, Imothep agreed to cooperate. He drafted the plans and took them to the Temple of Nubia, where Khufu received them.'

'Did he suspect Lord Khufu?'

'Imothep loved the Temple of Nubia: it was a link with our past. However, he always regarded Khufu as weak, a time-server. But as Imothep said, who was he to judge? Khufu was also being blackmailed and threatened. He likes his young women, does Khufu; perhaps he has even sipped at the same cup as your friend Shufoy, the empty-headed Lady Mataia?'

Amerotke remained silent.

'I suppose,' Sihera rubbed a hand down her cheek, 'that Imothep and I were distracted by our love for each other, by the threats, by the growing crisis in Thebes. We overlooked Parmen, fat and greedy; his resentment at being turned out of the House of the Forest must have rankled. The poison in his heart spread out. If I had been more attentive, I would have read the signs. It came like a thunderstorm on a summer's afternoon, sudden and violent. On that day I fell strangely ill and Imothep was murdered. At first I was distraught. I had to hide my lover's grief, but then, little by little, I began to question the entire plot. Why should the Arites kill Imothep? After all, it was me they had threatened, and they might have needed him again. Of course, Parmen and his accomplices committed little indiscretions: their grief was false, their mourning rang hollow. Those whispered conversations in corners. Secret meetings out in the garden. Other items disappeared from the house. Parmen was selling them. I began to wonder. I asked Parmen, when they moved, would they take me with them? He just laughed and said I'd have to fend for myself. A few days later, an itinerant hawker who sold baubles in the Temple of Nubia stopped by the house. I was fortunate, I met him by the postern gate. He asked about the two old beggars who had disappeared from the Temple of Nubia. I wondered about that corpse, and later about the other one you discovered. Parmen became busy with preparations for leaving. Openly he acted the mourning steward; secretly he was a thief ready to flee like a bat through the night. Imothep had a beautiful silver carving of an antelope: it disappeared. I went looking in the marketplace and saw it for sale. I remonstrated with Parmen, and he declared it was none of my business. He had to pay the expenses of the household. He would continue to do so until the House of the Forest was handed over to the Temple of Nubia.

'I used to lie on my bed and reflect about that fateful day: my sickness, the possibility of Imothep being dead long before the door was forced. The logical conclusion was poison. I went in to Thebes and visited the scorpion men. Eventually I discovered the truth. I wanted vengeance, justice. I was also determined that Parmen would not murder me. They organised last night's banquet. The usual hypocrisy, to celebrate Lord Imothep's life, to wish his ka safe journey to the gods. I was furious. Those evil creatures were in reality celebrating their murder of a generous kinsman who had even negotiated with the Arites to protect them. I waited until the servants had retired. Parmen acted very much the lord and master. He told me to bring fresh water. I did so, along with the almond powder I had bought from the scorpion man. I mingled it with the water and filled their cups. It was powerful, much more so than I'd ever, ever suspected. They became weak very quickly, with shooting pains; they could hardly move. I sat and watched them jerk, choke and die. I secured the red cloths around each of their throats, tight as a snare. Then I went down to my own chamber. I thought of destroying the almond poison, but I kept it just in case. I wondered if you'd find the truth, discover what really happened. Anyway, I aroused the saluki dogs, and felt happy enough.' She lifted her head. 'I'd carried out vengeance and justice against fat Parmen and his spoilt daughter, as well as that old rogue Rahmel. They never profited from their sin.' She paused. 'So, my lord, what will happen to me?'

'And the treasure looted from the Mansion of Silence?' Amerotke asked.

'My lord,' Sihera refused to meet his gaze, 'I do not know. I do not care.' She licked her dry lips. 'I wish to be gone – so, I ask you, what will happen to me?'

'I'll recommend Pharaoh's mercy,' Amerotke replied. 'You know what that means: a swift, painless death. I have one last question. Did you or Imothep ever suspect the identity of the Sgeru?'

Sihera shifted her gaze, staring at the door. She was about to reply when Asural walked in holding a small sack.

'Master, the poison . . .'

'Yes, yes,' Amerotke replied. 'Captain, please wait outside.' He continued to gaze long and hard at the woman. 'I asked you a question?'

'I suspected Khufu.'

'Is that why you denounced him anonymously to Lord Valu?'

'Yes, yes, I did.'

'But you have no real evidence to expose the Sgeru?'

'No.' Sihera crouched down opposite and pointed a finger at him. 'But I suspect you do, my lord, yes?'

Amerotke nodded. 'Like the river,' he whispered, 'when it breaks its banks. At first just a crumbling, just a trickle that swiftly turns into a torrent. Yes.' He chewed the corner of his lip. 'I am almost ready to expose the Sgeru.

CHAPTER 11

Sehbu: shouts of joy

By the following morning, Amerotke believed he had
prepared enough. He'd returned late the previous afternoon
from the House of the Forest. Asural had taken Sihera to
the prison beneath the Temple of Ma'at, where she'd be
held fast until Pharaoh confirmed sentence of death.
Amerotke had then spent the evening developing his suspicions and constructing his case until he'd reached the one
and only logical conclusion. The discovery of the malignancy
of the almond poison was, he realised, the key to all these
mysteries. He concentrated particularly on the death of the
Arites prisoner in the House of Chains beneath the Temple
of Nubia. He rehearsed the details of that fatal day and
revisited the cells. The keeper had been killed in the night
attack, but the guards were taken aside and closely questioned. One in particular recalled the events of that day,
showing Amerotke the cell at the far end of the corridor.

The judge went in and studied it carefully. The guard described precisely what had happened when the Arites was committed. Amerotke questioned him and, once satisfied, had the man detained in his own quarters.

Amerotke then visited the House of Powders. Its lector priest had also been murdered by the Arites, but an acolyte provided interesting answers to the judge's questions. He too was secretly detained. Amerotke refused to account for what he was doing. When Khufu came bustling down to complain, he immediately ordered the officer of the Isis regiment, camped outside the temple, to arrest both the high priest and his wife and detain them under house arrest until he was finished. Amerotke used Asural for other secret business, telling the captain to take his guards and ring the House of Myrrh, the temple hospital. Shufoy returned from the Malkata. He looked distressed, expecting the judge to lecture him on his prolonged absence, but instead Amerotke crouched by his friend and tugged at the new amulet Shufoy wore around his neck.

'Shufoy, listen! I want you to return to the Malkata. Tell the lady Norfret I will see her soon. You must then search out the lord Senenmut. Tell him I wish to formally question Lord Khufu and Lady Busiris in his presence and that of the Divine One.'

'For what?' Shufoy demanded.

'Treason!' Amerotke replied.

'Lord Khufu is the Sgeru?'

'I shall prove his treason,' Amerotke insisted, 'and Lady Busiris' tacit compliance. Do advise the lady Mataia that

270

her mistress will become hysterical; she must also be in attendance.'

'I will then join you?'

'No, Shufoy. Once Khufu and Busiris have been taken from the temple, search their chambers for any treasonable correspondence, anything I can use when I bring them to trial. Stay here in the Temple of Nubia and witness what happens. Please,' Amerotke gazed sadly at Shufoy, 'do this for me.'

At the ninth hour on that same day, Amerotke was ushered into the Chamber of the Leaping Gazelle, a spacious, opulent room at the heart of the Malkata. Hatusu and Senenmut, flanked by Nakhtu-aa in the full glory of their imperial livery, were waiting for him. Amerotke knelt on a cushion before the throne carved out of cedarwood, decorated with gold and silver foil and studded with precious jewels. The room was silent except for the swish of the flabella drenched with kiphye and the buzz of bees foraging amongst the brilliantly coloured flower jars: these stood beneath the open windows overlooking the Garden of Delights, which was filled with every type of plant and shrub, all thriving in the fertile black soil of Canaan.

Amerotke kept his head bowed for some time before Hatusu told him to look upon her face. He did so and intoned the usual courtly greeting:

As the deer longs for the coolest water,
So my eyes thirst for the face of the Divine One.
My eyes hunger for your favour, my soul thrills at your
    presence.

Hatusu, eyes hard as pebbles, glared back. She was dressed in the purest gauffered linen; her beautiful face, framed by a simple wig, was unpainted; no jewellery adorned her, nothing but the sceptre ring on the little finger of her left hand and those gold-edged sandals noisily tapping the footstool to show her impatience. She looked slightly thinner than usual. Amerotke realised that the crisis must have gnawed at her heart. He only hoped he could bring her peace. She continued to stare as if seeing the judge for the first time. Amerotke shifted his gaze. Senenmut looked worried, his burly face a mask of concern, eyes blinking, fingers restless as if impatient to be gone. He glanced sharply at the judge. Amerotke looked back at Pharaoh, who was still staring blankly at him, eyes clouded, lips twisted, as if she was suffering some inner pain. Amerotke had not told the Great House what he proposed; he dared not. Hatusu's temper was legendary, and she might strike before he wanted. He'd assembled Khufu, Busiris and Mataia outside and instructed Asural and Pharaoh's own standard-bearer not to admit anyone, including Shufoy. Only two witnesses and his wife would be needed.

'My lord judge,' Pharaoh spoke, 'look around, what do you see?'

Amerotke obeyed, gazing around that sophisticated chamber. On all sides the walls celebrated the beauty and speed of gazelles running and leaping over evergreen fields. The marble-hard floor was of glittering dark blue stone. The elegant furniture, caskets, stools and tables were all inlaid with special metals. The flower vases and jars boasted the full glory of summer, a stark contrast to the heavily armed bodyguards and, behind these, the Scribes of the Secret Cabinet along with their deaf-mute attendants. Shufoy called them the Vultures, the sinister harbingers of Pharaoh's wrath.

'You have brought us here, Lord Judge,' Hatusu declared, 'away from our pressing duties in the House of War. Why?'

'To hand you victory,' Amerotke replied in a carrying voice, 'to deliver to you, Almighty Horus, the neck of your enemy, the Sgeru, leader of the Arites. Foul fount . . .' Amerotke could not continue. Some of the scribes leapt to their feet. Senenmut's cry of surprise was almost drowned by the clatter of armour as the Nakhtu-aa turned to each other.

'Silence!' Hatusu's voice thrilled, cutting the air like a lash. 'Silence for the voice of Pharaoh. My lord judge . . . ?'

Amerotke lifted his head. Hatusu purred like a cat being gently stroked; colour brightened her face, her eyes sparkled, her lips no longer a prim twisted line.

'My lord judge.' If she could have Hatusu would have stretched out and caressed Amerotke's face. 'Such words gladden your Pharaoh's heart. Never,' she lifted her head, 'has a Sgeru been trapped. Killed in battle, yes, disappeared into the desert or jungle, but to be brought to Pharaoh's feet – tell us now.'

'Divine One,' Amerotke lifted both hands, 'I am your Chief Judge in the Hall of Two Truths. I beg you to let me plead in my own way and my own time.'

Hatusu blinked, then glared at him as if she was about

to refuse. Senenmut, forgetting all etiquette and protocol, leaned over and whispered. Hatusu nodded. Senenmut rose to enforce silence.

'Lord Amerotke,' the grand vizier sat down, 'we will wait on you.'

'I call on Lord Khufu, Lady Busiris and Chief Heset Mataia.' Cushions were quickly arranged as the doors were opened. Amerotke turned to face the three, who bowed before Pharaoh before taking their places on the cushions opposite. Khufu and Busiris looked dishevelled and broken. The high priest gazed fearfully at Amerotke; his wife simply sat back on her heels, head in hands, gently weeping Mataia looked as elegant as ever. Her face glowed like the purest ebony, her wig was short but festooned with small bright stones that matched her earrings, necklaces, bracelets and rings. She was dressed in a simple linen gown, cut low and tight around her chest to emphasise her full breasts. She smiled at Amerotke, one hand, the fingernails brilliantly painted, patting at a bead of sweat on her neck.

'My lord Khufu, you are guilty of treason,' Amerotke declared. 'You are high priest of the Temple of Nubia. Nonetheless, by your own admission, you allowed Pharaoh's enemies to blackmail you to look the other way. You did not do what the Divine One asked but what the Arites demanded. You were frightened that they might expose your indiscretions with a number of young women both in the temple and elsewhere, yes?'

'Yes, I, I . . .'

'True or not?' Amerotke repeated.

'True,' Khufu murmured, head bowed.

'And your wife,' Amerotke's tongue stung like a barb, 'was party to all this? She kept silent when she was duty-bound, if not paid, to tell all to Pharaoh.'

'I . . .' Busiris lifted her face, the paint all smudged with tears. 'I knew, but I didn't want my husband to be—'

'True or not?' Amerotke insisted.

'True,' Busiris conceded.

'True, you were frightened.' Amerotke moved remorselessly on. 'The Arites threatened to kill you, but you should have had more confidence in Pharaoh. She would have guarded you like the apple of her eye. But there was something else apart from blackmail, threats and fear. You, Khufu, were uncertain. You wavered. You acted the loyal courtier, warning Pharaoh, even saving her, but what if the Arites were successful? If Pharaoh's power was weakened?'

'Never!' Hatusu snapped.

'You stood at the crossroads,' Amerotke accused. 'You tried to walk both paths, as did Imothep, formerly Chief Scout of the Spies of Sobeck.'

'What is this?' Senenmut intervened. Calm and logical, Pharaoh's grand vizier now realised that Amerotke had uncovered more than the Great House had ever imagined.

'Imothep was also blackmailed and threatened,' Amerotke explained, 'forced to give up his secrets about the fortress of Timsah. Your Excellency,' he waved a hand, 'that must wait for a fuller explanation. Imothep's killers have been brought to justice. I shall report fully to the Great House, but it does not concern us now.'

'Strange,' Senenmut retorted. 'Lord Khufu saved the

Divine One from the assassins, yet now he does not mention it.'

'Because he dare not,' Amerotke answered. 'Your Excellency, Lord Khufu was told of the likelihood of the attack. The Arites sacrificed their men to portray Khufu as Pharaoh's saviour, to distract attention from both himself and the Temple of Nubia. True, they wanted to inflict danger on Egypt's prestige. More importantly, they regarded the Temple of Nubia as their nest, their lair, their secret stronghold in Thebes. They needed it, and didn't want Pharaoh to turn her heart against it. What does it matter if ten, twenty, thirty Arites died? They had struck at Pharaoh and depicted Khufu as her saviour. Only the cunning Lord Valu wondered if that was their real objective. The Sgeru and the Arites sustained their pretence, sending scarabs and red cloths as threats to Khufu and the rest, but that was only a means of diverting suspicion from what they really intended.'

'You are alleging Khufu was corrupt?' Senenmut asked. 'Is that what you are saying?'

'Khufu,' Hatusu leaned forward, 'you are finished.'

'Lair, nest?' Senenmut hastily intervened, fearful of Hatusu taking matters into her hands. 'You call the Temple of Nubia a stronghold of the Arites?'

'They wanted it kept open and free, a place where they could plot. Oh, Excellency, you placed troops in and around the temple, but how could they discern amongst the flow of visitors, not to mention members of the temple, who was loyal and who was not?' Amerotke stared across. Khufu and Busiris had their heads down. Mataia was looking at Amerotke, no longer smiling, her face tense, those lovely eyes watchful.

'Is he,' Hatusu jabbed a finger at Khufu, 'their creature, the Sgeru?'

'No,' Amerotke replied flatly, pointing at Mataia. 'She is.'

Amerotke's accusation was greeted with an astonished silence, broken by a piercing scream of protest from Mataia and an anguished cry from Khufu. Senenmut turned, gesturing at the Nakhtu-aa to stand behind the accused. Hatusu sat in shock, staring wildly at the heset. Mataia half raised herself up, arms outstretched to plead with Pharaoh, yet Amerotke caught the change, a shift in her eyes, a calculating look, followed by the realisation that she might be trapped. The Nakhtu-aa were now drawing their swords.

'My lord?'

Amerotke turned to Senenmut.

'This is a trial!' The grand vizier roared for silence, imposing it by his very presence.

'This cannot be true,' Khufu gasped. 'She is of peasant stock, she . . .'

'Deeper and deeper into the mire,' the judge riposted. 'You cannot even admit you have been fooled by a mere heset, a woman you've slept with!'

'You never tolerated an ill word against her.' Busiris, who had partially recovered her wits, was fearful about what was to happen. She turned on her husband, glaring at him with hatred.

'Peasant stock.' Amerotke held Mataia's gaze. 'That's not true!'

She glanced quickly over her shoulder. Escape? Amerotke wondered, or looking for a weapon to use on herself or him?

'Peasant stock,' he continued. 'Nonsense! The Arites were defeated by Pharaoh's father. Mataia was then a child, a scion of the royal line. What better way to ensure her safety, to guarantee her security, than by presenting her to the high priest of the Temple of Nubia, pretending she was some village girl when in fact she was a Nubian princess, daughter of the last Sgeru?'

'What proof,' Khufu sounded desperate, 'do you have of this?'

'What proof can you offer that she is not?'

Khufu glared sullenly back.

'I can,' Mataia declared coolly, though Amerotke noticed her shallow breathing, the sweat now lacing her neck and shoulders. 'I have not been to Nubia since I was a child.'

'True,' Amerotke agreed, 'but Nubia has come to you. You matured. With your charms and skills, both in bed and out, you became chief heset here in the temple. Undoubtedly your seduction of Lord Khufu helped. Anyway, you received many visitors from your homeland, including the Arites from their secret fortress at Bekhna. They revealed your true identity, your vocation, your mission. You would meet them, high-ranking officers who came into Thebes disguised as soldiers looking for work, or merchants, pilgrims, priests, holy men and beggars. They brought you the Sesher, the sacred chain of your coven, a girdle of discs, each bearing the head of your evil hyaena goddess. They invested you with that. Who would suspect? Even today, in your House of Myrrh, there are the sick, the poor, Arites posing as infirm, though not for long,' Amerotke declared. 'Officers and priest physicians from the regiment of Isis have now surrounded the hospital. They are going to examine each and every one of your patients. They will search for the sham injury, the make-believe infection, the beggar who is not spindly but has the body of a warrior. In a word, your followers.'

'But a female,' Khufu yelled, 'a mere heset, the Sgeru?'

'Where does it say that the Sgeru has to be male? The Arites worship a female goddess.' Amerotke paused. 'Do you remember when we first met? You asked Mataia to talk to us about the Arites. She mentioned the Sgeru and, interestingly, used the phrase "he or she" to describe the Silent One.'

The disgraced high priest, a haunted and broken man, could only shake his head. Amerotke turned back to Mataia.

'You were a spider at the centre of your web. You wove a tangle, then scurried here and there, and if not you, your faithful lieutenants.'

'So the Arites at the temple know the truth?' Senenmut asked.

'A few; I suspect their captains, high-ranking officers lurking in both the temple and the barracks. These helped spread the net, and drew others into their conspiracy. Messages came from Nubia and the plot bubbled as the cauldron was stirred. They needed the temple to be at least quietly acquiescent. Mataia could arrange that, the clever heset who'd seduced the high priest and kept careful watch on him and his lady wife. Khufu was threatened and blackmailed, as were you, Lady Busiris, to look the other way. Imothep was a different prize. He had precise knowledge of the wells, springs and tunnels of Timsah. He too was drawn in, coerced to copy his maps and bring them for Khufu to bury beneath that ancient sycamore where the Arites could collect them. In time the web grew more tangled. The revolt in Nubia began. The attack on the Divine One was plotted then betrayed to Khufu. The high priest and his temple could not fall under suspicion. If men had to be sacrificed, what did it matter?'

'Conjecture!' Mataia declared, wafting her hand before her face.

Amerotke gazed sadly at her and tried not to think about Shufoy's heartbreak. He quietly thanked the gods that the little man was not here to witness all this.

'Conjecture,' Mataia repeated. 'You have no proof.'

'I could say so much against you,' Amerotke retorted. 'My visit to Timsah? Did you wheedle it out of Shufoy? Or did you, Khufu, break your sacred oath to me and warn the Arites?'

'Never! Never!' the high priest muttered.

'Or did you, Mataia, realise what I was plotting and alert your coven?'

'Evidence!' she hissed. 'Produce your evidence!'

'You made three mistakes,' Amerotke replied. 'Excellency!' He beckoned to an officer of the Nakhtu-aa and whispered to him. The man bowed towards Hatusu, then hurried out and returned, murmuring into Amerotke's ear. The judge, holding Mataia's gaze, nodded. 'You made three very serious and very stupid mistakes,' he repeated. 'Lord Valu and I questioned one of your followers at the Place of the Skull. He agreed to cooperate. In truth, he was under orders to dissemble and mislead us. On that day Valu decided to send a messenger to the Temple of Nubia, saying we were bringing an important prisoner to its House of Chains. The messenger left. We followed shortly afterwards. During our journey through the city, the Arites attacked us. At first I thought this was to free the prisoner, but I doubt if you had the time to plot that. The real purpose of the assault was to weaken Pharaoh, remove officials she would use to probe your treason as well as bring her authority into public disrepute.' Amerotke paused. Khufu squatted, mouth open, as if he sensed where the judge was leading.

'The attack failed,' Amerotke continued. 'The prisoner was brought into the temple. You, Mataia, met us in the courtyard. You told us to hand the prisoner over to the keeper of the House of Chains. The Arites was taken down to the cell, where he was later mysteriously murdered, or seemingly so.'

'I was with you and Lord Valu,' Mataia retorted. No longer pretty-faced, the heset was beginning to panic, and Amerotke drew strength from this. 'Hush now,' he murmured. 'Let us first move to the death of Imothep.' He glanced at Hatusu and bowed. 'All this will be in my report to the Keeper of the Gate at the Great House. The Scribes of the Secret Cabinet will study what I have written.'

Hatusu's smile was cynical. She realised Amerotke had deliberately kept everyone in the dark so as to prepare his own deadly ambush. The judge had anticipated that

Hatusu did not really care about the hunt; she simply wanted to be in at the kill.

'Continue, my lord.' Pharaoh's voice, deep and throaty, carried a deadly menace.

'Imothep was not strangled by the Arites. He was poisoned by a powerful poison, the powder of the almond, which replicates the symptoms of strangulation. His assassins have already faced both judge and justice. However, his murder seemed to be the work of the Arites. It was certainly not. You,' Amerokte pointed at Mataia, 'also realised that. You were fascinated. How could that happen? You reached the same conclusion as I did: Imothep must have been poisoned and his death made to look otherwise.' Amerotke paused. 'I said you were a spider. You lurk deep in the shadows whilst your captains carry out your stratagems. You were very careful not to reveal your full malevolence. You were already well acquainted with poisons. Your followers mixed the tainted natron pellets for the Medjay and supplied the potions to drug or kill imperial couriers and messengers who camped at the Oasis of Sinjar. Potions are also given to your converts before they take the blood-oath. Poisons fascinate you – don't they, Mataia?'

She half smiled.

'So much so that you made a mistake. You were in a hurry to learn about a new poison. This time your officers did not consult the scorpion men. You yourself approached the House of Powders in the Temple of Nubia and asked the lector priest in charge if there was a potion that could cause such symptoms. He replied that there was, and you asked for some.'

'You have no proof of that.'

'You think so?' Amerotke retorted. 'You certainly did ask. You realised it was a hideous mistake: that is why the Arites, in their night attack on the Temple of Nubia, singled out that lector priest to silence his mouth. A strange assault,' he mused. 'Some chaos, a few deaths. Perhaps not what was planned, but there again, the assassins you'd hired from the slums had almost been annihilated by the Medjay during the attack on my mansion. No, the night assault on the Temple of Nubia was carried out only by the Arites lurking there. They had one task: to kill certain individuals. You were desperate to cover your hasty mistake. However,' Amerotke shrugged, 'the priest lector had already talked. Divine One, I wish to call a witness.'

Senemut agreed. A short while later, a frightened scribe from the House of Powders was ushered in to do full obeisance before Pharaoh. Amerotke led him with gentle questions before reaching the crux of the matter.

'Your colleague, the lector priest who was killed, he informed you that the heset Mataia asked him about the powder of the almond, yes?'

'Yes,' whispered the man, not daring to lift his head. 'He also gave her some. She maintained her request was on behalf of Lord Khufu.'

'It was not!' the high priest screeched.

'Silence!' Amerotke gestured at the scribe to continue.

'She said it was a confidential matter, not to be discussed. My lord, my colleague was intrigued. You see, some poisons, in small doses, may be used for medicinal purposes.'

'But not the powder of the almond?'

'No, my lord.'

'And is there any entry in the records of the House of Powders?'

'No, my lord. As I said, it was supposed to be confidential.'

Amerotke thanked the scribe, who scuttled out.

'Did you,' he asked, pointing at Khufu, 'make such a request?'

'No, no!'

'And neither did I,' Lady Busiris hastened to add.

'You then made your second mistake,' Amerotke accused Mataia. 'You were swept up by your own arrogance and apparent success. The poisoning of the Medjay, the unrest amongst the Nubian regiment, the revolt in Nubia, your success with Imothep, the seizure of Timsah, the attack on the couriers at Sinjar and your assault on the Divine One. On the day that Arites prisoner was brought in, you decided to manifest your power even further, with the death of an apparent traitor in the custody of Lords Valu and Amerotke at the House of Chains.'

'You took the prisoner down. I just watched. I had nothing—'

'Not then,' Amerotke interrupted, 'but you had before. Lord Khufu, when Valu's messenger informed you we were bringing an Arites to the temple, what did you do?'

'I asked her,' Khufu retorted quickly, 'the heset, to send a messenger to the keeper of the House of Chains, telling him to be ready to receive an important prisoner. I did not expect her to go there herself.'

'But she did!' Amerotke declared. Again he turned to the Divine One. 'I have a further witness.'

The guard from the House of Chains entered, trembling in his obeisance, though he remained stubborn in his assertion that Mataia had appeared in the House of Chains and talked confidentially to its keeper. She had also gone with him to indicate in which cell the Arites was to be imprisoned. He repeated, despite Mataia's objections, that what he had seen was the truth and could not understand why the heset should disagree with him. Amerotke thanked the guard and dismissed him, before turning back to Mataia.

'You went down there,' he said. 'You took the keeper of the House of Chains to inspect that cell. We too inspected it. Lord Valu scrutinised the water bowl. However, we then left. The keeper took the Arites in. Now . . .' Amerotke cleared his throat. 'I do not know the full truth here. The red cloth and the powder could have been hidden away in that cell. However, it is more likely that the keeper, as he allegedly confined the prisoner, powdered the water and handed the cloth over with the briefest of whispered instructions. A few heartbeats of time. If we had gone back, why should we check the water again? Or examine the prisoner? We thought he was safely confined. He was, but he was also preparing for death! Members of your sect in the face of death tie their so-called sacred red cloth around their throats. He did so, then drained the water bowl, which he dirtied further with filth from the ground to hide any odour.'

'But that would make the keeper of the House of Chains my accomplice,' Mataia hastily replied.

'He was Nubian; he was also one of yours. I saw him

285

take the prisoner to the cell. The message he whispered would only take a few seconds.'

'So he *was* my accomplice?'

'Yes, he was an Arites. You were flushed with pride. You wanted to deepen the mystery, and so you did. What did you care? You had learnt the secret of Imothep's death. What a startling way to proclaim how the Arites could go where they wished and do whatever they wanted.' Amerotke paused. 'Naturally there'd be an investigation, but what did that matter? Valu and Amerotke were already condemned to death; they would perish in those heinous attacks planned against their mansions. Pharaoh would be deprived of her Eyes and Ears. Who would think it was significant that you visited the House of Chains? – after all, you were only carrying out Lord Khufu's order. The keeper was your accomplice. Who would suspect poison? Why investigate when even greater murders, assassinations and crises become the order of the day?' Amerotke paused for effect. 'Valu died. I did not. The enormity of your mistake dawned, and as it did, you took whatever measures you could. You acted as if you, Khufu and Busiris were the inveterate enemies of the Arites. Hence the threats and menaces. You also took careful precautions. The keeper of the House of Chains must die. He knew your identity and what you had done. Arites or not, he had to be sacrificed, whilst the lector priest from the House of Powders would also die during that night attack on the Temple of Nubia. The entire purpose of that assault was the deaths of those two men.'

'You said she made three mistakes?' Senenmut broke the ensuing silence.

'Oh yes.' Amerotke shifted on the cushions. 'You hoped to rectify your mistakes with murder. When that failed, you suborned and seduced poor Shufoy, my friend: an excellent way of discerning what path I might be following. You also decided to act the innocent heset fleeing the temple, fearful of all these threats. Remember the day you left, emptying the contents of that sack to show you carried nothing suspicious? Saying Shufoy could look after your room, implying you had nothing to hide? Time was passing. You gambled that you could still survive your mistake. The military campaign would begin. The crisis in Nubia would deepen, as would that in Thebes. Once your followers launched fresh attacks to undermine the Divine House, you could hide in the Malkata, all protected, or slip away whenever you wished.'

'These followers in the Temple of Nubia?' Hatusu asked.

Amerotke gestured at Lady Busiris.

'Weren't you ever suspicious about those who came to the House of Myrrh, or the sturdy beggars seeking alms?'

'I . . . I left it to her,' Busiris stammered. 'She always said—'

'That she would take care of such dirty, dusty, poor and infirm creatures?' Amerotke finished the sentence for her. 'The flow of visitors to your temple concealed Arites, the Sgeru's messengers and assassins. Little wonder they could warn, threaten, kill and attack with impunity. They would emerge from the shadows to wreak damage, then quickly resume their disguise. Officers from the Isis regiment are now rounding up all such suspects, anyone who could be masquerading.'

Mataia swallowed hard.

'Most, I concede, will be innocent, but I am sure we will find a few jackals amongst the lambs.' Amerotke rose and bowed towards Hatusu. 'Your Excellencies, I must fetch one last piece of evidence.'

He left the room. Norfret was sitting on a stone wall-bench, staring round the antechamber filled with guards, their swords and daggers drawn. She caught sight of Amerotke and hastened across, clutching a leather sack. She placed this at Amerotke's feet, grasped his hands and kissed him full on the lips.

'Rumours flow thick and fast. There's disturbance at the Temple of Nubia. People are being arrested! Here in the palace, soldiers and Medjay throng around. You asked me to search Mataia's belongings? I brought you what I could.'

Amerotke pressed her hands, then crouched down and emptied the contents of the sack, half listening to Norfret's spate of questions and observations.

'She asked me to keep them safe for her. I received your message. I only brought the belts, girdles and sashes.'

Amerotke picked up the silver girdle and felt the hard surface beneath. He was sure Mataia had worn this when she left the Temple of Nubia. He called for a dagger from an officer, cut the ribbon and smiled at the silver-linked gold chain beneath. He freed it from its sheath and held it up.

'Beautiful!' Norfret murmured.

'The Sesher,' Amerotke breathed. He studied the exquisite gold chain, a string of wafer-thin pure gold medallions, linked by silver clasps. Each medallion was studded with the head of a hyaena, its eyes of precious stones, the clasps carved in the shape of two snakes, which fastened neatly into each other.

'A fortune!' Norfret whispered.

Amerotke gazed around. The sheer beauty of the chain was already drawing envious glances. He kissed Norfret and asked her to be patient. Then he placed the Sesher around his neck and went back into the Gazelle Chamber. He stood before Hatusu, who exclaimed in joy, hands going out to grasp the treasure. Amerotke took it off and laid it at her feet. Khufu and Busiris simply gaped. Mataia knelt, head down, shoulders shaking. Amerotke went and stood over her.

'You acted the innocent with nothing to hide when you left the temple. I glimpsed the silver chain around your waist. On reflection I could not understand why you wore it on such a hot day with a cloak wrapped about you. Later, in the House of the Forest, you took off both cloak and chain. I wondered afterwards why you insisted on wearing such items on a hot, dusty thoroughfare, only to remove them in the coolness of a mansion. You had to take the Sesher with you, and what better hiding place than the Malkata, in the lodgings of Lady Norfret, wife of Pharaoh's chief judge?' He went and knelt back on the cushions. Hatusu and Senenmut were busy examining the Sesher; a hum of conversation rang around the chamber. Amerotke gestured at Mataia.

'Throw yourself on Pharaoh's mercy,' he warned, and his words created silence. 'Do you want to be impaled, Mataia, at the Place of the Skull, your breasts torn off

289

and sewn to your mouth? Or do you want to be buried alive out in the Redlands? A jug of blood poured above you to attract the devourers, who will come at night to dig you out? And that is only after you have been tortured by the Scribes of the Secret Chamber. You are the Sgeru, yet you are no battle-hardened warrior, nothing but a plump heset girl whom the torturers would love to play with. Do you confess and plead for mercy?'

'Yes!' Mataia raised her head, eyes glittering. 'For mercy I confess. I also confess my fourth mistake. I should have killed you,' she hissed.

'Behold, Pharaoh, Horus in the North, Mighty Bull in the South, the Glory of Montu, the Beloved of Amun, Conqueror and Victor of the People of the Nine Bows, Lord of Battles . . .' Senenmut, dressed in the chief regalia of grand vizier, He-Who-Speaks-the-Words-of-Pharaoh, proclaimed Hatusu's titles from the top steps of the sweeping approach to the principal Temple of Amun at the heart of Ipet-Sut, the most perfect of places in Karnak. His words rang out across the great concourse, reaching the high crenellated walls where hordes of Medjay stood, powerful bows at the ready. The great parade area below was packed with soldiers. Along each flank were the Amun and Isis regiments, with the Glory of Ptah, an elite corps brought swiftly from Memphis, lining the gate wall. In the centre of this U-shaped formation stood the regiment of Nubia under full battle standards and pennants, officers to the front, all kneeling in anticipation of Pharaoh's imminent appearance. Facing these, going back up the steep temple steps, were rank after rank of Silver Shield bearers. At the top of the steps were ranged the Nakhtu-aa. The Nubian regiment had been mustered to hear what Pharaoh would say after she revealed her face. Had they been brought here to die? Was it true the Sgeru had been captured? Would Pharaoh bring them back into her love? The braying of conch horns, the wail of trumpets and the clash of cymbals rang out. Gusts of the most fragrant incense curled up as hundreds of pure white doves, like the souls of the blessed, burst from the darkened portico of the temple entrance. The chant of the priests rose and fell:

Show your face to us Divine One,
Loosen the bolts of the Great House,
Manifest yourself, Fair of Form and Lovely of Face.

As the words faded, a covered palanquin was brought out of the temple, surrounded by a swarm of fan-bearers, flunkeys, soldiers, priests and scribes. It stopped in a gap between the Nakhtu-aa on the top steps. The soldiers, drilled to perfection, moved back. The palanquin curtain was withdrawn to reveal Hatusu, the blue war crown of Egypt on her head, her shoulders draped with the Nenes, the Cape of Glory, over a long white linen gown. She was seated on the dazzling Throne of Majesty, a magnificent chair with gold-encrusted leaping lions, its legs decorated with the silver carved heads of Egypt's enemies. A trumpet blew. Senenmut demanded silence as Pharaoh rose. She stepped out of the palanquin and walked to the edge of the steps. The Keeper of the Stake, the executioners, torturers and

Scribes of the Secret Cabinet, all garbed in red, their faces hidden by Seth masks, moved out of the pillars. The Keeper handed Senenmut the sacrificial apron; his assistants the gold-handled war mace of Egypt with its diamond-shaped metal club. Hatusu just stood, terrifying in her beauty, as three captives, slightly drugged, were brought out, hands tied behind their backs, and were forced to kneel on Pharaoh's left. All eyes strained to glimpse the middle one. Hair shaved, her face a bloody mask, Mataia, former chief heset, now humiliated and exposed as the Sgeru. The other two captives were Arites caught during raids on the Temple of Nubia. Others had also been seized; they would die out at the Place of the Skull.

In a powerful voice, Senenmut proclaimed what had happened. The executioners moved behind Mataia, pulling back her head. Senenmut turned and asked her to confess. She nodded vigorously: it was all she could do, for her tongue had been plucked out in case she uttered further blasphemy against Pharaoh. A groan broke from the Nubian regiment, even the occasional jeer, but this stilled as Senenmut beckoned forward a flunkey and plucked the Sesher from a cushion. He held this up between his hands, turning it so the sun caught its shimmering grandeur.

'Behold the Sesher, the sacred chain of Nubia, now Pharaoh's by divine appointment and god-given victory!'

The effect on the Nubian regiment was astonishing: men just stood and gasped as Senenmut draped the Sesher around Hatusu's slim waist and fastened it tight. Trumpets bellowed.

'Behold Pharaoh's justice against the Sgeru and her accomplices!'

Hatusu, mace in hand, the sacred apron now about her, stood back as Mataia was brought to kneel at her feet. The mace was swung. Hatusu, with unerring aim, smashed the side of her enemy's head, a shattering crack. Bone, blood and brains spilt out in a gruesome trickle to drip over the edge of the steps. The two other captives were dealt with just as swiftly, then Pharaoh, standing in the blood of her enemies, mace raised, received the thunderous salute of her regiments, the Nubian included. Trumpets silenced the ovation.

'We know,' Senenmut proclaimed, 'that our sons of Nubia are still Pharaoh's children. Your hearts were turned by Seth creatures, phantasms of the dark. Some of these still lurk amongst you. Expel them now! Drive them from your midst! Accept Pharaoh's love or face utter annihilation!'

The line of Nubian foot and archers rippled like water under a strong breeze, then opened. Men were being seized, stripped of their weapons and pushed forward. Senenmut turned and smiled at Pharaoh. The revolt was over!

In the condemned cell of the House of Chains beneath the Temple of Ma'at close to Karnak, Amerotke heard the roar of the troops. He had been appointed as Pharaoh's witness. Now he sat on a stool and watched Sihera cradle the cup of swift-acting poison. Outside, in the ill-lit passageway, the keepers, in their dark kilts and jackal masks, also waited patiently. At the end of the passageway Shufoy crouched in a corner, sobbing uncontrollably.

'Glory and grief,' Sihera murmured as she lay on the palliasse, her back resting against the wall. 'All finished now, lord judge, yes?'

'True,' Amerotke agreed, 'all finished.' He paused. 'I have asked you this before; I do so again. The Scribes of the Secret Cabinet have searched Imothep's house.' He shrugged. 'They have indeed ransacked it. They cannot find the treasures Parmen stole from the Mansion of Silence, or, indeed, precious items from the main house itself. Parmen was truly greedy; he pillaged his dead master's goods. Do you know the whereabouts of such plunder?'

'It was Imothep's,' Sihera whispered. 'Let the House of the Forest keep it!'

Amerotke nodded. Sihera, if she knew, would not tell him. And what did it matter? That was the business of the House of Silver and the Scribes of the Secret Cabinet.

'Khufu and Busiris?' Sihera asked. 'What has happened to them?'

'Banned from Pharaoh's love, placed under house arrest. Disgraced and humiliated, both drank poison.'

'And Mataia?' Sihera smiled to herself. 'Who would have thought she was the Sgeru? The silly heset with the ornate wig and the short kilt, the lovely laugh and the swaying hips.'

'Did Imothep suspect her?'

'Never!' Sihera half laughed. 'He dismissed her as a simple empty-head, a temple girl, interested only in her dancers and her rituals.'

'Everyone did,' Amerotke agreed. 'Lady Busiris, before she took the poison, admitted that Mataia was allowed to go where she wanted and do what she liked. Khufu was fascinated by her, he spoilt her, but on reflection, he also ruefully conceded that Mataia had manoeuvred herself into a position of absolute power. She played the part so carefully: the innocent, the laughing girl, the dancer, the person always ready to help. She could go where she wanted, she could meet whomever she wanted, and no one ever suspected.'

'I am sure,' Sihera's voice grew sardonic, 'that Mataia in the House of Chains repaid the compliment to her former patrons?'

'Oh yes, she did,' Amerotke declared. 'Damning evidence about the high priest's real attitude to Hatusu, which eventually persuaded Khufu and his wife to take poison. I suspect Mataia seduced both of them. She certainly cursed Hatusu but she also confessed that Khufu entertained grandiose desires and chattered about them, showing off in front of a pretty heset. Sihera, as you know, we live in a man's world. Many in Thebes hide behind their masks and believe that Hatusu should not hold the flail and the rod. They are only too ready to rise in rebellion and depose her. Khufu, like many high priests, supported this in a secretive, treacherous way. He never really believed that the revolt in Nubia would succeed, but in the meantime, there was the possibility that Hatusu might be deposed. He allowed his dislike of Pharaoh to manifest itself, to make him dabble in treachery. Once that happens, you are committed: you either succeed or you lose. In the end,' Amerotke shrugged, 'Mataia was inexperienced. Her desire to appear invincible made her commit hideous mistakes and so exposed her.' He smiled thinly. 'Strange! Parmen and the rest understimated you and paid dearly for it. Khufu was equally dismissive of both Mataia and Hatusu, and lost everything.'

'And Nubia?' Sihera asked.

'General Omendap will sweep all before him. Bekhna will be destroyed and levelled, not one stone left upon another. The ground will be sown with salt and sand. The Nubian regiment will be purged, sent north to the Delta for a while to demonstrate its courage and loyalty. The Temple of Nubia will be closed to be purified, its priests replaced. Pharaoh will carry out bloody justice against all involved in the death of Lord Valu. The Churat, the Eater of Foul Things, has been promised even greater rewards to turn on the other gangs.'

'More blood will be spilt!' Sihera spoke as if talking to herself. 'Your Pharaoh, Lord Amerotke, watch her! Her heart will be coarsened by power and revenge. She will become like Sekhmet: nothing and no one will oppose her. Remember that, judge!'

Amerotke simply stared back.

'As for me,' Sihera continued, 'I am for the dark. I have confessed all my sins to a Priest of the Ear. Strange,' she mused. 'In a sense, Imothep's death brought the Arites crashing to ruin. He was always their enemy.' She raised her cup. 'To Imothep, Chief Scout of the Spies of Sobeck!' And in one swift gulp, she downed the poison.

Amerotke watched her slip into death, then rose and left the cell. He walked down the passageway and crouched beside the sobbing Shufoy.

'I had no choice.' He grasped his friend's hand and held it fast. 'I had no choice and you know that. Your heart breaks, Shufoy, and as always, that shattering can be so cold, so silent. You will not get over this, but you will come to terms with it. Come.' Amerotke was desperate to take his friend away from this place of blood. He helped the little man up, still clasping his hand. 'My friendship for you only deepens.' He smiled down at Shufoy. 'Such a little man,' he murmured, 'but such a great heart!'

He grasped Shufoy's hand tighter, then turned at the sound of footsteps. Asural came clattering down.

'Is she dead?' he asked.

'She's gone,' Amerotke agreed.

'Did she tell you about the treasure?' Asural asked. 'Hatusu, the Divine One, demanded that.'

'She did not tell me,' Amerotke replied. 'I wonder why. Perhaps she never had it.'

'And that priest of the Chapel of the Ear?' Asural asked. 'I asked him to stay, but he is gone.'

Asural stared down at Shufoy, who had now broken free from his master's grasp and was wiping his disfigured, tear-soaked face with the hem of his gown.

'A priest of the Chapel of the Ear?' Shufoy glanced up. 'Master, as you know, I was distraught. I still am. As we came here, I saw the priest leave. I dismissed him as just another priest.'

'But?' Amerotke crouched down.

'I'm not too sure,' Shufoy declared, 'but he may have been the Tcheser, a pious, sanctimonious creature; in truth, a scorpion man.' He swallowed hard. 'A confidence trickster . . .'

297

'Are you sure?' Amerotke asked.

'No, I'm not.' Shufoy smiled through his tears. 'But I want to confess myself. I wondered which temple to go to. So many tricksters swarm here. Liars . . .' He began to cry again.

Amerotke hid his own agitation. He stared up the steps at the lance of light pouring through the open doorway.

'But it's over, isn't it?' Asural asked.

'Is it?' Amerotke got to his feet. 'Is it truly, Asural?'

'The revolt is over.' The Devourer of Hearts and his surviving lieutenants sat on the coarse matting at the wine shop the Light of Horus, the Lord of the Sky, on the edge of the Mysterious Abode in the Necropolis. The assassin leader stared malevolently across at the captain of the Arites and his small cohort of followers. 'The revolt is over!' the assassin leader taunted. 'Your Sgeru is destroyed. The Sesher seized. Your followers now decorate stakes out at the Place of the Skull or the Wall of Death. So, what do you want from us?'

The captain of the Arites just stared back.

'Are you returning to Nubia?' The Devourer of Hearts, still furious at the ambush at Amerotke's house, fingered the handle of the dagger thrust through his waist sash.

'True, true,' the Arites commander refused to be provoked, 'the revolt is over. You know we cannot return to Nubia. Bekhna will be destroyed. Rewards will be posted against us, dead or alive.'

'So what?' the Devourer of Hearts taunted.

'We share a common fate.' The Arites captain smiled,

tongue going out to lick the sore on the side of his mouth. 'If we are destroyed, so are you! And yet,' he gestured around, 'we few have survived.'

'How did you?'

'We sheltered in Timsah,' the Arites replied. 'We escaped into the Redlands before Amerotke's troops ringed that fortress. We trudged for days under a malevolent sun, but we survived, as we will again.'

'How?' the Devourer of Hearts baited. 'Your stupid bitch of a leader has been sacrificed to Pharaoh's glory. Bekhna will be destroyed, so where will you hide?'

'Why, here!' the Arites replied. 'In the slums of the Necropolis.'

'I see,' the Devourer of Hearts sneered. 'And how will you do that?'

The Arites captain clicked his tongue. He peered over his shoulder and stared at his followers, who included the scorpion man who rejoiced in the name of the Tcheser, the Holy One, because of his innate genius at disguising himself as an exorcist, a priest of the Chapel of the Ear. He was a consummate trickster, skilled at being able to draw the most telling confessions from would-be penitents. A man whom the Arites had rewarded lavishly for his good services in the death cell at the House of Chains beneath the Temple of Ma'at. He had listened to Sihera's confession and brought the glad tidings he'd learnt to this most redoubtable of captains. The Arites nodded at the Tcheser and his other companions, then turned slowly back as if to continue the conversation, only to move as swiftly as a striking scorpion. He plucked the needle-thin dagger from the sleeve of his robe, his right hand cutting the air like a reaper's sickle. The dagger blade neatly sliced the Devourer of Hearts' exposed throat. The other assassins sat in shock as their leader, eyes blinking, mouth half open, simply rocked backwards and forwards, gargling on his own blood, before toppling gently to one side. A few of them recovered, hands searching for concealed weapons, but the Arites' leader had judged wisely. The assassins had no fight left in them. His own followers had already drawn daggers and clubs, whilst behind them, three more Arites, supposedly on guard outside, appeared in the doorway, powerful Nubian bows drawn back, arrows already notched. A deathly silence held the room, broken by the death rattle of the Devourer of Hearts, who was still jerking in an ever-widening pool of blood.

'Peace.' The Arites captain grinned, raising one hand, palm extended. 'Peace, brothers! We mean you no harm.' The good humour drained from his face. 'But him, brothers,' he gestured at the Devourer, 'are you going to die for him? What did he do but lead you and others into the Medjays' trap at Amerotke's mansion? He should have been more prudent. He was hired for a certain task, and he failed. If the Medjay sensed you, brothers, surely he should have sensed them!'

Nods of approval, even grunts of agreement, warmed the Arites' heart.

'Do you really believe the Divine Bitch will allow those who attacked and killed Lord Valu to escape unscathed? No, no.' He shook his head. 'Already our spies in Thebes and the Necropolis have alerted us. The Churat, the Eater of Foul Things, is to be well paid by the House of Silver to bring you down. He has already issued a proclamation. Bounty-hunters will swarm in from the Redlands, and what will you do? Your ranks are depleted, weakened by that disaster at Amerotke's house, and this, your so-called leader, would have led you from one defeat to another.' The Arites captain raised his hand again, gesturing at the archers behind him to put down their bows and his other followers to resheathe their weapons.

'What do you propose?' One of the assassins gestured at the corpse of the Devourer, which was now stiffening in its dark pool of blood.

'First, my name,' the Arites captain declared. 'I am Nema, the incarnation of my goddess's anger. I will be your Tedjen, your leader, your commander. Second . . .' He raised his hand and snapped his fingers. A large leather sack was handed over, which he placed between himself and the assassins. He opened this carefully, taking out Imothep's exquisitely precious statue of the hyaena, its base studded with gems, as well as the small boxes of ingots, silver and gold, and an array of other precious items. 'These are from the House of the Forest.' The Arites gestured. 'This is our House of Silver; with these we can buy weapons, bribe, recruit more followers.'

'How did you find it?'

'One of my companions,' the Arites murmured, 'posed as a Priest of the Ear. Sihera, housekeeper of Imothep, condemned to death for murdering her companions, found the treasure in Parmen's chamber and hid it deep in that overgrown garden. My companion, my friend,' he smiled at the Tcheser, 'persuaded her that such treasure should be handed over to the temple as an offering to the god for her ka and that of her master whose death she avenged.'

The assassins were now bought body and soul. They rocked backwards and forwards, whispering in praise at the cunning of the Arites. Such a leader would protect them from Pharaoh's vengeance and the ruthless pursuit of the Churat. They would do well to shelter under his shadow.

'And what shall we do?' One of the assassins spoke.

'Carry out my orders.' The Nema ran a finger around his bruised lips and stared at a point on the wall above the assassins' heads. He could not forget Amerotke, standing by that pool at the Oasis of Sinjar directing his men. That was where it had all gone wrong! The Sgeru had made a hideous mistake. Amerotke should have died!

'We will grow wealthy,' the Nema declared. 'Rich and powerful! One day, brothers, at the right place, at the appropriate time, I want vengeance, not only against the Divine Bitch, but against her judge, Amerotke. Vengeance is my dream, vengeance my prize!'

AUTHOR'S NOTE

Nubian resistance against Egyptian rule is a matter of history. Revolts and conspiracies were commonplace. Attempts by successive pharaohs to magnify their power in Nubia became a staple part of Egyptian foreign policy. In the end, during the last thousand years BC, Nubia had its revenge: a successful revolt did occur, and Nubian troops moved north to occupy Thebes and establish a Nubian dynasty in Egypt. One of the great contradictions of studying Egyptian history is that we know so little and yet we know so much. The Egyptians were intensely interested in life; they believed in good fortune, that everyone should be happy. Accordingly, they were reluctant to expose what I describe as the underbelly of Egyptian life. Their reaction to anything disgraceful was *damnatio memoriae* – simply to obliterate it, forget it and never mention it. Treachery and treason, however, are a staple of politics. Undoubtedly Hatusu faced conspiracy after conspiracy. We know from archaeology and written evidence that this was so. She must have been particularly vulnerable as a female pharaoh, and there must have been those who opposed her simply because of this. The same lack of evidence applies to the underworld of Thebes, which must have existed. The characters described in this novel were part of a great city, which, like any other, had a thriving underworld. The best example of this, and one the Egyptian authorities found difficult to obliterate, were the grave-robbers and tomb-pillagers. Egypt was very rich: the treasures of its tombs and the control of its busy markets could always be exploited.

As regards poisons, again, we must not dismiss the ancient Egyptians' experience in such matters. We know from several manuscripts that they had a very detailed knowledge of the power of certain potions and powders. The effects of cyanide are very clearly described in A. S. Taylor's marvellous work, *On Poisons*, published in 1848. I refer you to pages 774, 768 and following; it makes fascinating reading. A more modern account, *Deadly Doses: A Writer's Guide to Poisons* by Ms Stevens and Ms Klarner, carefully defines the properties of cyanide. How easy that poison is to distil and how deadly its effect, being described on page 14 as 'internal asphyxia'!

Paul C. Doherty
April 2008
www.paulcdoherty.com